THE CLASS REUNION

SAVANNAH BLAIZE

CONTENTS

I would like to thank the MRWG, my friends and family who have been a constant support on my writing journey.

Edited by Belinda Holmes

Print book size : 9 x 6

Cover designed by Jay Aheer www.simplydefinedart.com

www.savannahblaize.com

CHAPTER ONE

Lauren Taylor regretted this trip back to her hometown with every mile she drove. Despite the pleading, cajoling and begging, if Sarah, her childhood friend, had not gone through such a horrific time and survived cancer, she would not be making this trip. Excuses had already been formulated in her head for an early exit. Her fingers tightened on the steering wheel. The minute the reunion weekend ended she was out of there, like a bat out of hell. Distracted by an old song on the radio, she allowed her mind to wander back to the last phone call from Sarah. Tears welled in her eyes when she thought how close she had come to losing her only remaining friend in Clearwater Springs. A friend she had not kept in touch with as often as she should have until the last year or so. Regrets. Yeah, she had a few. Not that she cared about the town. No siree, it could disappear off the face of the earth for all she cared. Along with her so-called high-school "classmates". They were never "mates", more like enemies. Treated her with distain because she came from a broken home and hadn't two cents to rub together through high school most weeks. The car coughed and slowed a little on the road, making her sit up straighter and pay attention. A shudder, a loud bang, and the gradual loss of speed finally brought the car to a halt on the side of the road. Lauren switched off the engine and yanked out the key. The black night engulfed her.

"Goddam piece of junk! You could have at least got me into town." She thumped the steering wheel, and slumped forward till her head rested on the cold metal. Bone tired didn't begin to describe the way her body responded to this new depressing situation, in a seemingly never-ending run lately of bad luck.

Pelting rain had seeped through her shirt and jeans before she had taken two steps in the direction of the trunk. She struggled to find the lock in the inky darkness. The toolbox tucked into the corner contained a set of jumper cables, a flashlight and assorted tools, all of which looked completely foreign to her. She remembered a conversation she had with her father when she bought her first old bomb of a car; or rather, a lecture her father had given her, warning her of the dangers of not servicing your vehicle regularly. *Why didn't I pay attention, instead of hoping a knight in shining armour would sweep me off my feet, marry me, and take care of mundane things like car repairs.* "Yeah, right. You're doing it on your own, sister." She shuddered. Her voice sounded eerie even to her.

The flashlight had difficulty illuminating anything in the storm, she had no idea what she was looking for, but she had little choice. *Onward and upward.*

Lauren wrenched up the hood and propped it open as she inspected the dark and murky interior. Everything looked normal. Or as normal as an engine could look to someone who was not used to poking about in the belly of the beast. No loose or protruding twisted parts that should could see, no flames. *That had to be a good thing, right?*

In the distance, twin shafts of light cut through the storm and illuminated the sky. Then a vehicle thundered down the road in Lauren's direction. She had time to register the truck was nearly upon her, obviously travelling faster than the speed limit on the deserted back road allowed. The wall of freezing water the tow truck threw up as it flew past her and drove through a puddle took her breath away and had her gasping for air. *Moron!*

TOMMY SLATER HAD BEEN SINGING ALONG TO THE DULCET TONES of Kenny Rogers on the country music channel when he rounded the bend and almost sideswiped the broken-down car on the side of the road. He glanced over, and had barely registered the figure of a woman under the hood when the tires sliced through a patch of water and completely drenched her and the car.

His father didn't bring him up to ignore someone in need, and he certainly didn't encourage walking away from a problem Tommy had caused. He swung the truck around at the first opportunity and headed back to see what he could do. He drove up on the wrong side of the road, and parked facing the car, with the intention of jump-starting the engine. His headlights illuminated the scene and the rear view of a woman with a very shapely derriere bent over the engine.

She turned toward him, shielding her eyes.

Oh fuck, it's Lauren Taylor. Why did you stop, you idiot? You should have kept on driving and sent someone else back to get her.

"HEY BUDDY, THANKS FOR THE SHOWER BACK THERE. YOU SEEMED hell-bent on getting somewhere in a hurry. But thanks for coming back. Any chance you could get her started?" Lauren peered at the approaching figure backlit by the truck headlights. Something in the way he walked had her heart pounding. *No, it couldn't be. Not Tommy. Life couldn't be this cruel.*

"Tommy Slater!" She took a faltering step back, suddenly nervous, nearly dropping the flashlight in the process. "I didn't know you were back in Clearwater Springs. Didn't you move to play baseball across the other side of the country?" *My God, he looks great. Muscles on muscles. Hard to hide that body with a rain-soaked denim jacket and jeans.* Her mind raced through memories as sharp as broken glass, and twice as deadly, remembering how close they once were. Her heart pounded.

"Lauren." He gave a curt nod in greeting. "Came back at the start of the year after the old man had his heart attack." Tommy moved closer, bending over the engine, but not before she had a chance to get a good look at the man he has become. He's taller than she remembers. Strong shoulders fill out his denim jacket. It's hard to see his eyes beneath the shadow cast from the bill of his baseball cap. His jaw is firm and square, with a layer of stubble. His nose, still crooked from a few nasty tackles in football, gives his handsome features a more authentic appeal. *He'd be too pretty otherwise.*

"You here for the reunion this weekend?"

"Yeah. I came back for Sarah Harper. She talked me into it."

"You don't sound too happy with your decision."

"Been a long time, Tommy. Nothing for me to come back for. No family here. Except for Sarah, everyone I cared about has either died or left town." *Or so I thought.*

Suddenly conscious of his intense stare, and what he must be thinking of her, she pulled away a little into the shadows, out of the arc of the flashlight, crossing her arms over her chest. All too aware her hair is plastered to her head, and her sodden clothes are clinging to her body. The cold and biting wind whipped around them. Clamping her jaw tight to stop her teeth from chattering, she wished the ground would open up and swallow her. And the damned car.

"Nothin' I can do here. I'll hook her up and have a look back at the garage."

"I don't know how much you charge, but I can't afford much, Tommy. I'm doing this weekend on a budget. I can't stay with Sarah; she's got enough on her plate. I can sleep in the car and use the three night's motel money for repairs, if you can do just enough to get me back to the city on Monday?"

"I won't know until I take a good look, but I'll do the best I can. Why don't you climb up in the cabin where it's dry, and let me hook her up, huh?"

He unhooked the abandoned car he'd collected, reversed the truck around and secured her vehicle. He climbed into the cabin, and pulled some towels out of a sports bag and gave her one. "Don't worry, they're clean." He removed his sodden cap and used one himself to get the worst of the rain off his drenched head, and to stop the icy water running down the back of his neck and into his collar. Glancing over at her, he watched her dry her hair and run the towel over her face. He remembered so clearly what it was like to taste that rain-soaked skin. Lost in the memory for a few seconds, he had to swallow down the groan that rose in his throat. One night in particular came to mind, when they had been caught in the rain after a football game, and they had sheltered in an abandoned building. *The night that changed everything.* His body tensed automatically, as the blood flowed south just thinking about it. *Fuck! A few minutes in her company and I'm like a fucking sex-mad teenager.*

He never saw her again after prom night. Being a popular guy, he was crowned Prom King and Maggie Cuthbert was crowned Prom Queen. When Maggie kissed him on stage, with tongue, he caught a glimpse of Lauren watching from the audience, a horrified betrayed expression on her face. He immediately knew he'd been played. He tried to get off the stage but everyone crowded around them, and when he broke free of the well-wishers, Lauren had already left the hall. He searched everywhere for her before his friends had dragged him back to the celebrations, but she had disappeared. She didn't answer his calls. He heard later in the week that she had left town that night. She didn't even say goodbye. So much for friendship.

Truth be told, he had never forgotten her. Every woman he had ever met had been compared in one way or another to Lauren. None of them ever made the cut.

When they got back to the garage, he hooked a thumb in the direction of the office upstairs, where it was dry and warm. "Go on up to the office. There's a comfortable couch and blankets upstairs now. The old man sometimes slept there if he had an early start, or a late- night poker game. You can't sleep in the car."

"Are you sure? I don't want to cause problems with your father."

"It's only for a few hours. I'm the boss here now. He's not around much."

He flicked on the lights and allowed her to go first up the stairs. He had an ulterior motive. He wanted to see if her ass was as firm as he remembered. She didn't disappoint.

Upstairs, she could not help but be drawn to the wall of family and client photographs his father had collected. He suspected that subconsciously he had planned she would see this. She found many photographs of them both, taken at football games and in school events, and happily pointed them out to him. It brought lots of memories rushing back, some good, some painful. There were a few pictures from prom night. Lauren stopped talking, and stared at the image of him and Maggie on stage. "I'll be back in a few minutes." He retreated, uncomfortably aware of the painful ones.

As he rummaged in a cupboard for something dry for her to wear, he heard her soft chuckle. She must have found the ones of him as a child. He found some clean coveralls and a sweatshirt. "Not glamorous, but dry and clean." He handed them over and showed her where the washer dryer was in the back so she could dry her wet clothes, and left her to it.

DOWNSTAIRS, THE CLOCK INCHED FORWARD INTO THE WEE SMALL

hours of Saturday morning. The only sounds in the open space were metal on metal as Tommy replaced the worn and damaged carburettor, fan belt and alternator using spare parts from the old abandoned car he had gone back and picked up.

Tommy slid out from under the car, rose stiffly to his feet and arched his back. He pulled a crumpled rag from his back pocket and wiped the oil and grease from his hands. The cold and damp had seeped into the garage, drifted across the concrete floor and permeated his exhausted body, causing his joints to ache.

Despite the depressing weather, his spirits had lifted in the last few hours while reminiscing about the good times with Lauren as a teenager. What had started out as friendship in junior high had slowly turned to something deeper, something only they were privy to, far away from school or town or friends. They had been good together. No denying it.

She had been there for him when his older brother Rob died, when he hated the world and couldn't face another well-intentioned condolence speech. She had been there for him when he didn't make the cut in football, and applauded him when he began to make runs in baseball.

He had been there for her when her mother ran off and her family fell apart. He thought of her now, upstairs, just a few metres away, wearing his coveralls and his old sweatshirt that had worn soft with constant wear. He imagined her getting changed, pulling the sweatshirt down over her head, the fabric bunching up over her naked breasts, getting caught on her tiny pebbled nipples, before it fell to her bare thighs. Those nipples he had licked and knew so well. Those nipples he had sucked while he worked his fingers inside the edge of her cotton panties as they sat in the back seat of his first car. Those nipples he had hovered over as she took him in her warm, soft hand and slowly stroked him to orgasm. *Fuck.* No way he was going to sleep tonight with this raging hard-on. Better get back to fixing the car.

CHAPTER TWO

TOMMY WASN'T THE ONLY NIGHT OWL. LAUREN HADN'T HAD A wink of sleep since she pulled the blanket up over her in a vain attempt to try and stop shaking. She couldn't get warm enough to sleep. Or was it nerves that kept her awake? She couldn't stop her mind from racing. *God, who was she kidding*? She wasn't going to get any sleep tonight with Tommy working on her car, and that hard-muscled body only a staircase away.

The wooden stairs didn't creak as she crept down in her bare feet, but to her surprise the workroom was empty. The lights were on but there was no one home. *Where the hell was he?* She bent down and searched under the car, just in case. Nope. She picked up a baseball hat from the floor. His name had been stencilled inside. She ran her finger over the writing. When he came up behind her, she experienced his arrival before she heard him. The hair on the back of her neck and arms stood up, and her stomach did a little tumble. He smelled of rain and motor oil, a familiar smell she remembered, and one he could never completely get rid of. The downside of helping his father in the garage after school. She didn't have to turn around to know he had bent his head down to smell her hair. The closer he leant in, the more her body responded. A delicious shiver ran up her spine.

"You're still using that coconut shampoo."

"Some things never change." She turned to see he was holding two takeaway cups of coffee.

"You have. You're all grown up now." His eyes wandered a little over her body. "Even in those coveralls you look all woman."

"Talking about coveralls, I notice Slater & Son on the back. Did your father have problems after the heart attack?"

"Yeah, he knew he couldn't work here like he used to. He had open-heart surgery. He changed the name from Slater & Sons when Rob died, but he transferred the ownership to me earlier this year. I guess there is no need to change the name again for the moment. He has to take it easy. Still helps out from time to time with advice, but the heavy work is down to me and Don. Remember Don Cooper? He was a couple of years below us. Used to hang out with us at the diner sometimes. His family lived down near the river."

"He was a quiet kid from memory. Big for his age. And strong. I felt sorry for him. He got teased a lot. Struggled a bit with school, if I remember correctly. Always playing hooky and going fishing."

"Most people thought he was a bit slow. He's a quiet guy alright. Keeps to himself. Turns out he's a miracle worker with car engines. Or anything mechanical. He's a good worker. Takes a lot of the stress off the old man knowing we can keep the business goin'." He motioned to the table in the corner. "Do you want to have a seat?" He handed her a coffee. "I don't know how you like it, you weren't much of a coffee drinker, but I took a guess on white with one."

"Let me guess. Yours is black, double shot. Yeah?" The crooked smile he gave her just as he lifted the cup to his lips told her she was right. That crooked smile had been her undoing many times in her youth.

"Did you sleep?"

"Not a wink. But thanks for the use of the couch."

"I think the car is fixed. I'll take it out for a test drive once the sun comes up. Could you follow in the truck just in case?"

"Sure. I'll get dressed. My things should be dry."

"No rush. Drink your coffee. The sun won't be up for another twenty minutes. So tell me, what sort of work do you do?"

"Oh. I'm not working at the moment. Between jobs. You know how it is. It's tough out there."

"Yeah. What were you doin' when you were employed?"

"I was in journalism. Had a column in the paper under a pseudonym."

"What was the name of the column?"

"The Bitter Pill."

"No way. You're Pippa Stone? I followed that column every week when I was in New York. Hell, you were good. I enjoyed the articles on travel." He sat back and grinned at her. "I noticed the column disappeared. Why did they pull the plug?"

"Some people in high places didn't like me delving into their private lives. *C'est la vie.* I travelled around a lot since I left Clearwater Springs. A perk of the job to be honest."

"No kiddin'! And here I was thinking I had travelled a bit, going over the other side of the country to play ball in New York State."

"Times have changed though. No one is hiring. Or they have been warned off. As I said, I ticked off some very influential people. The money is running out fast, what with rent and expenses. I hadn't prepared to be out of work. So I thought I would write."

"Write, huh. What?"

"A novel, actually. I'm halfway through. It's about a small town, like this one."

"Let me know when it's out there. I'll buy a copy."

"Sure." Lauren dropped her gaze to her fingers wrapped around the takeaway cup. A frown creased her brow.

"Being out of work is tough. I don't see a wedding ring. But I guess your boyfriend is helping you out?"

"No. No ring and no boyfriend. I have enough to get by for a little while if I'm careful. I had a good teacher when it came to making money last."

"Yeah, your dad was a tight-fisted old sod."

"Well, he's gone to a place where money is no object now, hasn't he."

"Yeah, I heard he passed away. You okay? Did you ever find your mother?"

"Nope."

"Sorry, I know it was a sore point. I just thought . . ."

"She doesn't want to be found. Best leave that one alone." The steely look she gave him shut down any further questions.

THE SUN'S WATERY RAYS FILTERED THROUGH THE WINDOW. TOMMY pushed back his chair and tossed the coffee cup into the trash.

"Let's take her out on the road."

"Give me five minutes to get dressed."

"We can drive by Jake's Diner out by the lake and I'll buy breakfast."

"Driving down memory lane, Tommy?"

"Sure, why not? That's what this weekend is all about, isn't it. Taking a step back to the past. The class reunion get-together, seeing old friends."

"Some things I don't want to remember."

He reached out and grabbed her arm as she passed him. "Some things I can't forget."

The few inches of air between them vibrated with emotion. He watched her lick her lips, the tip of her tongue sweeping over from one side to the other and then darting inside. He longed to bend his head and place his whiskered cheek against hers, and close his eyes in anticipation of the slow glide of his lips to find their mate.

Heavy footsteps shattered that fantasy. A man appeared at the garage door, carrying a paper sack advertising the local fast-food restaurant. He stopped mid stride, and turned around to leave.

"Hey Don, come back."

"Don't wanna interrupt anythin'."

"You remember Lauren? We're just about to head out to test drive her car, and get some breakfast. You can get started on the abandoned car I found out by Silversmith Lane. I've taken a few parts, but you can strip off the rest. Keep anythin' you think we can use."

"Hey, Lauren. Back for the reunion?" Don kept his head down. He shuffled from one foot to another and clutched his takeaway close to his chest.

"That's right, Don. A flying visit."

Tommy could see the wheels turning inside Don's head as he glanced up and his eyes skittered over the coveralls she wore, and then down to Lauren's bare feet. *Fuck.* News travels fast in this small town, and he didn't need this getting back to his old man before he had a chance to explain.

"Let's go. Okay?" Tommy hooked a thumb in the direction of the car.

"I'll be back in five." Lauren took the stairs two at a time and disappeared into the office.

"I'd appreciate it if you would keep quiet about Lauren being here, Don. I'm helping her out. Her car broke down on the way into town last night."

"Sure, Tommy. You're the boss."

Lauren appeared at the top of the stairs wearing her crushed shirt and jeans, and tugging on her ankle boots. She had pulled her dark brown hair back into a ponytail, accentuating her high cheekbones and long neck. His daydreams of her had put her on a pedestal, but now she was here, in front of him, and he saw that the picture he had in his mind was real. Flesh and blood Lauren was everything he had imagined. And more.

THE REPAIRS PROVED TO BE SUCCESSFUL. LAUREN'S CAR PERFORMED as it should and it wasn't too long before both vehicles pulled up at Jake's. Lauren noticed the diner had been given a fresh coat of paint, and the sign above the door had been replaced, but most of the external appearance hadn't changed much at all. The shiver that ran down her spine had more to do with the fresh morning air, and less to do with the memories this place evoked in her. At least, that was the line she was telling herself as she opened the front door and stopped dead in her tracks.

Maybelline Jones stood behind the laminated counter, pouring coffee into a customer's mug, her cheeks as full and rosy as Lauren remembered, her snowy-white hair pulled up into a soft bun on top of her head. She wore the same tortoiseshell-framed glasses; the same cotton-candy pink-striped uniform with the white Peter Pan collar, albeit a little larger. The moment she looked up and spotted Lauren, her smile became almost as wide as the arms she stretched out to welcome her. She rushed forward and hugged Lauren so tight, holding her to her ample bosom. It took Lauren's breath away.

"Lord, will you have a look at who just walked back into my life! Lauren Taylor, you are a sight for sore eyes, you sure are." Maybelline took a step back, holding Lauren at arm's length as she looked her up and down. "You're all grown up. And such a beauty too."

"Maybelline, you sweet talker! You haven't changed at all. I didn't think you'd still be working. Weren't you close to retiring to help look after your grandchildren?"

"Tried that. Didn't last long. Angie's husband got a job in Texas, so when they moved away I came back here. Best to keep busy. As for looking the same, my chassis has gained a few pounds over the years." She patted her tummy, and chuckled. "Looks like I am going to have all my schoolkids back for the reunion this year. Isn't it great."

"Hey Maybelline. Don't mind me. I don't get that kind of

welcome with my coffee." Tommy pulled out a chair and sat by the window.

"Tommy Slater, you hush now. How come you didn't tell me Lauren was coming back this year?"

"It was news to me too."

"No one knew I was coming back except Sarah Harper. She kept phoning till I had to say yes."

"Ah, Sarah. Such a terrible thing to have happened to her. She's got two young kids to look after too. I hear she is in remission though."

"Yes, things are looking up for her at last."

"What can I get you? Breakfast? Or are you just here for coffee?" Maybelline picked up a menu from the next table and handed it to Lauren. She pulled a pad and pencil out of her apron pocket.

"I promised you breakfast. So what takes your fancy?" Tommy tried to hide the cheeky smile, but the wink he gave Maybelline, and the twinkle in his eye gave the game away.

"Is that your way of saying coffee, tea or me? Back in your box, hotshot."

"Can't fault a guy for tryin'."

"I'll have pancakes please, Maybelline, with strawberries and blueberries on the side. And a glass of orange juice."

"No coffee?"

"I've had my fix of coffee for the morning. Juice will be fine. Thanks."

"And you, young fella?"

"I'll have the same. But with coffee." Tommy handed the menu back to Maybelline, who headed for the kitchen.

"So what's the damage? How much do I owe you for the car?"

"I took the parts from the old car, so it's just labour really. Since you're having a bad time, let's say you owe me."

"I pay my debts, Tommy. How much?

"Tell you what. I don't have a date for the reunion dinner. So how about you come along with me and we'll call it even."

"I don't think that's a good idea."

"Why not?"

"People will talk. And I know they already have such a high opinion of me. But you don't want to be dragged into it. You have to live here, but I go back to the city on Monday."

"As long as you don't leave town as suddenly as the last time, I think I can live with the talk."

The memory of that night suddenly surfaced, and Lauren tried hard to retain her smile.

"When you left with Brett Hagar, I gotta tell you, it was hard . . ." "What?" Lauren's face drained of colour. "Left with Brett Hagar . . . what makes you think I left with Brett?"

"You didn't answer my calls. You left town that night and so did Brett. It was pretty obvious. Everyone was talkin' about it."

"Well everyone, including you, was wrong. I left on my own." Lauren pushed back her chair. "Don't worry about the breakfast." She rummaged in her bag and pulled some bills out of her wallet. "Will this be enough for the repairs?"

"Why are you getting all riled up? Shit. I'm only repeating the talk back then. If you say you didn't then I believe you. You must admit it's strange. A few people saw you with him at the prom, they said you looked pretty cosy."

"If you believed everything you heard in this town, I would have had a few teenage kids in tow by now. I was supposed to be pregnant every other week. To somebody new. Those stuck-up bitches, and you know who I am talking about, had me dating every guy in school. Did you ever wonder why Maggie Cuthbert hated my guts, Tommy?"

"Oh, she wasn't that bad."

"She had the hots for you all through school, and she couldn't get you fair and square, so she did everything she could to come between us. She knew what she was doing at the prom. Kissing you. Practically swallowing you whole on stage. And you loved every minute of it. Admit it. It's every man's dream to have women fighting over them. The only thing was, I wasn't fighting *her* for *you*."

"Well, you made that pretty obvious when you left without saying goodbye."

"I had my reasons. And no, I don't want to talk about it now." "Okay, calm down. I didn't mean to upset you. Stay for breakfast. Please."

Maybelline brought the plates of steaming pancakes to the table, ending the tense conversation. Lauren picked up her knife and fork reluctantly. She had to admit that a lot of water had flowed under the bridge in the last fifteen years, but there was no reason to take it out on Tommy. Returning to this town brought the ghosts out of the woodwork. She could see the frown lines on Tommy's brow as he chewed, and she knew without a shadow of a doubt that he would bring it up again. He was like a dog with a bone when he wore that stubborn expression.

The question she was asking herself now was how much should she tell him.

A loud argument outside the diner had people swivelling in their seats.

The door opened and the police chief entered, clutching a scruffy- looking man by his collar and forcing him ahead of him. He let him go at the counter.

"Caught this guy going through your rubbish again, Maybelline.

Give him a takeaway sandwich and a coffee on me."

"I don't want your charity, Chief." The man appeared to shrink into himself when the police chief released him.

"It's only a sandwich, Marty. About time you went back to the mission and tried to clean up your act, don't you think. People are worried about you."

"Everyone should mind their own business. Thanks, May." Marty took the brown paper bag Maybelline held out, picked up takeaway coffee and shambled out the door.

"Who is that?" Lauren stared at the retreating figure, trying to place him.

"Marty James. Colin's father. Remember he was Rob's best friend in high school?" Tommy shook his head.

"Yeah I remember Colin. God, what happened to him? He can't be more than fifty-five and he looks about seventy."

"Lost his job a few years ago. Seems he was fond of gambling and booze. Got hooked when he travelled for work. Gambled away any money he had in the bank. Lost the house, his wife left him, took the kids."

"Looks like he sleeps rough."

"Yeah. He stays at the mission a few nights on and off when he's sober. Picks up some work from time to time, but nothing permanent."

"The police chief looks familiar. He was a sergeant, wasn't he?"

"Yeah, Greg Bailey, he's been around a few years. He left school before us and joined the force. He picked us up that night the car broke down after the game."

"Thought I remembered him. He's gained a few pounds." Lauren chewed her pancakes and glanced at the counter. The police chief had turned around to eat his breakfast. Another memory surfaced of him holding out his hand to help her off the ground, after she had passed out. She buried it again. Quickly.

CHAPTER THREE

LAUREN MARCHED UP TO THE FRONT DOOR AND RANG THE BELL. She could hear kids running around inside squealing and giggling. She rang the bell again. The door opened suddenly. A girl of about four, with long blonde curly hair tumbling over her shoulders, and big blue eyes, dressed as Wonder Woman and carrying a wooden spoon, gazed up at her. A boy slightly older with similar features and sporting a blond buzz cut pushed in front of her, obviously preparing to take the lead on the interrogation. He placed a hand protectively around the little girl's shoulders.

"You shouldn't open the door to strangers, Milly. You know that. Who are you, and what do you want? If you are selling anything we don't want it. If you are collecting for something we haven't got any money. Bye!" He promptly closed the door.

Lauren rang the bell again. She tried not to smile as the small man of the house opened the door and puffed out his chest. "Go away, or I'll call the police."

"I've come to see your mom. Is she home?"

"She's upstairs . . . Mooooom . . . there's a lady at the door . . . what's your name?"

"Lauren. I'm a friend of your mom's."

"Mooooom . . . there's a lady at the door. Says she's Lauren, and she's your friend."

Footsteps could be heard and squeals of laughter, as someone came hurrying down the stairs. Two small people stared wide-eyed at the woman who had caused such a ruckus. The door was yanked open wide, and Sarah joyfully hugged Lauren, dragging her inside.

"Milly and Jake, meet Lauren. My friend from high school. Lauren, these two are my little superheroes. Now go play Wonder Woman and Batman or whoever out back so we can catch up, okay. I'll fix some snacks and come get you." Sarah gave Jake a playful shove in the direction of the kitchen. The kids took off, with Milly's cape flying behind her.

"It is so good to see you. When did you get here? Where are you staying?"

"I got here last night, but the car broke down. As of this morning, I'm staying in town at the Holiday Inn."

"Why didn't you call me to pick you up? Where's your car now?" As she closed the door, Sarah peered behind Lauren at the car parked beside the curb. "Whose car is that?" She took Lauren's arm and guided her into the sunny open-plan kitchen and family room.

"That's mine. Tommy found me out on Cedar, and helped me get her up and running again."

"Tommy? Tommy Slater? Oh my, Lauren. That must have been very interesting."

"Yes, you forgot to tell me he was back in Clearwater. A deliberate omission by any chance?"

"No. Well . . . maybe. I wanted you to come back for the reunion. If you had known he was here you wouldn't have. Would you?"

"Very sneaky, Sarah. I shouldn't forgive you. But I will. He's turned into quite a hunk, hasn't he?"

"That he has. He's filled out in all the right places for sure. But more importantly, he came back to help his family. Which means he goes up in my estimation. He wasn't a bad kid at school, but he was a bit full of himself. So eager to get out of town and make it big. I heard he had an injury. His game wasn't as good after that. Talk in town was that he came home before they got rid of him. But then, talk in town is never favourable, is it?"

"You and I could write a book on how many things they 'got wrong' over the years. Matter of fact I've started writing one already. I've changed the location and names to protect the innocent, of course. But there was so much material I could use from my childhood here. I couldn't pass that up. And since I'm not working, it makes sense to keep busy."

"Yeah. How's the job hunting going?"

"Nothing out there as yet. I'm not giving up though. Just changing my approach for a while."

"You look good, Lauren. Being a starving journalist is working wonders for your bone structure."

"Ditto. You're rockin' the short hair. Who would have thought it would grow back curly?"

"One of the perks of chemo, I'm told."

Lauren reached out and hugged her friend tight. For a few seconds neither woman spoke. Sarah broke free first.

"Right. Let's get some coffee and cake. I made a ton of food knowing you were coming. I hope you're hungry? I made a chocolate mud cake. It was always your favourite. I hope that hasn't changed?"

"I would never turn down some of your chocolate cake." Lauren pulled out a stool at the high bench. "Sarah, I'm impressed." Lauren looked around her at the warm and welcoming kitchen and family room layout. "This is lovely. You've been here a few years. Did you renovate?"

"Yeah, Sam's grandfather was a carpenter, so he inherited that gift. And he's enjoyed making things with wood. Even though he's a maths teacher, he's really good with his hands. Saved a ton of money doin' things ourselves. I used to help out until I got sick. It came as a bit of a shock. No time is a good time to get cancer, but we were struggling to make payments on the house, so it couldn't have come at a worst time. But things are good now. Sam got a promotion, so we're doin' okay."

"Must be nice to own your home, put down roots."

"You need to find a good man and settle down too. Hint, hint." Sarah cut the cake and handed Lauren a plate.

"You don't need to find a man to own a home. You just need to have the cash."

"Settling down is not all about the house. It's about finding someone who has your back. Someone you can rely on to be there for you. So that you can *both* make a home together."

"I'm changing the subject now. What are you wearing tonight?" Lauren dipped her finger in the chocolate frosting and licked it off. She took a large forkful of cake and closed her eyes as the gooey chocolate melted on her tongue. "I might not fit into my dress after I eat this cake, it's divine!"

"Thanks. But you're not getting off that easy. I'll come back to this subject later. As for the frosting. I took a class in cake decorating. It's nice to get to show off my new skills now and again."

"I haven't baked for years. Can't remember the last time I used my oven, actually. I am more of a microwave kinda gal these days. Take-out meals are easier."

"I don't know how you keep your figure if you don't eat well, Lauren. But it's your health I worry about. The rubbish they put in packaged foods these days. You should try to eat fresh unprocessed foods and vegetables and fruit. You shouldn't take chances with your health. Take it from one who knows."

"I hear you."

"Lecture over. To answer your question, I picked up a dress on sale. It was a bargain. The upside to being a stick-thin woman is I can pick up small dress sizes. They are usually the last ones on the rack."

"I bought my dress especially for this evening too."

"Are you trying to impress anyone in particular?"

"When I bought it, I just wanted to look good and stick it to those bitches that gave me a hard time all through school. But now I'm hoping Tommy might be impressed. He's taking me as his date to the reunion dinner."

"Hey girl. You work fast."

"It was his idea, actually. He asked me to be his date in lieu of payment for fixing my car. Although I think there will still be payment required. But it's a fee I can handle. He has grown into quite a handsome man."

"Don't be surprised if all eyes are on you. There are a few women in this town trying to get Tommy Slater's attention. I will take great delight tonight, watching them turn green with envy."

"I'd better get back to the hotel and try to get some sleep. It was impossible last night."

"Anything you want to share?"

"No, nothing happened. I tried to sleep on the couch in Tommy's office. But I was too wound up."

"I'll see you later at the school. About seven. Dinner starts at seven-thirty." Sarah followed Lauren to the door.

"Okay. And Sarah, I'm kinda glad I came back for the reunion." Lauren leant over and hugged her friend.

"Yeah. I thought you might be. Make sure you relax enough tonight to enjoy your date with Tommy. Don't let the jealous bitches get under your skin."

"Believe me, I'll try."

LAUREN HELD ONTO THAT THOUGHT ALL THE WAY BACK TO THE hotel. Her stomach clenched with both nerves and excitement at the thought of attending the reunion with Tommy. When she pulled the curtains shut and set her alarm, the main thing on her mind was getting some beauty sleep, to get rid of the bags under her eyes. She needed to look her best. Not to show off to those gossiping women.

To show Tommy what he had been missing these last few years.

But sleep evaded her. Instead she tossed and turned, her mind filled with images of her younger self, the insecure young woman she thought she had left behind. That last year of school had been a disaster. She didn't relish revisiting the place that caused her such pain. She didn't like sneaking out to meet Tommy. Or the fact they had kept their relationship secret. She had wanted to shout it from the rooftops but Tommy had wanted to keep it quiet. She had never understood why, and had put it down to the fact that she was unworthy. Feeling unworthy meant she had been unable to argue with him. Any time they spent together had been a bonus for her. Any time she had spent out of the house had been like freedom from prison. Her father had not taken the last few years without her mother well. He had become mean in many ways. Mean with money, mean with the time he spent at home, and mean with his affection towards his only daughter. It was as if he blamed her in some way for her mother abandoning them. Truth be told, Lauren blamed herself as well. She rationalised that if she had been more helpful around the house, if she had been a better student, a better daughter . . . then maybe her mother would have stayed. Another plain and simple fact was that she looked so like her mother that her father hardly glanced at her. She saw the pain in his eyes when he did, and so she stayed out of his way as much as possible.

With a sigh, she wrenched the covers back and gave up her illusive quest for beauty sleep.

She pulled a royal blue dress from the closet and laid it on the bed. Her fingers ran over the soft fabric, imagining what it would be like to be dressed up tonight, her hair done, make-up on. What it would be like to dance in Tommy's arms, lay her head on his shoulder. Would he hold her close? Her fingers trembled. She checked her watch. *Time to have a shower and get ready.*

The warm water running over her skin relaxed her, and as she soaped her body she thought of how nice it would be to feel a man's hands on her again. It had been a long time since anyone had held her, let alone made love to her. Wait a minute. *You are getting ahead of yourself here. He's taking you to a dance. No one said anything about making love.* No one said anything about fucking either . . . but that was clearly on her mind.

CHAPTER FOUR

By the time she'd dressed, added a sweep of black liner and mascara, a coat of deep red lipstick, attached a necklace and bracelet and took a step back from the mirror, she had five minutes to tidy the room before he arrived. She smoothed out the covers on the bed and put away her jeans and shoes in the closet. She plumped up the cushions on the couch, telling herself it was because she wanted to make a good impression. *Yeah, it's not about getting him in the sack.*

Nope. Not at all.

A knock on the door stopped her halfway to the bathroom. She slipped into her heels and pulled the clip from her hair, allowing the cascade of chestnut curls to drop to her shoulders. One more quick glance in the mirror and then she opened the door. The moment she saw him, desire flared in her stomach, and her fingers fiddled with her necklace in an attempt to distract her and hide the nerves that had surfaced. He looked so damned sexy. *Whipped cream with a cherry on top never looked that good.*

"Come in. I'm ready." She stood back to allow him to enter. Spicy aftershave, and the heady aroma of warm male skin wafted towards her. Her nostrils couldn't get enough of him. She rose up a little and kissed his cheek, inhaling deeply. Then stepped back before she got carried away. Pleasure gathered between her thighs. Her fingers itched to touch him. *No need to rush. We have all night.*

"Wow, you look great. That dress . . . it clings to all the right places. No doubt about that." He took her hand, raised it above her head and twirled her around. The soft chiffon skirt floated around her knees.

"I'll take that as a compliment. Thank you. I bought it especially for this occasion."

"I'm feeling a little underdressed now. I should have brought a jacket."

"A white shirt looks good on you. Always did." Her eyes were drawn to the snug-fitting dark navy pants and dark brown tooled cowboy boots. *Smokin' hot, just as he was. No jacket required.*

"Shall we go? I brought the old man's car. It's more comfortable than my truck. Wouldn't want to get grease or oil on that dress."

"Hang on, I'll grab a wrap."

"I don't think you'll need one. It's pretty warm out there tonight."

"It might get cold later."

"I'll make sure you won't get cold. I could warm you up . . . I mean, I'll have you back in the car before you get cold." His cheeky grin told another story.

"You never were very good at poker, were you, Tommy." She smiled at him, glad they were on the same wavelength. She straightened his tie, and fought very hard to keep her hands from wandering all over his impressive shoulders.

He reached out and tucked a curl behind her ear. "I'm hoping I get very lucky tonight."

Lauren melted a little more as his fingers rested on the soft skin beneath her ear for a heartbeat or two.

"We'd better get going. Sarah is keeping a seat for us at her table." Lauren reluctantly pulled away to open the door. *Go now or you never will.*

Tommy reached around her and opened it first. "Ladies first." Lauren couldn't help but be impressed with this older version of

Tommy. Courteous, kind and a gentleman.

She couldn't wait to explore his other grown-up qualities.

THE CROWDED SCHOOL HALL HAD BEEN DECORATED IN THE STYLE and fashion of their final year. Banners on the walls announced the latest crazes, the popular bands and the fashions of the time. Sarah and another old classmate, Justin West, manned the welcome table positioned just inside the main door. Badges with student's names and quotes from their yearbook adorned the table. Sarah ticked off names and handed out badges. Justin lassoed the men into buying raffle tickets and selecting numbers for door prizes. Many local businesses had got into the swing of things and offered donations of produce or services. There was even a weekend at the local Rendezvous Hotel, with a complimentary romantic dinner for a very lucky couple. Tommy bought a small book of twenty tickets.

Lauren helped Tommy attach his name badge to his shirt pocket, and then pinned hers in place.

"Would you like a drink? There's a bar set up over in the corner."

"Sure. I'll have a beer."

"A beer? I thought you would want a glass of wine, or champagne."

"Isn't this reunion supposed to be taking us back to our youth? I used to drink beer."

"Don't let that cat out of the bag too loudly. You were underage back then. Police Chief Bailey over there might arrest you." Tommy took Lauren's hand and pulled her in the direction of the bar.

"He was a few years ahead of us in school. What's he doing here?"

"He married Maggie Cuthbert."

"No way. I would never have taken her for the kind of girl to marry a cop."

"Well, when you get yourself pregnant straight out of school, you don't have a lot of choices."

He handed her a bottle. "I'll go get a glass for that."

"Don't rush, I can cope. It's not the first beer I've downed straight from the bottle."

"I'll get you a glass, Lauren." He shot her a concerned look.

"Yeah, maybe I had better act more like a lady tonight. The tongues will be wagging."

They worked their way through the crowds to the table on the edge of the dance floor, where they were joined by Sarah and her husband. Once the introductions were made, Sam pulled the chair out for Sarah, and held her hand on top of the table. Lauren could see the love he had for his wife in every gesture.

"Some turnout, nearly everyone's here." Sarah proudly announced. "The money raised from tonight is going to extend the children's ward in the local hospital."

"I bought a book of tickets." Tommy waved the small book of blue tickets at Lauren.

"Did the weekend at the Rendezvous Hotel and a romantic dinner for two have something to do with it?" Sarah flashed a smile in Tommy's direction.

"It might have. But who would I take to a romantic dinner for two?" He raised an eyebrow and shot Lauren a questioning look.

"What a pity I'm going home on Monday. But you're counting your chickens. You haven't won it yet." Lauren sat back grinning, and crossed her arms over her chest.

"I've already told you. I'm feeling lucky tonight." Tommy winked at Lauren. He gave her his trademark lopsided grin, and her heart fluttered. Like her fifteen-year-old self. Back then a look from Tommy, or a secret wink, brought tingles to places untouched by a boy. Warmed her flesh and brought her imagination to life. No one had ever had the same effect on her most powerful erogenous zone since.

More classmates arrived to take up positions at their table. By the time the entree had been served, Lauren was on her second beer and Tommy was telling tales of his time playing ball in New York. The conversations flowed around jobs and children and hobbies and cars. Lauren had begun to relax and enjoy the evening. Much to her surprise. She ordered a whiskey and soda from a passing waiter.

"I like this song. Would you like to dance?" Tommy leant in close and whispered in her ear. Zings of pleasure rippled through her when his lips touched her lobes.

Lauren would never have taken Tommy for a dancer. He never showed any talent or interest in that regard, when they were at school. They would just sway to the music, she figured. Good humour and a couple of beers meant she played along. But, she couldn't have been more wrong. From the moment they took to the floor, he held her in such a way that demonstrated he knew what he was doing. Every move appeared effortless, yet with every twist, with every turn, he danced her into a state of amazement.

His hand placed exactly in the right position on her back, guiding her with slight pressure to turn left or right, his strong torso and arms supported and twirled her with minimal effort. *I have underestimated this man.* He lifted her off her feet at one point, as if she weighed nothing at all, and without breaking a sweat. His lips curled up in a smile that was all for her. Impressed could not convey her emotions on that dance floor. Blown away was more like it. All her defences started to crumble. A man who could dance, *really dance*, in this day and age, was a rare thing indeed. Tommy had somehow managed to move further up in her estimation. Tonight was shaping up to be very special indeed. Her insides quivered with longing.

Tommy held her elbow to guide her back to the table. She drank her whiskey greedily.

"I'd say by the look on your face you enjoyed that." Sarah clapped softly as they re-joined the table. She turned to her husband. "Maybe dance lessons would be a good anniversary gift next year, hey?"

"They're going to draw the grand prize." Tommy turned his chair around to get a better view of the stage, and Principal Martinez at the microphone.

"I'd like to thank you all for returning tonight to mark this fifteen-year reunion. Some people have come all the way across the country for this celebration. It pleases me to see so many familiar faces. We have raised a substantial figure for the children's hospital tonight. I won't announce the amount yet as there are still some fundraising activities tomorrow at the time capsule unveiling. A cake stall is being set up by the reunion committee, and a barbeque, with the meat supplied by Jake's Diner, will be provided afterwards for anyone wanting to stay on at the school to socialise. Families are welcome."

"Without further ado, I'd like to draw the grand prize of a weekend at our wonderful Rendezvous Hotel and a dinner for two lucky people. Drum roll if you please."

Principal Martinez's secretary held up a cardboard box. He rummaged around in the box and extracted a blue ticket.

Lauren squeezed Tommy's hand. "It's blue."

"I can see that." Tommy winked.

". . . and the winner is . . . Tommy Slater. Come on up here and collect your prize." The principal shook Tommy's hand and gave him the embossed envelope.

Tommy returned to the table, and pulled out the voucher and accompanying letter.

"You're going to have to come back and help me use this voucher. Look at the list of extras." Tommy waved the voucher in Lauren's direction.

"You want me to drive all the way back here for a weekend at a hotel."

"Not just a weekend at a hotel. A weekend with me, at a hotel. With dinner for two. Plus a list of extras. Beauty spa. Champagne on arrival. Chocolates. A fruit basket. Come on. How can you say no to this?"

"It's a pretty good deal, for sure." Sarah said.

"Say you'll think about it." Tommy fanned her face with the voucher.

"I'll think about it." Lauren reached over and took Tommy's hand. Across the table, Sarah was grinning at their exchange. She lifted an eyebrow. Lauren shrugged her shoulders. "I will. I'll think about it."

IF SHE THOUGHT DANCING WITH TOMMY HAD BROUGHT OUT THE need in her . . . Sitting with him on the long drive back to the hotel, without touching, without talking, with only one thing on her mind . . . *hopefully on his too* . . .

"It was a great night, don't you think?"

"Sure."

"You're mighty quiet. Tired?" Lauren turned a little to face him. "No, not tired. Thinkin' about how good you looked in that dress tonight. How all the guys were wishin' they were me on the dance floor."

"I think you have that whole scene wrong. All the women were wishing they were dancing with you tonight. You sure kept that quiet all through school. Where did you learn those moves?"

"I never liked to dance in front of people, always felt uncomfortable. But I took some lessons in Boston. The teacher said I was a natural, so I took some more. Reckon I spent a ton of money on those lessons. Worth it if I got your attention."

Oh, you got my attention all right. "I haven't danced that much in a long time. So if you asked me, I would say the lessons were worth it." Lauren shivered remembering how hard those muscles felt, smack up against her for their time on the dance floor. It made her think of the many and varied ways in which she could experience those hard, rippling muscles back at the hotel.

"Are you cold? I'll turn on the heater." Tommy flipped a switch and the car warmed up instantly.

No, honey, I'm not cold. Not cold at all. Lauren slid down a little in the seat, and turned her attention to traffic flashing past. Anything to get her mind off the ache low in her belly.

And the desire to reach over and put her hand on his thigh.

CHAPTER FIVE

His hand sitting at the base of her spine, gently guiding her, burned through the thin fabric of her dress. Warmth flooded her limbs and although every fibre of her being wanted to turn around and melt into his embrace, she held back. *Not in a public car park*. The walk to her room gave her time it took to argue with herself that going to bed with Tommy was not a good idea. It would stir up old wounds, would cause her to doubt herself, doubt where she wanted to be. Because she sure as hell did not want to be back in Clearwater Springs. The time for that had passed. Oh, she had considered returning years ago, before he left, mainly because she wanted to see if he still cared. But returning to a town where everyone knew your intimate business stifled and suffocated her, to the point of hyperventilation, when she allowed those negative thoughts to invade her mind.

She had difficulty fitting the key in the lock. Her fingers shook. He reached around her and gently took the key from her grasp, slid it into the lock and pushed the door wide. She walked ahead, acutely aware now of the absence of his hand and the lack of heat that accompanied it. She turned to see him standing on the threshold. A question in his eyes, in the way he held his body, proudly, warily, gave away his intentions.

"Would you like to come in for a nightcap?" She wobbled slightly. A little unsteady in her heels after a few drinks. A little giddy with lust, if the truth be known.

"I don't think I need any more alcohol tonight." Tommy remained at the open door, pushed his hands into his pockets and stared intently at her lips. "I don't think you do either." The set of his jaw conveyed the internal battle he fought.

"Oh. Well. Would you care to come in for a coffee . . ."

He took two giant steps forward, kicking the door closed with a bang on his way, and crushed his lips against hers, removing all doubt, removing all rational thinking from Lauren's mind. Her hands sought his face, running her fingertips over the stubble on his chin, then delved into the mane of soft dark hair as he bent his head to hers. Had she been asked to describe his kiss before then, she would have been using words like sweet and loving and tender. But this. This was not sweet, this was not tender; this was carnal. Visions ran amok through her brain. Hot-red spikes of passion flashed behind her eyes, which had fluttered closed the moment he had touched her. Every nerve ending, every cell had become alert to this touch, syncing to the weave of his arms and the muscles that rippled in his stomach, as he held his body in check and barely controlled his ardour.

His lips broke away from hers to explore her neck, one large, warm hand sweeping aside her hair and the other cupping her cheek, to inflict a torturous row of tiny nips and kisses all the way down to her collarbone. His tongue dipped into that hollow and feathered upward, eventually resting just below her earlobe. Lauren waited; anticipating his next move and wishing like hell he would hurry up and kiss her again. Tommy pulled away, and Lauren's eyes flew open and she gasped in surprise as he turned her around and tucked her body into the curve of his. His hard torso and her soft curves fused together. In this position, his lips roamed her exposed neck, his hands roamed her body and his obvious attraction pushed hard and urgently against her warm and willing posterior.

"Lauren baby, you sure feel good. But I'm not about to go any further unless you tell me that's what you want."

Lauren snuggled her bottom more firmly into him, lifted his left hand from her waist and placed it over her right breast. His hand slipped inside her dress, cupping and supporting the heavy weight of her, his thumb and first finger pinching her nipple to a tight peak. A delicious tingle of desire ran through her, tugging at her core with every tug of his fingertips. She heard a low moan and realised it was her desire bubbling to the surface. His free right hand had gathered and inched up her skirt until his fingertips grazed her mound. She pushed forward against his hand. Torn between wanting to remain snug against him to feel his arousal and wanting to move towards his searching fingertips, she moaned again and decided being held against him was the better option for now. Squirming, she reached out her hand to lean forward, supporting their combined weight on the back of the small couch, her mind already jumping three steps ahead to accommodate a better outcome.

TOMMY INCHED UP HER DRESS TO REVEAL A SCRAP OF LACE wedged between her cheeks and not much more. The sight of her exposed in this manner notched his desire higher. He hooked his fingers into the sides of the flimsy garment and pulled it down until she wiggled a little and her G-string slithered to her feet. She kicked it aside. Her round bottom presented itself to him, just as lush and perfect as he remembered. He bent down and pressed a kiss to her skin, which was as soft as silk, his lips quirking up at her sudden intake of breath. "Hold on." Tommy ran his hands over her pale, unblemished derriere, revelling in the position in which he now found himself. He counted himself lucky to be given another chance with Lauren.

He reached into his back pocket and removed the condom from his wallet. The sound of the foil tearing appeared loud, even to his ears. He hurriedly sheathed himself making sure of the fit. "Oh no!"

Lauren tried to turn around but he placed a hand at the base of her spine, pushing her forward onto the back of the couch, and held her in her position. "*Oh no* is the last thing a woman wants to hear when her bare butt is in the air, and she is in a very vulnerable position. What's going on?"

"Having some problems with the condom. It split."

"Use another."

"I only have one in my pocket."

"Expecting a big night then were you?"

"I didn't want to be cocky. Do you have any?"

"No. I wasn't expecting to be the one to provide them. I never did before."

"No, I guess I was always the lucky guy that had to appropriate them from the drug store, without Mr Schwartz catching me."

"This is not quite what I had expected." Lauren began to laugh. "Please don't do that." Tommy said.

Oh dear. I've done it now. "I forgot laughing causes a slight alteration to your physical attributes. Let me help." Lauren laughed louder. She groped around behind to grasp him. He pulled away.

"Not helping." Tommy pulled up his underwear and trousers. "Don't put it away." She turned around and yanked Tommy towards her, and overbalanced. They both tumbled over the back of the couch, landing on the seat in a tangle of limbs. Tommy saw the funny side of it and laughed along, until he realised Lauren was now quietly sobbing.

"What's wrong? Why the tears?"

"I had wanted this night to be perfect. I tried, I really did.

Why does it always get screwed up, Tommy? Why do I always screw everything up? I'm a disaster!"

"Don't cry, Lauren. Shhhhh. You *are not* a disaster." Tommy held her tight to his chest, his heart hammering. He had always hated to hear her cry. Her sobbing subdued, and as he stoked her back, he heard a slight snore and realised with regret that she had fallen asleep. *Oh baby, you had one too many drinks, didn't you? Maybe it was better this way.*

Disappointment came crashing down around him.

He carefully moved her to the inside of the couch, got up, tucked in his shirt and fastened his trousers. He pulled the cover off the bed and wrapped it around her, cradling her head against the cushion.

"Sleep tight, sleeping beauty." He bent and gently kissed her forehead. She smiled in her sleep, and squirmed down further into the cushions.

It wasn't surprising. Neither of them had slept the night before. Adrenalin had kept him going. But if he was truthful, he would rather enjoy their first time sober and in bed, after all these years. Not three sheets to the wind, and not in a hurry. He wasn't after a quick fuck on the couch. He wanted to spend the night making love to Lauren. And that thought both excited and scared him.

. .

THE BLINDING LIGHT IN HER EYES, SHINING THROUGH THE OPEN bathroom door, announced that morning had well and truly broken. She struggled to sit up, trying to recall how she had ended up on the couch. *Alone.* It came rushing back to her. The scorching hot kisses, the feel of him nestled against her. *Oh yeah. The broken condom.* The laughter that had ended any attempt at lovemaking. She cast her mind back to the one sure thing that had the power of ruining any sexual games with Tommy back when they were young. He had explained about the teasing,

37

and his brother and his brother's friends' ridicule when he was becoming a teenager and couldn't control the surge of hormones and random erections. Laughter had the ability to stop dead any action in an instant. No amount of reassurance from Lauren that she was not laughing *at him* had made any difference in the past. Looks like it was still an issue. She searched her memory. Did they talk before she passed out? He must be pretty pissed off with me. After all, he had left her, and gone home.

She found her abandoned underwear beside the couch, and tucked it into her dirty laundry bag in the wardrobe, peeled off her rumpled dress and bra and added it to the pile. She headed for the bathroom. The thump, thump, thumping inside her head might quieten down with a hot shower and then some coffee. Maybe a pot or two, or maybe three might do the trick.

THE WAFT OF WARM AIR HIT HER, AND THE SMELL OF GREASY FOOD rolled her stomach, but she marched forward to the counter and took a seat. She removed her sunglasses, placed them on the counter and massaged her temples.

Maybelline appeared from the back, holding a huge tray of powdered sugar donuts.

"Lauren honey, you don't look so good."

"I don't feel so good. Coffee please, May. Keep 'em comin'." She rested her head in her hands.

Maybelline poured her a cup of coffee, and pushed it in front of her bowed head.

"Cream and sugar. I remembered. Do you want some breakfast? . . . or should I say lunch, cos in fifteen minutes it'll be noon."

"Maybe some eggs. Some toast too, please."

"Fried or scrambled?"

Laurens stomach rolled again. "Scrambled please, May. No butter on the toast."

"Watchin' your figure? I heard everything is in its place, and you were lookin' mighty fine last night. Got the lowdown at the breakfast shift, from a few attending the reunion after-party. Heard you left with Tommy."

"Is that a question? Or are you telling me?"

"Don't get snippy with me cos you're hungover, young lady. You're not too old to put over my knee."

Lauren took the first sip of her coffee. The hot liquid and comforting warmth of the cup in her hands momentarily lifted her spirits enough to see she had stepped over the line. "Sorry, May. I am being a grouch today."

She ate her eggs in peace, the diner continuing to operate around her like white noise, her mind going over and over the events of last night until she wanted to scream.

"Penny for your thoughts?" Tommy leant in, his lips brushing her earlobe and sending pleasant shivers through her.

His smile, slow and genuine, reassured her he had not left in anger last night.

"I'd want more than a penny. There's a lot scrambling for attention right now. Like why did you leave?"

"I thought it was better I go home and let you sleep. We were both tired. We can take a rain check if you're up to it after the ceremony tonight?"

"The time capsule?"

"Yeah. They are digging it up at four pm. A blast from the past. Can you remember what you put in there?" Tommy sat down on the stool beside Lauren.

Maybelline appeared with a pot of coffee and another mug. "Can I get you anything to eat Tommy?" She poured him a cup without checking, and slid it towards him.

"You know me too well, May. No. I've eaten. Got to get back to the garage, Don and I are clearing out the old cottage out the back. I might take a spot on your community board and advertise rooms for rent." He turned in Lauren's direction and winked at her. "I spotted Lauren's car, that's why I stopped by."

"I'll see you there at four o'clock then."

"I'll pick you up."

"No. I'll meet you at the school. I'm going to drop by and see Sarah first."

Tommy raised an eyebrow. "Sure." The smile had disappeared from his face.

"I'll catch up with you later, Tommy. I want to see Sarah. Girl talk about the reunion. The dresses, the music, the money they raised."

"Yeah, later. Bye, May. Thanks for the coffee." He placed a bill on the counter, and dropped some change in the tip jar.

Lauren glanced around as he left. Tommy passed a couple of guys at the door without stopping to say hello, and climbed into his truck. *What's his problem? Is he mad at me? Maybe if he had waited until morning, I could have put a smile on his face regardless of the condom fiasco.*

TOMMY THREW THE CAR INTO REVERSE AND GUNNED IT OUT OF THE car park. Lack of sleep and a hangover wasn't helping his current state of mind. His mood had turned sour. All because she brushed off his offer of a ride. Or was it? *Where did the Lauren from last night disappear to? Maybe she has ulterior motives.* Maybe she didn't really want to fuck last night and is making excuses. *She'll be back in the city soon. No point in getting into something again, even for old time's sake.*

WHEN HE ARRIVED AT THE GARAGE, HE DUCKED IN THE SIDE DOOR. He took the stairs to the office two at a time.

His phone rang and he glanced at the screen, and shook his head. He considered turning it off or chucking it into the office and walking away.

"Yeah, what?"

"What the hell are you so ticked off about? You took off like the devil himself was at your heels. Just because I said I wanted time with Sarah, and wouldn't go with you to the time capsule reveal."

"Not just because of that. I got to thinkin'. Maybe it was best we didn't go through with it last night. Maybe it's best we learn from mistakes and keep the libido under wraps. Stay friends."

"Huh? . . . friends. Okay, if that's what you want."

In all honesty, he didn't know what he wanted. Part of him wanted to walk away from whatever had been going on last night, but another part of him wanted to drive back and apologise for being such a hothead and make things right. He wanted another chance with Lauren.

THE AFTERNOON DRAGGED BY. THEY PULLED APART THE SMALL cottage, throwing out all but the bare essentials. Some of the old furniture still looked okay and only needed a facelift, and the walls could do with a coat of paint, but hopefully they could get a few bucks for the space. He locked up and left the garage at three pm to go home and have a cold shower, hoping that his mood would improve. It didn't work. He took a hit of bourbon to see if that helped. Nope. He sat down heavily on the couch. He had finally come to the realisation that it was disappointment sitting like a lead balloon in his gut. He'd messed up big time, and he knew it.

There were only a couple of spots left in the crammed parking lot, indicating a good turnout. The mayor's car was parked beside the entrance. His daughter had been in Lauren's class, so he was officiating. The local police had shown up, and two police cars were parked on the grass in front of the administration building. The music blaring from the speakers drew him to the other side of the football field at the back of the school. The bleachers were filled with friends and family, and the reunion students queued beside a podium to await the unveiling. A ditch had been dug and a pile of dirt stood beside it. Joe, the groundsman, bent over in the hole, shovelling out the last remaining inches of dirt. Tommy noticed Sheriff Bailey standing nearby, arms folded across his broad chest, legs spread, surveying the crowd. *Hardly an event for police presence.* Then he remembered the chief's wife was one of the few by the podium.

The clang of the shovel hitting metal had everyone peering in the hole, smiling and reminiscing with each other about what they would unearth in the treasure chest they had buried. It had been the senior year's decision to bury a large treasure chest rather than an official metal time capsule. They were able to fill it with more exciting memorabilia.

"Ladies and gentlemen, take your seats while we pull out the time capsule and unload it on the table," the mayor announced.

The two rows of folded chairs were quickly filled and another handyman helped Joe out of the ditch with the metal box. The mayor produced a key and upturned the treasure trove onto the long table. The students strained forward to catch a better view. The envelopes with students' names tumbled out. The mayor stood back to allow Principal Martinez and his secretary to spread out the envelopes. Laughter intermingled with quiet exclamations around the table. The names were announced, and the mayor gave a speech. Friends and family came forward and joined the throng of people to view the assorted contents.

Tommy spotted Lauren and Sarah making their way towards his end of the long table as the envelopes had been laid out in alphabetical order, S for Slater siting right alongside the T for Taylor.

"Tommy." Sarah approached Tommy, and squeezed his arm. "This is exciting, don't you think."

"Guess so. Can't remember everything I put in this envelope." He plastered a smile on his face, picked up his packet, and moved back to let Lauren grab hers.

"Hi Tommy." Her curt greeting stung. *Well, what did you expect after that phone call?*

"Lauren." He nodded, his smile frozen in place. Her eyes bored right through him.

"KIDS, GET OUT OF THAT HOLE. YOU'RE GETTING FILTHY." MAGGIE Bailey marched over to where her two youngest boys had made a mess out of the pile of dirt and were now jumping around in the ditch. "Rich, give me your hand and get out of there now. You hear." She pulled six-year-old Richard onto solid ground and started brushing off the dirt from his jeans. She gave him a little push in the direction of his grandparents and turned to help Jordan scramble out.

The scream that tore through the air immobilised half the reunion class and bystanders. The others were hurrying in the direction of the screaming woman to see what the commotion was about.

Maggie Bailey's terrified eight-year-old son Jordan sat a few inches from an excavated portion of a human skull, the rest of which was wedged firmly beneath in the dark brown earth.

CHAPTER SIX

"STAND BACK, PEOPLE." CHIEF BAILEY MOVED THE BYSTANDERS out of the way to get to his hysterical wife and traumatised son. He hugged his wife to his chest, and wrapped an arm around the bewildered child clinging to his thigh.

"Call it in, Deputy." He yelled over his shoulder to his second-in-charge. He ushered his wife and sons away from the grisly site and towards the administration building. "Move people back." He gave orders as he moved through the crowd. "Keep the children away from that hole in the ground."

Tommy leant over the hole to get a better look, only to be shoved back into the crowd by the deputy. "Get back, people. You heard the chief. No one goes into the hole. The coroner is on his way."

"Well, this was not what I expected to happen this afternoon." Sarah guided her children away from the scene. Jake strained his little neck trying to get a glimpse of the skeleton someone had announced was in the hole. Milly, dressed in powder pink with white socks and dainty shoes, did not need any persuading to get well away from the pile of dirt.

"I imagine it's not what the school wanted either." Lauren

grabbed Milly's hand, and noticed the little girl was shivering. No doubt worried by all the adults frantically rushing about and yelling. She picked her up and hugged her to her chest. "How about some nice hot chocolate when we get home, kids. I have marshmallows in my bag." Milly nodded enthusiastically.

"Where is Daddy?" Jake asked.

"He'll be along soon. He's helping the deputy guard the . . . em, the hole in the ground."

Lauren glanced back after she had secured Milly in the car and shut the door.

Looking grim, Tommy stood with his back to the hole, shoulder to shoulder with Don, Sam and the deputy assigned to guard the gravesite. Police were herding up the onlookers and guiding them back to their cars, encouraging them to go home. Another policeman returned the envelopes to the time capsule and handed it over to the principle. A few metres away from Sarah's car, the mayor tried to get into his limousine. The local press, on site for the reveal, huddled around him. They fired questions at him but his consistent answer was, "no comment until the police investigate the scene."

***

"I WONDER HOW THEY'RE DOING AT THE SCHOOL. I THOUGHT SAM would be home by now." Sarah tugged Milly's pyjama top down over the little girl's head.

"A car just pulled up." Lauren continued to pour water from a large jug into tumblers around the table, while Jake placed the knives and forks on the woven place mats. The children hadn't left the adults' sides since they'd returned home, so Lauren and Sarah hadn't had a chance to discuss the discovery of the body.

The front door opened and Sam ushered Tommy ahead of him into the living room.

"Tommy gave me a lift and I invited him to stay for supper." Sam bent down and kissed his wife and chucked his daughter under the chin. "Can Daddy have a hug?" Milly launched herself into her father's arms.

Lauren wished she could turn back the clock and launch herself into Tommy's arms. She noticed he was carrying a bottle of wine. "Can I take that from you?" Lauren smiled at him and accepted the bottle, hoping to remove the strained atmosphere vibrating between them. His expression softened, and he smiled back.

"Hey kids, why don't you go watch TV in the other room while Mom gets dinner ready." Sam put Milly down on the floor, and gave Jake a little nudge in the direction of the family room.

When the kids were safely out of earshot, the adults congregated around the breakfast bar to discuss the afternoon's discovery.

"They think the body is Brett Hagar. They found identification." Sam announced. "Looks like he has been there a long, long time. Chief says the last time anyone remembers seeing him was on prom night."

Lauren's cheeks drained of colour. Brett's face, contorted with anger, flashed before her eyes. She reached out to steady herself against the counter, and sat down on the barstool before her legs gave way.

"What's the matter, Lauren? You look as white as a ghost." Sam turned to Sarah with a questioning look. "I'll get her a brandy."

Sarah put her arm around Lauren's shoulder. "She's upset because the rumour mill had her leaving town with Brett after the prom."

"Well now they know why he couldn't be found." Tommy sat on the barstool next to Lauren.

Sam handed the glass of brandy to Lauren and waited until she took a sip. "Didn't his parents try to find him?"

"He lived with his grandparents from when he was orphaned as a toddler. They tried for years to track him down, till they passed away within eighteen months of each other. Some say they died of broken hearts." Sarah announced.

"He wasn't the nice guy everyone thought he was." Lauren took another small sip of the brandy.

All conversation stopped and Sarah, Sam and Tommy turned towards Lauren. *All too polite to ask the question hanging in the air.*

"And why do I say that? You are all dying to know. Because Brett Hagar assaulted me on prom night, and knocked me out because I wouldn't have sex with him." Lauren put down the brandy with shaking hands.

"My God, Lauren. Don't say that to anyone else. They'll put two and two together and come up with five."

"You think I don't have the same thought? If he's been gone since that night, and if I was the last one to see him alive, then I'm the prime suspect."

"Maybe they'll find some other clues. They're sifting through the gravesite now. They put up search lights." Tommy never took his eyes from Lauren's face. His concerned frown etched into his forehead.

"At least I know I'm surrounded by friends. None of you have asked if I did it." Lauren sighed.

"Of course we know you didn't do it. Right, Sam? Right, Tommy?" Sarah reached over and squeezed her friend's hand. "But how terrible for you. So is that why you left town? Why didn't you tell me? Did he. . . did he?"

"Rape me? No. But he told me not to struggle as no matter what happened he swore he would tell everyone he had *enjoyed* me. That no one would believe me. That I was a tease. He had me pinned down on the grass. I started screaming and he tried to shut me up, then he punched me in the face and I must have blacked out. When I came to, Chief Bailey, who was only a sergeant then, was talking to me and helping me up. He took me home in the back of the police car. My underwear was still intact. But I had dirt and grass all over me, scratches on my neck and arms, and a black eye swelling nicely. My own father didn't believe me, I'm sure. He was furious. Sergeant Bailey had to tell him to calm down. I left that night because I couldn't take it any longer. I wasn't popular at school, and I wasn't popular at home. There was nowhere I felt safe. I knew Brett would spread the word." Lauren looked into Tommy's eyes. "I didn't want to face anyone. I didn't think anyone would believe me."

"When you left, didn't your father come looking for you?" Sam put his arm around Sarah's shoulders.

"He was probably happy I'd gone. He didn't have to deal with me anymore. I was a constant reminder of my mother. She wasn't there to make his meals and do his laundry, so he transferred his anger to me."

"Look, I have to get supper served for the kids, but you should stay here tonight, you shouldn't be on your own." Sarah walked around the breakfast bar and kissed Lauren's forehead, then began to prepare their meal. "Sam, would you set another place. It's pot roast and baked potatoes and greens, Tommy. Your wine will go nicely, thank you."

With the children present, talk around the supper table concentrated on the reunion dinner and on Tommy's work on the weekend. "Don and I cleaned out the old cottage behind the garage. My old man used it for storage when they renovated their house. Some good pieces of furniture are being thrown out if you want to take a look, Sam. Maybe strip them down and give them a coat of varnish. Thought I would offer them to goodwill if you weren't interested. I'm going to put an ad on the noticeboard in the diner and see if I can get a few bucks rent for the place. Furnished, of course. Once Don and I give it a coat of paint and a bit of a clean it will be liveable. It has hardwood floors, a fireplace and the plumbing is intact. I've got a spare refrigerator in the garage we can install."

"Sure. I'll come by and take a look tomorrow or the day after." "Would anyone like dessert? I have some cherry pie." Sarah started to clear the plates, and Sam got up to help.

The doorbell rang. Everyone stopped. Frozen on the spot.

"I'll go." Sam squeezed Lauren's shoulder as he passed. They all knew what was coming.

Chief Bailey and his deputy stood on the porch, backlit by the flashing red and blue lights of the police car. "Good evening, Sam."

"Evening, Chief. What brings you out at supper time?"

"Is Lauren Taylor here with you?"

"Yes, we're having supper."

"Don't have the police chief standing on the doorstep, honey. Invite them in." Sarah appeared at Sam's side. "Evening, Chief. Evening, Deputy."

Lauren got up from the dining room table and joined the others in the living room.

"Hello, Lauren. I assume Sam and Tommy told you that the body we discovered today is Brett Hagar. We found identification under the body to confirm his identity, but we will have dental records checked to be sure. I have some questions I'd like to ask about prom night. That was the last time anyone remembers seeing Brett Hagar. People have said the last time they saw him he was with you."

"He followed me out of the hall, yes."

"And then what happened?"

"We had an argument."

"An argument. About what."

"He wanted more than a kiss."

"And when you didn't give him 'more than a kiss' . . . what then."

"I don't know. He knocked me out. I remember you helping me up off the ground and taking me home."

"When I found you, there was no one else there. I thought you'd fallen over."

"Come on, Chief. I was covered in dirt, my skirt was around my waist and I had a black eye. You saw the look on my father's face. He didn't think I had fallen down. Neither did you. When you left my father made me tell him what happened. He was furious."

"I had no idea who you were outside with that night. But now, until someone proves otherwise, you were the last one to see Brett. You had an argument. He disappears and turns up fifteen years later with what looks like a fractured skull." Chief Bailey stood. "So you see the predicament I'm in here. All the evidence points to you being the last one to see him alive. I need to take your statement down at the station."

"Chief, please. You can't think Lauren had anything to do with this." Sarah looked genuinely worried.

"It's alright, Sarah. I didn't do anything wrong."

"Can't the statement wait until the morning? She is staying here tonight. I can vouch for her. I will bring her into the station in the morning."

"Sorry, Sarah. It's procedure."

"I'll come with you." Tommy announced.

"Don't worry, Sarah. Chief, can I go back to the hotel after I make my statement?" Lauren gathered up her belongings.

"You can go back to the hotel. But it's best if you don't leave town."

"For how long?"

"For as long as it takes to find out what happened, Lauren."

"I'll call my lawyer for advice." Tommy took her hand. Squeezed it.

They all walked out to the police car, and watched as Lauren drove away.

"I'll call you both tomorrow if we find out anything. Thanks for supper." Tommy gave Sarah a quick kiss on the cheek, and climbed into his truck.

Tommy followed the police car into town. He called his lawyer and arranged to meet him at the station.

CHAPTER SEVEN

HE COMMANDEERED A CHAIR OPPOSITE THE BOOKING DESK. THE haphazard thoughts flying around in his head were making him dizzy. She was assaulted. By Brett fucking Hagar. He tried to rape her. Where the fuck was I? Oh yeah, enjoying Maggie Cuthbert's tongue rammed down my throat and the pats on the back for making Prom King. Yeah, a big fucking hero!

When the door to the interview room finally opened and Charlie Alexander, Tommy's family lawyer, guided Lauren through ahead of him, he could tell by the shadows under Lauren's eyes that the session and the shitty day had taken its toll.

"Can we go now, Chief?" Tommy jumped to his feet.

"Remember to leave your contact details with the desk, and I expect you to stay in town until we investigate this further." The chief hooked his thumbs into his belt and addressed Lauren.

"I'll be at the hotel until tomorrow. Then I'll have to find something cheaper." Lauren crossed her arms over her chest and rubbed her arms. She shivered.

"Here, have my jacket." Tommy removed his jacket and placed it around her shoulders. "Better?"

"Better, thanks." Lauren snuggled into the jacket, which was huge on her small frame, and slipped her arms inside the sleeves. She wrote down her details and gave them to the duty sergeant at the desk.

"Here's my card with my cell on it, Lauren. Call me if you need anything." Charlie gave her a business card, patted her shoulder, shook Tommy's hand and left the building.

"Let's go. My truck's out front."

Tommy opened the passenger door and Lauren stepped up into the cabin, laid her head back against the headrest and closed her eyes.

He headed for the hotel. He didn't try to talk. He let her rest for the few minutes it took to reach their destination.

"I'll walk you inside."

"Could you stay? And before you say anything, I'm not making a pass." Lauren opened her eyes and turned to Tommy. "I just don't want to be alone tonight."

"Sure."

"In the morning we can talk. I could really do with climbing into bed and having someone hold me, if that's not too much trouble."

"Hey, you're asking a lot of me, but what are friends for, huh?" Tommy tucked a lock of hair behind her ear, and was rewarded with a tired smile.

It took all of five minutes for Lauren to undress down to her bra and undies and climb into bed, and one minute for Tommy to be right behind her in his boxers. She scooted back until her chilled body was snuggled into his warm muscled chest and her bottom was tucked into the curve of his raised thighs.

Think about baseball, think about baseball, think about baseball. How many runs did you make in the last year. "Are you alright?" Tommy whispered.

"Mmmmm."

"Getting warmer now?"

"Shhhhh Tommy. Just hold me." Lauren took his arm and wrapped it around her middle. "I knew I shouldn't have come back. I just knew it." In a few minutes her body relaxed and he figured she had fallen asleep.

Tommy didn't sleep for some time. He kept going over what had happened, what he could do to help, who he could talk to, and if his father knew of anyone he could talk to at the Coroner's Office. After all, he played poker with some of the guys from the County Court. He'd been fixing the judge's car ever since Tommy could remember. By the time he fell into a dreamless sleep, he had worked out he would offer Lauren the cottage at the back of the garage, if she had to find somewhere to stay.

He tried not to smile when he thought of the chief demanding she stay in town.

"GOOD MORNING." TOMMY MURMURED SOFTLY.

Lauren opened her eyes and looked into the dark grey depths of Tommy's. She hadn't been aware of his arm under her neck until that moment. Hadn't been aware of her leg thrown casually over his either.

"Good morning. How'd you sleep?" Lauren yawned and stretched, removing her leg and relocating from the tempting heat of his groin.

"I got a few hours in. You were out like a light. Hardly moved all night." Tommy's chin had the dark shadow of stubble. His hair was tousled, soft locks falling onto his brow. His chest, also scattered with dark hair, drew her eyes. He watched her watching him.

"Thanks for staying. I don't remember anything after my head hit the pillow." Lauren rolled onto her back and stared at the ceiling, acutely aware of the short distance between them.

He swung his legs over the side of the bed and pulled on his pants. "Where are you going?"

"To the bathroom."

"Why did you put on your pants?"

"I would have thought that was obvious. I am male. It is morning."

"Oh, yeah. Sorry."

"Don't be. I'm used to morning glory." He closed the bathroom door.

"I was thinking about the cottage behind the garage. What if I helped you paint it and fix it up, would you rent it to me while I'm forced to stay in town? I honestly cannot afford much." She called out through the wall. She heard the toilet flush, and the door opened suddenly.

"I've been thinking about that too. But you can stay there for free if you slap some paint on the inside walls and give it a clean. It's not fancy, but it's only temporary. I'm sure they'll find out what happened soon and you can go back to the city, and then the old man can get some rent money out of it. What do you think?"

"I'd be happy to paint it. I never shy away from getting my hands dirty. A least it'll keep me busy."

"Good. A win-win then. I'd better get going." Tommy headed for the door, pulling on his shirt, buttoning it and shoving his feet into his boots as he walked.

"I'll take a shower and pack my things. I'll come on over when I check out and you can show me the place. I don't need fancy, Tommy. As long as it has a lock on the door, a bed, running water and a toilet, I'll be fine."

"It's not five star for sure. But the roof doesn't leak, and it's not run-down. My old man stored furniture there when they remodelled the house. Mom decided she didn't want most of the old furniture back. He never got around to selling it. Everything is covered with dust covers."

Lauren got out of bed, stood on tiptoe and kissed Tommy's cheek. "Thanks for all you're doing to help me."

Tommy looked a little embarrassed and tried to shrug it off. "I mean it. I will repay you."

Lauren watched him walk down the hall, from her position tucked behind the door. She closed it, allowing a sigh to escape before she laid her head on the cold, hard surface. *Get a move on. Pack up before they charge you for another day.*

CHAPTER EIGHT

TOMMY WAS NOWHERE TO BE FOUND WHEN LAUREN ARRIVED AT the garage. Don came out of the small kitchen with a takeaway cup of coffee and sandwich. He stopped dead in his tracks when he saw Lauren. He lowered his gaze to his coffee cup and shuffled past her.

"Hey, Lauren. Tommy left you a coffee and some breakfast in the kitchen. He's gone to Walmart for some paint."

"Thanks, Don. I could do with a strong coffee."

She almost inhaled the coffee, wishing there was more in the cup, and nibbled on the breakfast sandwich Tommy had left on the counter. She glanced around the small room, taking in the neatly stacked containers, the stacked cups, plates and paper towel on the shelf. The scrubbed kitchen table and battered kitchen chairs had seen better days, but everything was unusually clean for a working garage. *Someone keeps this place tidy*. She made her way out the back of the garage when she heard a car pull up.

"I got some white paint and a couple of rollers. Don can manage the work in the garage this morning and I'll help you give it a lick of paint." He unlocked the cottage door and pushed it wide to let in some fresh air. He pulled up the blinds and opened the windows.

"It's a good size." Lauren walked from room to room. She appeared from the bedroom. "You should get some decent rent money for this, when we give it a freshen up."

"I bought a couple of pillows, towels and some sheets and blankets. The bags are in the car, with some other stuff you might need."

"You'll let me know how much they cost." Lauren lifted off the dustcovers and took them outside to shake and fold.

"I'm going to rent it furnished so you don't have to worry about paying me back. I had to buy them anyway."

"Where do you want to start?"

"Let's sort out what needs to stay. I'll get Don to help me move the extra furniture out onto the porch. Sam's coming later today or tomorrow to take a look, and if he wants any furniture he can take it off my hands. Otherwise I'm going to give it away. The stuff we are keeping we can move into the middle and cover again with the dustsheets so we can paint the walls."

"They say less is more. It will make the place look bigger if we keep only the essentials in each room."

Once they had decided on what could stay, Tommy made a list of the furniture to give away.

"I'll start cleaning the kitchen." Lauren found a bucket under the sink and some rags in the garage. "The water is cold. Do you have any matches and I'll light the pilot light for the hot water."

Don appeared at the kitchen door. "I'll light it."

"My God, Don, I didn't hear you come in." Lauren clutched her chest, her heart hammering against her ribs. "You're light on your feet for a big guy."

He disappeared as soundlessly as he had arrived. Lauren shook her head and got down to business, filling a pot with water, and placing it on the stove to heat. She noted there were cups and plates in the cupboard over the sink and silverware in the drawers. She'd wash them all later.

Tommy and Don began arranging the furniture Lauren chose to keep into the middle of the rooms, and carried the surplus onto the porch. She selected the cleaning products from the paper sack Tommy had dumped on the kitchen counter. It wasn't too long before the kitchen and bathroom were clean enough for the time being, and it was time to start painting. The day flew by as they worked companionably side by side, going from room to room, Tommy concentrating on the walls and woodwork, and Lauren doing most of the cutting in and the ceiling with a long-handed roller.

Lauren's stomach grumbled. Glancing at the clock, she couldn't believe how the time had passed. The only real food they had eaten were the midmorning sandwiches, apart from the corn chips and soft drinks from the vending machine in the garage.

"Time to call it a day. I'm glad that was the last room that needed painting. There's very little paint left in this can." Tommy headed for the laundry room and rinsed out the tray and the roller. "How about a pizza and some beer?"

"Sounds like my kind of dinner." Lauren cleaned up her roller and left it to dry.

The garage was locked up and empty. Don had left the light on in the office.

"Let me check that everything is turned off, and we can go get something to eat. Leave your car here. We'll go in mine." Tommy took the stairs two at a time, checked the office and flicked off the light. Moonlight illuminated the garage workshop from the skylight above. "All good. Let's go."

The drive to the local pizza parlour took less than five minutes. Pizza Delight's car park was half full already. Tommy pushed open the shop door to allow Lauren to enter. The aroma of garlic bread and hot salami wafted out, enveloping them in a cloud of spicy anticipation.

"Table for two?" The waitress grabbed two menus and showed them to a table by the window. The restaurant had dark timber tables, and booths with red fake leather upholstered seats. The walls were adorned with Italian posters, the lighting was subdued and the atmosphere homely and welcoming. Combined with the delicious aroma of garlic and herbs, you could be forgiven for thinking you were in Italy.

"This place is new, I don't remember what was here before."

Lauren flipped open the menu and selected her favourite pizza combination.

"It was a vacant block of land for years. This restaurant only went up about two years ago."

"It's busy. Must be good."

"Yeah, busy most nights. Monday and Tuesday night specials keep it busy through the week. Family deals make it reasonable for most folks. What do you fancy?"

"I like anything except Hawaiian. Although my choice would be Capricciosa. With extra anchovies. On the side, if you don't approve." Lauren closed the menu and pushed it away, as the waitress approached their table.

"You've got a deal. Family Capricciosa with extra anchovies. And two beers." He passed his menu to the waitress. "Thanks."

"I made up the bed, and turned on the fridge while you were painting the front room. I'll grab some essentials from the 7-Eleven on the way back. I'm good to go."

"What about the paint fumes?"

"They weren't strong. Should be gone by now. We had windows and doors open all day."

"I guess if you're happy, I'm happy."

"If you come by early, we can move the heavy furniture back in the morning."

"Sure. Don is usually there at the crack of dawn."

"Maybe I can help a little in the garage. To take some off my tab?"

"I don't know what you would do. There's enough work for me and Don, but not much more."

"Take calls. Make bookings. Order spare parts. I could write up the ad for the cottage to rent. Besides, I need to be writing my book, so I could bring my laptop into the office, answer phones at least. What do you think?"

"I haven't told my folks you're here."

"Is that going to be a problem?"

"Don't think so. But let me run it past the old man first."

"Just trying to repay your kindness." Lauren reached over and placed her hand on his. He placed his other hand on top.

"And I appreciate what you're trying to do."

Their food arrived and talking took a back seat to the importance of shovelling in hot fragrant pizza and washing it down with cold refreshing beer.

Lauren pushed away her plate, a self-satisfied grin on her face. She drank the last of her beer.

"Now I can die happy."

"Nothing feels as good as a full belly and a cold beer." Tommy finished off the last of the pizza.

"If this place had been here back in the day, Jake's Diner might have had to close up shop."

"Jake owns this place too. And the fancy restaurant on the hill. So he wins no matter what folks want to eat." Tommy called for another two beers.

"So he's doing alright. I noticed a few changes in town. Some stores gone. Some still the same. Not bad for a small town. A lot of small towns like this are ghost towns, with folks moving off to the cities."

"Are you glad you moved away?"

"There have been good times. There were times when I thought about Clearwater Springs. But not with affection. Too many bad memories outweighing the good ones. You were gone, to the other side of the country. Or so I thought."

"You wouldn't have come back for the reunion if you had known I was here, would you?"

"No."

"Was it that bad between us?"

"Actually. It was that good."

"Huh?"

"There has never been anyone who could hold a candle to you, Tommy. I didn't want my face rubbed in the fact that we never made it. But I've never forgotten what we had."

Tommy did not take his eyes off hers. "Neither have I. I realised too late I wasn't honest back then. I should've treated you better."

"Water under the bridge now."

"Except seeing you again, having you here, has brought it back. I'm not proud of what I did. Keeping our relationship secret was crazy. I thought I was one of the cool kids. I should have been a better man, instead of a scared idiot."

The waitress brought their beers. They lapsed into silence, each deep in thought.

"I could never understand why I wasn't good enough for the other kids to hang with once my mother left town. It was as if I had a big L on my forehead. And no one mentioned my mother. It was as if she had never existed."

"You were very outspoken. And so angry. You stood up for yourself and folks didn't know how to react. You were scary."

"You're saying that was why I wasn't invited to parties. Why people crossed the street when they saw me coming?"

"Pretty much. And when I think back, I was as bad as the others. I was selfish and happy not to have shared you with anyone else. Spending time together, in our own world. Away from everyone else when I could escape from the old man and learning the ropes in the garage."

"Your father was the only adult who didn't talk down to me. But he didn't seem to be impressed that his only remaining son was spending time with the girl from the wrong side of town. He wanted more from you. He wanted Maggie Cuthbert for you. Little Miss Prom Queen."

"Look how that turned out. Three kids down before she was thirty. Wouldn't be surprised if there are more to come."

"I sure didn't expect her to be married to Chief Bailey." Lauren twisted her napkin on the table.

"So here we are. Sitting together, having a nice meal, and

discussing things like two reasonable adults." He picked up his beer and held out his bottle. "To new beginnings. What do you say?"

"To friendship." She clinked her bottle against his. "That wasn't what I meant."

"I know. Give me some time. Let's start with friendship. See where it goes."

"Fair enough. But you do know that if I get invited back into your bed, I won't be there just to hold you."

"If I invite you back into my bed, I won't expect anything less than your best game." The thought of having him in her bed sent butterflies spinning in her stomach. Heat rose in her cheeks.

"Now that I can do. Next time I promise to come prepared." Tommy sat back in his chair. His wide grin could not be hidden as he took a slug of his beer. A little trickled down his chin. "Now look what you made me do. I can't hold my liquor."

"But I can." Lauren giggled at her attempt at humour. She noticed the eager puppy look on his face. "Sorry, not funny to tease you."

"You are taking me down a track you may regret with that comment." The waitress appeared and Tommy asked for the bill. "Shall we go?"

The drive back to the cottage was quiet and Lauren left Tommy with his thoughts. They pulled up around the side of the garage.

"I'll walk you to your door." Tommy came around and opened the door of the truck and took Lauren's hand. His strong fingers were warm and he continued to hold her hand to the door of the cottage. He pulled the key from his pocket, opened the door and switched on the light. He handed Lauren the key on a key ring advertising Slater & Son. "I'm happy you're back in town. Even in these circumstances."

"I can't say I'm happy to be in town. But, if I'm honest, I am happy I've got to spend some time with you."

Tommy pulled her into a sweet and gentle kiss that drew a

sigh from her lips, and a longing for the kiss to go deeper. It was over far too soon. He stepped away.

"I'll be reporting for duty bright and early." Tommy headed for the car, his hand raised in a salute.

"I'll be waiting," Lauren called out. She closed and locked the door, and looked around the room of stacked furniture. "I guess I've nowhere else to go."

Lauren picked up her suitcase and carried it through to the bedroom. That was when she remembered she had intended to pick up some bottled water and supplies from 7-Eleven on the way back from dinner. She couldn't even get a cold drink from the garage next door. She changed into a long cotton T-shirt and cleaned her teeth in the small bathroom.

The knock on the front door startled her. She had no intention of opening it. "Who's there?"

"It's me. I thought you could do with these." Tommy called out.

When she opened the door, he handed her a paper sack full of assorted cold drinks, a litre of milk, jar of peanut butter, and a loaf of bread. "That should do you tonight. That's all I could get from the gas station." He glanced at her bare legs, and turned to walk away.

"You're aiming for a gold star, aren't you?" Touched he had remembered, and a little sorry he was leaving so quickly, she opened the door a little wider. "What's the rush? Don't like what you see?"

Tommy walked backwards. "No. I *do* like what I see. I told you. Next time I'm invited in I can't guarantee I will be on my best behaviour. Friend."

Warmth spread through her body, followed by a delicious shiver of anticipation. She pressed her thighs together and reluctantly watched him get in this truck, back it down the alley and disappear around the corner.

Maybe it's time to rethink this friendship gig.

Lauren tossed and turned, mad as hell for allowing her mind to wander down a lust-filled track. A one-way track of frustration for sure. Her trusty battery-boyfriend was back in her apartment in the city, so there was little hope of putting out this fire with any certainty tonight.

TOMMY FOUND HER SITTING BY THE OPEN FRONT DOOR ON AN upturned crate, eating peanut butter sandwiches and drinking a glass of milk when he returned at six am. He noticed dark circles under her eyes. *She hadn't slept either by the looks of things.* Sleep had evaded him until the early hours of the morning. Flashes of bare legs and creamy skin swirled around him in his dreams. An elusive seductress dancing just out of reach held out her hand and called his name. His morning shower had been an intense release of pent-up frustrations.

"You're up early." He handed her a takeaway coffee he had purchased on the way, and took a sip of his.

"Couldn't sleep." Lauren finished the sandwich and rose to place the dishes in the kitchen sink. "Thanks. This coffee smells divine."

"I'm going over to see my folks this morning. I need to tell the old man you're staying here."

"Is it okay if I take my laptop over later and work in the office? Do you have internet?"

"Sure. Don will get you the password and log-on details."

"Let's get this show on the road then." Lauren disposed of her empty coffee cup and rolled up her sleeves.

"I'll get Don and we can move this furniture back into place."

As Tommy headed for the garage, a utility pulled up in the drive. Sam climbed out and shook Tommy's hand, and raised his free hand in greeting to Lauren.

"Hi Tommy, hi Lauren. I've come to take a look at the furniture."

"Sure. Take all you want from this stack here. The rest is going to Goodwill."

Don appeared as if on cue, and between the four of them the furniture was moved around the small cottage and put in place. Sam left with several pieces he could use now, some he could repurpose, and the few pieces remaining were earmarked for collection later that day. Tommy took off to see his parents and Lauren settled into the office for a catch up on her email and the life she left back in the city.

CHAPTER NINE

JEFF SLATER DIDN'T ENJOY ENFORCED RETIREMENT. HE AWOKE EACH day with a sense of dread. Those idiots who said that retirement years were the best years of their lives had rocks in their heads. Or they were thirty-something young guns with plenty of work to keep them busy all day, with no thoughts in their head of dying. You see, that was what Jeff woke up to every day. Death constantly hovered at the edge of his thoughts. His life was drawing to an end. Brought on very quickly if he didn't take it easy and stop stressing about providing for his family and what his one remaining son was doing with the business he had kept going all these years.

There had been times when there was barely enough to pay his workers, pay bills and put food on the table. He didn't take a wage so that his workers could be paid. He had to put off one young mechanic, and that did not sit well with him as this fellow had been a part of Slater's since he left school. Helen, his wife, had offered to find a job, but she worked hard enough looking after their family all her life. She deserved to enjoy her time at home. In a small town where every year more people left for the bright lights of the city, small businesses suffered.

But his business had picked up several years ago when a few locals had returned and set up factories and manufacturing in the area. The bank account had grown substantially. Slater & Son had more regular towing and maintenance jobs than they'd had in years, as well as servicing the vehicles owned by the companies in the area. Things were turning around for sure. Then the bottom dropped out of his world when he had the heart attack. If Tommy hadn't returned to take over the garage, his lifelong work would have gone down the toilet.

Now Lauren was back in town. He knew what that meant to Tommy. No mistaking the connection between those two when they were younger. He found it interesting that his son hadn't called in to see him over the last few days. Especially since he had heard Lauren had been taken to the sheriff's office in the back of a patrol car. He knew about the body they found. The grapevine had been working overtime this past weekend.

Jeff was facing the bedroom window when he saw Tommy's car pull up in the driveway. He finished getting dressed. He heard his wife greeting their son at the front door. He tucked in his shirt and resolved to keep his opinions to himself, and to let the boy tell him what was going on.

"Hey Tommy, you're here early. Helen, is that coffee cake I can smell in the oven?"

"Yeah, I thought I would come by and tell you what we've done with the cottage. It's looking great. I don't think we're going to have any problems renting it. I'm going to advertise around town."

"Why don't you boys sit down and I'll bring you some coffee and cake in a few minutes. Tommy, I hear they found Brett Hagar's body on the school grounds. Isn't it terrible? That poor boy." Helen returned to the kitchen to make the coffee.

"That must have been a shock on Sunday. He was in your class, wasn't he?" Jeff eased himself into a recliner rocker. His arthritis was making itself known this morning.

"Yeah, he was in my senior class. Explains why he disappeared all those years ago."

"His grandparents are no longer here to find out what happened to him. They wore themselves into an early grave looking for that boy."

"Lauren Taylor came back for the reunion. She was the last person anyone saw Brett with that night. They questioned her down at the station. She's been asked to stay in town, so I let her use the cottage. It's just for a short while, till they get this sorted out. I just wanted to let you know."

"Lauren Taylor and you had a thing going, if I remember. How do you feel about her being back in town?"

"She's changed. More confident. She's a journalist. Or at least she was. She lost her job, so things are tight. That was why I let her stay in the cottage."

"You didn't answer my question."

"I like having her back, truth be told."

"She had guts, that girl. Her father was a troublemaker. No loss to the town when he passed."

"She didn't have the family life every girl dreams about, that's for sure. He was a real piece of work. Never had a kind word for her. From the time his wife walked out on him."

"She stayin' around, or going back to the city?"

"The sheriff wants her to stay around till they work out what happened to Brett. She doesn't have to get back to the city."

"No husband, family?"

"Nope."

"I liked her. She had spunk. Maybe you could bring her over for dinner this week. Your mom could make your favourite pot roast." Jeff watched Tommy struggle to keep his smile in check.

"I'll ask her."

Helen appeared with a tray. "Here you go. Coffee and cake for my two favourite guys. Now what were you two talking about?"

"I was telling Dad Lauren Taylor is in town. She's stayin' in the cottage, and he suggested I bring her round for dinner one night. He offered your pot roast as a bribe." Tommy took the plate from his mother.

"I would be happy to cook a pot roast. Have you rented the cottage already?" Helen sat in the recliner opposite her husband.

"No, she helped me paint it, and she is staying there for free at the moment. She did offer to help out in the garage. But there's hardly anything she can do."

"It's a terrible thing, this young man being killed. The talk around town is he had a fractured skull. Have you heard any more about it?" Helen sat forward, an eager expression on her face. "This murder has been the most exciting thing to have happened in town for a long time."

"If I hear anything I will be sure to keep you posted. I'd better get back to the garage." Tommy took a big swig of his coffee and finished off the last of his cake. "Thanks for the coffee and cake. The pot roast sounds great. I'll call you later and let you know."

They all walked to the front door and Tommy hugged his mother and gave his father's shoulder a squeeze. While they said their goodbyes, Helen rushed off to the kitchen and returned with cake wrapped in silver foil. "There's a piece for Don, and one for Lauren too."

Helen wrapped her arm around her husband's waist as they stood on the front porch and waved goodbye. "You think he's still sweet on Lauren Taylor, don't you?"

"I'd bet my last dollar on it."

"In that case, I'd better look for a good dessert recipe to make with the pot roast. I can't remember the last time he brought someone to our table. I might be entertaining the mother of my future grandchildren."

"Why do women always think of weddings and babies? I just think he still likes her. I don't know if he is going to propose."

"A mother can hope, can't she? A daughter-in-law and a grandchild or two would be a lovely addition to our family."

That pleasant thought kept Helen smiling for the rest of the morning. Jeff hadn't seen her look as happy for a long time. Maybe this was what they needed to remove the spectre of death from the household. A wedding would do it. And he was not going to stand in Tommy's way this time, if that was what he wanted.

CHAPTER TEN

LAUREN HAD SET UP HER LAPTOP ON THE ANCIENT DESK, WHICH had belonged to Jeff Slater for over thirty years. The chair leather was worn and comfortably softened with decades of use. She had deliberately left the door of the office open as she felt like an intruder in someone else's space. There was so much of Jeff Slater's life scattered around this room. Tommy hadn't really made his own impact, other than a few bits and pieces of sporting memorabilia. The room could do with a lick of paint and some tidying up. There was a filing cabinet in the corner, but most of the paperwork had been piled on top, or on chairs, or still lay scattered on the desk. *Maybe this was a way to repay Tommy?* She could make this office a more agreeable space. *How the hell did they find anything?* Receipts, bills, spare parts and invoices lay strewn in front of her. There seemed to be no organisation in this space, but downstairs the kitchen and workroom had orderly and clean stamped all over it.

Lauren hung over the landing at the top of the stairs. Don had his head under the bonnet of a utility.

"Hey Don, do we have any white paint left?"

"I'm pretty sure there's one full can. Tommy was going to return it for a refund."

"Great. I'm thinking this office could do with a lick of paint, and a tidy up. Why is everything so tidy downstairs, when this is a shambles?"

"I guess you'll have to ask the boss. Not my area upstairs. Only my responsibility down here."

"So you're the neat freak down there. I wondered. I've never seen a garage as tidy."

⁂

WHEN LAUREN HEARD TOMMY RETURN, SHE CALLED HIM UP TO the office.

"How would you feel if I gave the walls a lick of paint and freshen the place up? I could sort out the paperwork too, if you like."

"Office paperwork is not my strong point."

"So if it is okay with you I'll start on the paint job. While you're here, will you help me take down this corkboard of photographs? I don't want to damage them or get paint on them. I don't want to remove them either as some of them are so old I am sure they would crack or split when I took out the pins. This is a collection of your father's history on this wall."

They each took hold of an end and lifted the corkboard off the hooks and moved it into the bathroom. It was cumbersome and too big. They couldn't close the door.

"Nope. That's not going to work. Could we store it in the garage? . . or what about if we put it in the cottage until I finished painting. It would be safe along the wall behind the couch." Lauren hated the thought of ruining Jeff's memories.

"I guess that would be the best option." Tommy walked the corkboard backwards to the top of the stairs.

"Hey, Don. Come help me move this to the cottage."

Don took the stairs two at time, wiping his hands on a rag he pulled from the pocket of his coveralls. He lifted the heavy board and descended the stairs with it raised over his head and disappeared out the side door.

"You've got to admire a man with muscles." Lauren laughed at the look on Tommy's face. "It's alright, champ, I know you have muscles. But Don is seriously strong. He lifted that as if it weighed nothing."

THE DAY COULDN'T HAVE GONE ANY BETTER. LAUREN GATHERED up the paperwork to attend to later, pulled on a spare set of coveralls, and concentrated on prepping and painting the walls. She finished with half an hour to spare before Don and Tommy closed the garage for the day. Don was lowering the roller door when she returned from the local supermarket.

"Could I interest anyone in some homemade spaghetti? Don? Tommy?" She held up the bag containing ingredients for an evening meal.

"Got plans. Thanks." Don dipped his head as he passed Lauren, and took off down the road.

"Doesn't he like me? He never looks me in the eye."

"Don't mind Don. He is a bit of a loner. Maybe he's shy around women. Come to think of it, I've never seen him with a woman."

"So can I tempt you with my famous spaghetti bolognaise?" Lauren wiggled her eyebrows.

"Don't want to eat alone, I presume?"

"You got it. It's great you letting me use the cottage, but it's a bit creepy. I feel as if someone is watching me."

"Must be your imagination, given why you are still here in town."

"No, I really feel 'watched'. Spied on. Not in my imagination."

"You've been watching too many movies. It's Clearwater, not New York City. But I'll keep you company. You've twisted my arm with the offer of food. I'm going home to shower and pick up a nice bottle of red. Be back in an hour."

Lauren dumped the bag on the kitchen table, and scrounged around in the cupboards for the pan and dishes she needed. She sautéed the onions and garlic, seared the meat, added spices and put all the ingredients into a large pot to bubble away while she had a shower and washed the paint spots off her skin.

There were no wine glasses, but she found some glass tumblers in the cupboard. She set the small battered table with a mishmash of plates and odd cutlery, but everything was clean, so what difference did it make. She was having a nice dinner with a friend. Who was bringing wine. Who was at home at that moment having a shower and probably putting on cologne. And who was she to talk. She had even taken time to shave her legs. *No expectations here.* No, none at all.

TOMMY HAD FORGOTTEN WHAT IT WAS LIKE TO BE EXCITED ABOUT having dinner cooked for him. By a woman. By an attractive single woman, who consistently brought his thoughts back to sex. No matter what they were discussing, no matter where they were, vivid images flashed in his head of Lauren in stages of undress, under him, on top of him and lying beside him, her hair spread out on the pillow, and her cheeks flushed with the afterglow of a damned good fucking.

He took his time getting dressed, selecting a nice shirt, adding some spit and polish to his best boots. He shaved real close and splashed on some aftershave his mother had given him last Christmas. She said some Hollywood actor had been advertising it, so it must be good. The red wine he had picked up on the way home was a favourite. He hoped Lauren enjoyed it too, but just to be on the safe side, he bought some white wine as well.

By the time he pulled up at the cottage, he had convinced

himself he was not going to make the first move. *Let her come to me*. If she was interested, he wasn't going to walk away tonight. No siree. There were only so many cold showers a man could take.

When he got out of the car, Lauren pulled aside the curtain and then opened the door. The loose sleeveless dress she wore skimmed the tops of her knees. *Bare legs and no shoes. That's a good sign*.

"Hey. I hope I'm not too early?"

"Nope, just finished my shower." Lauren took the bottles offered to her, and stood on tiptoe to kiss his cheek. "You smell delicious, by the way." She lingered a little longer, sniffing his collar. Her soft breast pushed against his bicep. Every inch of his body had tuned to high alert when she came near.

"So do you. I can smell coconut shampoo and something else. Something fruity."

"Strawberry lip balm."

"Good enough to eat."

"Mmmm. Yes. Well. Dinner is ready, so *shall* we eat? You could open the red wine if you like." She handed him the bottle of merlot.

"My pleasure." He poured two glasses of the red.

"How hungry are you?" Lauren returned to the stove to serve the meal.

"Very hungry."

"Would you like to taste this?" Lauren approached with a spoonful of pasta sauce and held it up to his lips.

Tommy took the spoon into his mouth, swallowed, and licked his lips. Lauren watched. The weight of her intense stare pressed against his skin.

"Delicious."

"You forgot a bit." Lauren stood on tiptoe and licked the drop of sauce from his bottom lip. She took a step back. "Yes, delicious."

No, he wasn't going to misinterpret this signal.

He lowered his lips to hers. Gently. Slowly. Her breath

feathered across his mouth. Their lips met with only a slight pressure, broke away, and then became more insistent. Hands became part of the game. Eager, testing, searching, cupping, until bodies were so close their arms wrapped around each other. Lauren walked backwards, pulling him with her into the bedroom until the backs of her thighs touched the bed. She broke away, crossed her arms and reached down, pulling the hem of the dress up and over her head. He had a flash of full breasts spilling over the top of a lacy red bra. Then her arms were around him again, and her warm body pressed into his. Concave to convex. Hard against soft. His heart swelled with longing.

All thoughts were now zeroing in on her body's responses to his touch, to his kiss. Holding her, touching her, actually experiencing the hunger in her kiss. His job, his focus was on pleasure. Pure and simple. Hers and his. Because as sure as his heart was hammering in his chest, he was at the gates of heaven right now. *Don't fuck this up.* She whimpered when his teeth grazed her neck and his lips locked on her earlobe, sucking gently, and teasing the plump flesh with his teeth and his tongue.

His forefingers hooked in her bra straps and slid them off her shoulders. He lowered his head and dropped scattered kisses along her collarbone, returning to capture her mouth as if he couldn't bear to be away from its sweetness for such a length of time. She moaned into his kiss and moved closer. Tried to climb inside him. Possess him. He felt powerful, invincible; he had never experienced desire such as this from a woman. His body pulsed with the need to bury himself deep inside her. But he had to back off a little or it would all be over before either of them planned.

Think football. Think cars. Think engines . . . no not engines . . . think taxes. Yeah, that'll do it.

Lauren pulled away a little, and blew out a breath. "Wow. It was never as passionate as this when we were kids."

"We grew up."

"You sure did." Lauren placed her hand over the bulge in his jeans.

"Let's slow this down a little, Lauren honey, or neither of us will get lucky tonight. I want you to enjoy this. I want you to enjoy this very much."

"I am enjoying this, believe me. I need you inside me. It feels like I've waited an eternity for this to happen, and I don't want to wait any longer."

Lauren unbuttoned Tommy's shirt and pushed it from his shoulders. It slid to the floor. He started to unbuckle, but she patted his hands away and removed his belt and pushed his jeans down his thighs. As she rose back up, he hooked one finger in her bra, between her breasts, and drew her to his bare chest. Both hands reached up to cup her face. His kiss started off gently exploring and tentative, and became more urgent, his tongue probing her very willing mouth. With every swipe of his tongue, his erection, confined within his underwear, twitched against her stomach, eager and restless. He located the clasp of her bra and tugged it off. She surged against him. *At last. Skin to skin.* He toed off his boots, put one heel on the toe of the opposite foot and removed his socks. He kicked off his jeans. All without breaking his kiss. Her hands moved to his chest and she pushed him away a little. He stood tall in a pair of fitted black boxers.

"That is a sight to behold. May I unwrap the package?" Lauren grabbed the elastic and Tommy sprang free.

"Hell, that is impressive. I want you inside me even more now." Lauren licked her lips wickedly. She eased off her red silk underwear, and lay down on the bed. "You don't have to woo me. I'm all yours."

Shit. There's only so much a man can withstand. Silk and lace and a smoking hot woman is definitely my Kryptonite.

Tommy needed no further encouragement. He joined her on the bed, his lean hard body covering hers. He nudged her legs wider and she rose to meet him. The kiss they shared intensified the pleasure as he eased inside her until he could go no further. She cried out, her fingers digging into his shoulders. Her legs wrapped around him possessively.

Thus began the familiar rhythmic dance they both knew so well.

THE SUN CAME UP AND LAUREN'S EYES FLUTTERED OPEN. TOMMY, inches away, watched her intently. A smile played on his lips.

"Good morning, sunshine." Lauren cupped his face. His chin, rough and stubble-coated, grazed her palm.

"It's a great morning. I was hoping you would wake up early so we could have breakfast and some time together before I had to go to work."

"You mean you want to 'get up close and personal' with the hired help *again*. Take advantage of a girl down on her luck? I thought you would have had enough last night. And through the night." Lauren inched a little closer. "There seems to be something coming between us."

"Perhaps we should do something about that. You know I'm good at problem-solving, don't you?"

"You're good a few things. Fixing cars, selecting wine, painting . . . ah . . . I'm having trouble remembering what else you are good at." Lauren grinned.

"Come here. Let me remind you what else I am *very* good at." Tommy's big hand clamped possessively on her hip and dragged her over to his side of the bed.

Breakfast was forgotten in lieu of pleasure.

CHAPTER ELEVEN

Lauren stayed in bed when Tommy left to shower and change at home. She snuggled down into the warmth, pulling the cotton sheets up around her face and inhaling the smell of Tommy's cologne and unique body odour. And sex. Her muscles ached a little, a pleasant reminder of long hours of nocturnal and early morning activity with a very capable lover. The carnal images flashing through her brain had her grinning. *Oh boy, there certainly were things he was very good at.*

No rush to get dressed. Maybe take a cup of coffee back to bed to consider her plan of action for the day. She rose, pulled on some underwear, slipped a long cotton T-shirt over her head and scooped up her discarded clothes from the floor to place in the laundry basket. Today she would use the washer dryer in the garage while she worked in the office. She didn't bring much with her and her supply of clean clothes was dwindling again.

In the kitchen, the scattered remains of a hasty late-night spaghetti supper were congealing in the pots and on the plates. Her nipples pebbled at the thought of the dollop of sauce

Tommy had smeared on her breast and licked off. *That man can do wonderful things with his tongue.*

The knock on the front door surprised her. She edged aside the curtains an inch and came face to face with Chief Bailey. "Hang on." She returned to the bathroom, slid a pair of jeans off a hook on the back of the door, and pulled them on. She glanced in the mirror. Her hair looked as if she had gone through a wind tunnel. *Hells bells, it was seven o'clock in the morning. What did anyone expect?* Lauren opened the door and stood back to allow him to enter.

"Chief. It's early. What's up?" Lauren crossed her arms in front of her chest, suddenly aware she wasn't wearing a bra.

"Sarah told me you were living here. Just wanted to see for myself. This place hasn't been lived in for a while. I'm impressed. Looks like you've worked on it."

"Tommy and I painted the walls and cleaned it up. It's surprising how big it is, now the extra furniture has been cleaned out."

"So this is your address for the duration?"

"Until you tell me I can go back to the city. Do you have any news?"

"There are no new developments. Don't worry. You'll be the first to know. But you said you weren't working. What's the rush to get back to the city?"

"I'm more interested in knowing who put Brett in the ground. I am presuming the rumours are still going around that I left town with Brett. I didn't. You took me home. I left town on my own. So what now? Do they think I snuck back into town attacked him and buried him? Or do they have another theory?"

"You're always going to get rumours, Lauren. Small towns are famous for spreading rumours."

"One of the main reasons I left." Another sharp knock made her jump.

"I'm pretty popular today." Lauren pulled open the door.

Tommy held a cardboard tray containing two cups of takeaway coffee.

"You okay? I brought you coffee." Tommy handed the cup to her.

Looked past her and nodded, "Mornin', Chief."

"Mornin', Tommy. Checking up on Lauren's new address." Chief Bailey hooked his thumbs into his belt on either side of his buckle. He rocked back on his heels and arched his back. "Anything new to pass on?"

"We haven't heard anything new." Tommy came to stand beside Lauren.

"No news isn't always good news. Has the coroner's report come back yet?" Lauren put her coffee on the kitchen bench and crossed her arms again.

"It shouldn't be much longer. They're waiting on some more test results. I'll be in touch." Chief Bailey made his way out the door, glancing at the large pin-board of photographs leaning up against the wall. Something caught his eye and he moved closer. "There are some pictures here of prom night. Who took these?"

"Not sure. I'd have to ask my old man. This was in his office. We took it down to paint the office walls." Tommy peered at the board.

"Hmm. Ask him and let me know." Chief Bailey let himself out.

Lauren let out a breath, she wasn't aware she was holding. "What was that about?"

"I didn't know what to think when I saw the car out front." Tommy put his arm around Lauren's shoulder, concern etched in his face.

"Bloody early for a social call. I wonder if he was expecting to find you here?"

"Why would that be something the police were interested in?" "Maybe not the police, but the rumour mill in this town would love it. I've a feeling any dirt on me would be good. If he tells Maggie, then it will be all over town by noon."

"I better get on over to the garage. You comin'?"

"Sure. I'll have a shower and make breakfast. Have you eaten?"

"Grabbed a doughnut when I picked up the coffee. I'm good. See you later."

THE MORE SHE THOUGHT ABOUT THE EARLY VISIT, THE MORE SHE wondered what the chief was up to. She dropped her laptop bag on the floor by the door, knelt down and peered at the corkboard filled with images, until she found the ones of prom night. A picture of a beaming Tommy and Maggie, flagged by admirers, and a few of Tommy and his friends on the stage, random images around the hall, and another of Tommy's father in the background, on chaperone duty at the exit. There was something in these photographs that drew the chief's interest. But what?

The next few hours flew by. Lauren added another coat of paint to the office walls, the last of the paperwork was filed and the office had been turned into a bright and tidy space. When Tommy stuck his head in the door at the end of the day, Lauren was typing furiously, too focused to even notice him.

"What a difference. You've done a great job. The old man's going to be so impressed." Tommy took a couple of steps into the room. Lauren didn't look up.

"Earth to Lauren. Time to leave. We have to lock up."

"Two minutes, I'm on a roll."

"I'll let Don lock up. I'm going home to shower. Pizza for dinner? I could bring it back? Or we could go out?"

"A pizza would be great. Bring it back. Sounds good." Lauren shot Tommy a quick smile and returned to her typing.

After about fifteen minutes, she packed up her laptop, picked up the notes from the table and made her way downstairs. Don was in the kitchen, texting on his mobile phone.

"Okay, Don, you can lock up now, I'm off. See you tomorrow."

"Yeah, tomorrow." He didn't look up.

Lauren scooted under the half-closed roller door. Don pulled it down and secured the locks. He took off down the street without a backward glance.

Without the garage lights, the alley to the cottage was dark and uninviting. Lauren flipped on the torch on her mobile phone to see where she was walking on the cracked concrete. Goosebumps appeared on her arms. That creepy feeling she was being watched resurfaced. She glanced behind her, but no one was there. When she got inside, she locked the door, and scanned the alley through the lounge room window. *Too many shadows to see anything.* She pulled all the blinds down and closed the curtains before she turned on the lights. Her heart thudded in her chest. *Stop it, you're scaring yourself. There's no one there.*

By the time Tommy drove up, she had showered and changed and her mood had lifted. The two pizzas and the box of mixed salad he brought were quickly devoured and they settled on the couch with the remainder of a bottle of red wine and a block of dark chilli chocolate.

"You do know the way to a woman's heart." Lauren broke off some chocolate, popped it into her mouth and closed her eyes, savouring the chilli heat.

"Are you going to share?"

"Sure." She picked up a large piece of chocolate and held it between her lips, edging closer, offering it to him. He took the chocolate and also captured her lips, pulling her into his embrace and scooting down further onto the couch, until he was above her. He pulled back smiling as he ate the treat.

"Chocolate-coated kisses are the best." He plundered her mouth, licking, tasting, consuming every last vestige of melted chocolate from her lips before his tongue entered her mouth with slow and deliberate precision. She moaned. He had already discovered his deep kisses were her weak spot.

Shivers of pleasure skittered up her spine and she arched her body towards his. His fingers slipped under her top, searching for and finding her breast, cupping it and teasing the now sensitive nipple to a peak. Liquid heat flowed through her as he settled his body on hers, his erection cradled in between the tops of her thighs. Every tiny movement created a delicious friction against her mound. Her jeans became a barrier she no longer needed or required. She squirmed beneath him, trying to wriggle out to get undressed.

The thump on the outside wall stopped her in her tracks. "What was that?"

"A cat in the alley probably." Tommy tried to kiss her again. "Bloody big cat to make that noise. Go have a look. Pleeeeease."

Lauren tried to sit up.

"You really are spooked here, aren't you?"

"Someone was in the alley when I came home, I'm sure of it. I couldn't see anyone, but I felt someone out there."

"I'll go take a look. Don't worry." Tommy pulled the door closed behind him and headed for his truck. He switched on the headlights, illuminating the space between the cottage and the garage, and grabbed the metal torch from under the seat. He walked around the cottage and returned to the truck to turn off the lights and lock up.

"There's nothing unusual outside. Here, keep this torch with you. If nothing else, it's heavy enough to give someone a very sore head." Tommy pulled her over to the couch. "Come here and stop worrying about it. Tell you what. I'll install a sensor light on the porch tomorrow. Okay?"

"Okay. I'd feel better with a light outside. At least it would give me a heads-up that someone's out there."

"Now, where were we?" Tommy took her hand and kissed the back of her fingers.

"Let's go to bed. I'm suddenly not so keen to make out on the couch."

"I won't turn down that offer. Ever."

"Can you get a deadbolt for the front door when you're

picking up the porch light?"

"Maybe we should rethink you living here, if you are this worried."

"I've nowhere else to go, Tommy. I can't afford a hotel."

"What about moving in with me?"

"That's sweet of you. I'm just being paranoid. I'll be okay. Surely they will find out something and I'll be able to go home soon."

"Well, if you change your mind, the offer's there."

"And I appreciate it."

"By the way, my parents have asked me to bring you over for dinner one night. So how about tomorrow?"

"Your parents? Really?"

"I was over there telling them you moved in here and my old man suggested Mom make a pot roast and invited us both over for dinner. He even said he liked you. That you had spunk."

"A dinner with your folks. That's a surprise. Sure. Why not."

"Great, I'll call Mom in the morning."

"This trip back to Clearwater was not at all what I expected."

"Not all bad, I hope."

"No, not all bad. I have definitely had some good things happen to me. Now come here, you good thing." Lauren eased off his shirt as he unbuckled his belt, kicked off his boots and dropped his clothes beside the bed. He pushed her down on the quilt and helped to pull off her jeans and top, throwing them over his shoulder. She laughed at his haste to get her undressed. "Don't leave tonight. Stay with me."

"I won't leave. I'll be here when you wake up."

She buried her face in his neck and took solace in his strong arms around her. She was safe tonight. Safe here in his arms. But what about tomorrow and the night after that? She was becoming used to having Tommy in her life. *Can I go back to being alone again?*

CHAPTER TWELVE

TRUE TO HIS WORD, TOMMY STAYED. HE HAD NO INTENTION OR desire to be anywhere else. If someone had told him a month ago that his day-to-day thoughts would evolve around a woman he would have laughed out loud. However, here he was trying to imagine what he could do to make this woman stay in town. To stay *with* him.

Loneliness had not occurred to him until now. He hadn't even been aware of what he was missing. Friends had hooked up, got married, had a few kids, but he had never felt the pressure to follow in their footsteps. When he returned from New York State he had fought the feeling of failure, burying himself in the business and trying to forget his dreams of being a successful baseball player with money in the bank and a way forward in life. He came back for all the right reasons. He couldn't let his father's life's work go down the drain. Guilt would have driven him insane if his parents had to give up what they had worked all their lives to achieve. But that did not eradicate the fact that if his brother had still been alive he may not have had to be the one to give up his plans and take over the business. Perhaps he was deluding himself. The injury he had sustained had benched him. Although he had been prepared to work his ass off in rehab, the doctors had not been hopeful for a return to his previous form in the game he loved. Mediocre in baseball did not sit well.

There had to be something he could do to show Lauren that fate had brought her back, and fate had pushed her into the oncoming path of all this bullshit about Brett. If he could turn back time, he would have searched harder on prom night, found her and dragged her back into the hall. Then maybe they could have made a go of it. *Hell, who was he kidding?* He was a messed-up know-it-all kid back then, who wanted to prove to everyone he could make it in the sport. Women were not part of that equation. Lauren certainly was further down than most because of her background and popularity. What kind of a jerk would treat the girl he cared for like that, keeping her a secret, meeting in the shadows, never telling her how much she meant to him. *I was that fucking jerk, wasn't I.*

Lauren stirred beside him, snuggling into his neck. Her warm body pressed closer, the scent of her stirring something in him, the smile appearing on his face as an automatic reaction to her proximity. Can you fall in love with someone twice? *Maybe I never fell out of love.*

"Surely it's not time to get up? Tell me it isn't so." Lauren's hand wound its way down his spine to rest on his well-defined glutes. "Did I ever tell you your butt was one of your best features?"

"No, that never came up. Unlike other parts of me you seem fond of now."

"I will say that there are several parts of you that are very appealing. Such as your smile, the twinkle in your eye when you want to kiss me, those dimples at the base of your spine, like two giant thumb prints, your tongue when it dances over mine, your sense of humour . . . and oh yes . . . this." Lauren wrapped her fingers around his erection, her thumb gliding over the sensitive tip. "I have found this part *very* appealing."

She bent down and ran her tongue from the base of his cock

to the tip and back again. He arched in anticipation before her mouth descended on him, enveloping him in a soft warm embrace. His eyes closed with the sheer perfection of that sensation. Her lips worked their magic, making him rock-hard in record time. She slid her leg over his and raised herself above him, hovered for a few seconds, waiting until his eyes met hers, and then descended. Taking him lovingly inside her until she could take no more.

Tommy reached up to brush the hair away from her face as she swayed back and forth, the friction between them building, her breath coming faster. He cupped her face in his hands. He loved looking at her in the throes of passion. His thumb touched her lips and she sucked it in, the motion mirroring the rocking of her pelvis. His hips rose, keeping in time with her, eager now to finish. As her peak drew nearer, she ground herself against him and bent forward so their lips could meet in what was a ragged and disjointed kiss. Her muscles contracted around him, pulling his release from him on a groan of pleasure.

He held her against his chest, running his calloused workman's hands down her smooth fair skin, amazed at how easily she fit into the shape of his body, how at ease and at peace he felt, and thanked his lucky stars Brett's skull had appeared in the earth when it did. If she had left town without them being able to make love . . . . whoa . . . 'make love' . . . since when did this change from fucking to making love?

Okay, big shot. Deny you're in love with her.

CHAPTER THIRTEEN

"I MESSAGED MY FOLKS AND SAID WE COULD MAKE IT TO DINNER tonight. Mom suggested we arrive about seven. I'll buy some wine on the way to pick you up. Do you have a preference? Mom likes white wine. Dad drinks red, or bourbon."

"I'll stick to white wine with your mom. I thought I would pick up some flowers from the market." Lauren stood on tiptoe and kissed Tommy goodbye at the front door. Her arms wrapped around his neck and pulled him in tight.

"Are you trying to get me to leave, or stay? Cos if you keep kissing me like that I know what's gonna happen next."

"Can I help it if your kisses are so damned addictive?" Lauren opened the door and gave him a little shove. "Go on then. Get to work."

She watched as he backed his truck down the alley.

She showered, dressed, and set the cottage to order in record time. Then decided to drop by Jake's Diner to see if Maybelline had heard any more gossip about the discovery of Brett's body.

Jake's car park was pretty busy, due to their legendary early morning breakfast special, which could keep you going through a whole day if you were on a budget.

Lauren slid onto a stool at the counter. Maybelline appeared from the kitchen with a fresh pot of coffee, and a plate piled high with bacon, sausage and eggs, which she deposited on a customer's table by the window. She beamed when she saw Lauren.

"Hi there, Lauren honey. So nice to see you." Maybelline hugged Lauren to her ample bosom. "I know you don't have a say in it, but I'm happy you're still here. I should imagine Tommy is too. Little birdies are telling me you've been spending a lot of time with Tommy in the last couple of days."

"Well, for once the little birdies are correct. Tommy and I are enjoying each other's company. I'm staying in the cottage behind the garage. It's basically two tiny rooms and a bathroom, but it's a roof over my head and it'll do till they tell me I can go back to the city."

"I'm pleased for Tommy. That boy has been on his own since he came back from New York State. He took on a lot, you know, when Jeff had the heart attack. The garage wasn't doing so well. He's been building the business up again. Got a couple of corporate deals, I hear. Jeff and Helen think the world of him. I know that, because Helen drops in now and again for coffee and a chat. We went to school together. She told me you and Tommy were invited to dinner this week."

"Tonight, actually. I'm really surprised they invited me over. Although his father was always nice to me when I hung around the garage with Tommy after school. He talked to me like an adult. He didn't have much to say about my old man, I don't think he liked him. I figured he knew my mother when they were growing up. He always had nice things to say about my mother. Although at the time I didn't want to hear it. I guess I was pretty bitter back then."

"Yes, your mother went to school with Jeff and Helen. And me."

"What? You went to school with my mother. I never knew that."

"I was older than them, a few years ahead, but I remember Alice at school. A bit shy then, and skinny. Always had her head in a book. She grew up to be a good-looking woman, your mother. Long brown hair, neat little figure. Smart as a whip if I remember correctly. Married your father straight out of college. Had you a few years later. Your father wasn't from around here. Came here to work. I never knew what she saw in him, to tell you the truth. If you ask me, she regretted it as soon as she got married. I always thought he treated her badly. Had a black eye once and I asked her about it. She didn't take kindly to that question. She stopped coming into the diner as much. I don't know what happened to make her leave town, but your father was never the same. He wasn't very outgoing or pleasant to be around before, but he turned into a recluse."

"He turned into a mean old sod. Couldn't stand to be around me. It was like he saw her every time he looked at me. I hated her for leaving. I hated what my life had become. The gossip, the way I was treated. My old man turned into a drunk."

"I'm so sorry, Lauren."

"Water under the bridge, May."

"Can I get you some breakfast? I'd better keep moving. We're getting busy now. I need an extra pair of hands in the morning."

"I'll have the special. That way, I won't need to eat until I go to Tommy's folks."

"The special it is." Maybelline wrote out an order and clipped it beside the grill for the chef to assemble.

LAUREN FINISHED HER BREAKFAST AND PUSHED AWAY HER PLATE. She pulled the newspaper someone had left on the counter in front of her. The door opened behind her and she heard Chief

Bailey arrived with his deputy. You couldn't mistake the deputy's nasal twang. They slid into a booth by the window. Lauren dropped some cash on the side plate with the bill and made her way over to take advantage of the opportunity.

"Chief. Deputy. Can I sit for a minute?" Lauren slid into the booth beside the deputy, opposite the chief. "Do you have any updates?"

"Cause of death, a fractured skull. But we already thought that. No one has come forward with any more information. Did you find out who took the prom photographs?"

"I'm going to Tommy's folks for dinner. I'll ask them tonight. What was it that you saw in the photographs, that caught your eye?"

"There were photographs of before the crowning and then photographs during and after the crowning. Maybe the person who took them has some more. We can piece together what happened after the crowning."

"Well, you know where I was after the crowning. Out cold on the grass behind the gym and then in the back of your police car."

"Ask him. Get back to me. I'm trying to help you."

"And I appreciate it. I do." Lauren stood to leave. "Enjoy your breakfast."

"Bye May." Lauren called out.

Maybelline left the table she was cleaning came over and squeezed Lauren's hand affectionately. "Bye. Don't be a stranger."

CHAPTER FOURTEEN

When Jeff Slater opened his front door, Lauren struggled to hide her surprise. His health scare had aged him considerably.

His hair, once dark with a touch of grey at the temples, had turned to snowy white. His sunken cheeks were sallow, and his appearance was one of someone who had lost a lot of weight, quickly. His navy slacks and white shirt hung loosely on his frame. He still had that twinkle in his eye though. Tommy gave Jeff an enthusiastic hug, and placed a gentle affectionate kiss on his mother's cheek. Tommy's mother wasn't as familiar to Lauren, so the change in her was not as noticeable. She smiled, waiting for Tommy to introduce them. A slim, older woman, with fashionably styled salt-and-pepper hair, wearing a string of pearls, a dark grey dress, and a pink gingham apron fastened over the top. Lauren had a flashback to watching the reruns of *Happy Days*. They reminded her of Richie Cunningham's parents.

"Mom, Dad, you remember Lauren, don't you?" Tommy put his arm around Lauren's shoulder.

Lauren held out the flowers to Helen. "Thank you for

having me over for dinner. These are for you. I hope you like them. Tommy wasn't much help with suggestions of your favourites."

"They are beautiful, dear. So bright and colourful. You didn't have to bring anything. We're happy to have you and Tommy for dinner. We don't see enough of him since he came back. He works too hard."

Jeff took Lauren's hand in between both of his, a wide smile appearing on his face when he greeted at her.

"So nice to see you again, Lauren. Please come in." Jeff tucked Lauren's arm in the crook of his and walked with her into the lounge room. "Have a seat. Tommy has been keeping us up to date with what's going on. It's a terrible thing to have happened. But at least the mystery of where that boy had disappeared to has been solved."

"Only part of the mystery, Mr Slater. No one knows how he got to be in the ground." Lauren sat beside Tommy on the couch.

"Jeff and Helen, please. We're all adults here now." Jeff eased himself into a leather recliner beside the fireplace. Helen perched on the edge of the couch beside her son, still holding the bunch of flowers.

"Okay. Jeff and Helen it is."

"I hear you've worked wonders and tidied up the office at the garage. I'll have to drop by and take a look."

"She sure has. I can actually find invoices and customer quotes now without swearing, kicking the desk and digging through the piles of paperwork for hours." Tommy winked at Lauren and leant back, his arm along the back of the couch, touching her shoulder reassuringly. Lauren enjoyed the warmth of his skin through her top.

"I was anxious to do anything I could to pay you back for letting me use the cottage."

"The cottage is looking good, Dad. We'll get a decent rental price for it now that we painted it, got rid of some of the extra furniture, and cleared out the boxes."

"I have to ask you something before I forget, Jeff. We moved the photo-board from the office into the cottage while we were painting. Chief Bailey saw it and asked who took those prom night photos you pinned there."

"I took those. I was a bit of an amateur photographer in my younger days. I took most of the photos I pinned up. And Helen took some." Jeff paused. "There would be more in the attic. Along with my old camera, tripod and projector. We used to have film nights when the boys were young . . ." Jeff paused, staring off into the corner. His eyes glistened and he blinked it away. "All that stuff is old-fashioned today. It's all wide screen movies and pay TV now."

"Would you mind if Tommy has a look later? Chief Bailey was quite insistent, and I think he is on to something."

"It's probably a good time to put these flowers in water and serve up dinner. I hope you like pot roast, Lauren?" Helen disappeared into the kitchen.

"I love pot roast. It sure is a treat to have any kind of home cooking Mrs . . . Ah . . . Helen." Lauren called out to Helen's retreating back.

"Your mother has been looking forward to tonight. We couldn't remember the last time you brought a young lady to dinner."

"Jeff, don't embarrass Lauren. Or Tommy for that matter." Helen appeared in the dining room adjacent to the living room. She loaded the dining table with dishes of steaming vegetables, creamy mashed potatoes, a jug of aromatic gravy and a serving plate containing a large piece of prime rump steak.

"Tommy, can you pour the wine please. Jeff, do you want to carve the meat?" Helen placed the crystal vase of flowers Lauren brought at the far end of the table, and untied the pink and white gingham apron from around her waist. "Come sit over here, Lauren, opposite me, so we can have some girl talk. I'm sure the men will be discussing sports and business. Like always."

Tommy and Lauren had been grilled about their friendship, as only parents can do. By the time empty coffee cups and chocolate-smeared cake plates had been removed, Jeff had begun to fade. He appeared really tired, his shoulders sagged, and his eyes kept closing for a few seconds at a time when they were talking. Although he hadn't stopped smiling all evening. Everyone agreed it was time to call it a night.

Tommy kissed his mother goodbye, shook his father's hand and opened the car door for Lauren. He dropped the box of photographs they'd found in the attic into the back, and climbed into the driver's seat. A sense of wellbeing swamped him. He could no longer pretend that this was just a casual thing. What had occurred tonight felt more like a permanent relationship, complete with the third degree from his parents. *It felt so right, being there with Lauren. Like she was already part of the family.* He glanced over to see her reaction. She hadn't said a word since they had left the house.

"You're very quiet. You okay?" Tommy reached over to take Lauren's hand in his.

"They surprised me. I had a nice time. Your mother thinks we're a couple, you do realise that."

"I figured as much." His grin was hard to hide.

"She asked me all sorts of questions. She doesn't think I had anything to do with Brett Hagar's death. I know you had something to do with that. What did you tell your folks? I had a feeling she was sizing me up for daughter-in-law status."

"How does that make you feel?"

"Confused."

"Tell me to shut up." Tommy pulled over to the side of the road. "But tonight felt good, babe. My folks really liked you, I could tell. You've only been back a short time and it's early days . . . but I don't want you to leave. No matter what happens."

"What are you saying?"

"I'm asking for a chance to make a go of this. A second chance." Tommy kissed the back of her hand. He eased out into the traffic. "When we were kids I didn't treat you right. I want a chance to be better this time. To be a better man."

"My life is back in the city. My apartment, my friends, opportunities for work." Lauren closed her eyes. "I remember what it was like living in a small town. Everyone knows your business." She opened her eyes and turned towards Tommy. "I don't know if I can do it again. The memories of growing up here still haunt me."

"Give us a chance. Please. Maybe this was fate."

"I'd like to take it one day at a time. I can't make any promises. I believe I'll be able to think more clearly when this mystery has been solved."

They turned into the alley and the porch light activated, illuminating an arc around the front door.

"Oh, when did you install the light?"

"This morning, when you were out buying flowers. Cool, eh."

"Very cool."

"I fed it through the roof and it's plugged into the mains. It has a timer and a battery backup."

"You thought of everything. I'm impressed."

Lauren unlocked the cottage door as Tommy collected the box from the back seat and locked the car. "Come on. No time to waste." She closed and locked the door behind him and noticed the new deadbolt. *He remembered*. She slipped it on.

"What are you talkin' about?" He put the box on the kitchen counter and brushed the dust off his shirt.

"I haven't kissed you properly for over four hours. I need to make up the time." She took him by the hand and pulled him into the bedroom, where they fell onto the bed. "I need my Tommy fix." He braced himself on his elbows above her, taking some of his weight off her torso. She scattered kisses all over his throat and up under his chin, working her way towards his mouth. His lips tasted of coffee and chocolate frosting. His smile disappeared as his mouth covered hers. He deepened the kiss, and his body settled onto hers, the solid weight of him both a comfort and a pleasure.

They shed their clothes quickly, happy and eager to be skin to skin, mouth to mouth, heartbeat to heartbeat. Tommy eased Lauren's leg over his thigh and snuggled in closer. As they lay side by side under the covers, his fingertips gently touched her temple and ran down her cheek. His intense stare caused butterflies to tumble through her insides.

"You're beautiful. So beautiful." Tommy whispered. His fingertips traced the fullness of her lips.

She kissed his fingers. "Being with you like this is a dream come true."

"Then stay. Stay with me, Lauren. It will be different this time. I promise you." Tommy leant forwards and kissed her so softly, her heart melted. "I love you."

Lauren cupped Tommy's cheeks in both her hands, and looked into his eyes. "I have always loved you. From as far back as I can remember. Loving you is not the issue. This town, and all the small-minded people in it, is the problem."

"Surely I can make up for that. You could have a good life here with me. My folks were so happy to have us both there tonight. I make a good living and you wouldn't have to rush into anything. You wouldn't have to worry about work. I'd take care of you. You could write that book you were talking about."

"Don't pressure me. Please. Just love me. Make love to me." Lauren rocked her hips, and Tommy moved closer still. The tip of his erection edged inside her, his hand flat at the base of her spine encouraged her forwards. He lifted her leg higher and hooked it over his hip. She was so ready he had no problem slipping inside.

Tonight, their lovemaking was slow. Slow and steady, prolonging the pleasure, prolonging the moment where they could kiss and look into each other eyes as they edged towards release. Lauren's heart beat faster and her breath became ragged, the pleasure building quickly. Tommy's tongue danced over hers, his mouth and lips sucking gently, and her muscles began to contract, pulling him deeper and deeper inside her. She moaned into his mouth as she came. He eased her onto her back, guiding her legs up and around his waist. He drove deeper, concentration etched into his features until, with one final thrust, he lowered himself into her embrace, his heart pounding against her chest, his lips finding hers again. *Stay with me Lauren. Please stay.*

CHAPTER FIFTEEN

"I'M GOING TO GO THROUGH THAT BOX OF PHOTOGRAPHS TODAY before I call Chief Bailey." Lauren switched on the coffee machine, leant against the kitchen counter and watched Tommy pull on his boots. "Then I might drop by and see Sarah and the kids."

"Maybe we would go together this evening. Take pizza. I'd like to see what Sam did with that furniture."

"I'll call Sarah and see if she has plans."

Already deep in thought about what she'd find in the box of photographs, Lauren absentmindedly accepted the quick kiss Tommy placed on her lips, and the squeeze to her bottom as he left.

Eager to get started, she spread a dustsheet on the floor and got to work unpacking and sorting the contents into piles. She had promised Jeff and Helen she would take good care of their memories. There were photographs of different sizes and quality, in black and white and in colour, envelopes of negatives, small boxes of slides and a viewer. So many family photographs to sort through. She extracted one of a very young Tommy and his brother Rob at the County Fair. She ran her finger lovingly over the image of Tommy, his smile so wide and innocent, his crew cut so sharp and neat. Such a beautiful boy. His brother was the yin to his yang. Where Tommy was dark and small, Rob was blond and lanky. Five years between them made a difference. Lauren unearthed more photographs, showing him catching up. In their teens Tommy had grown to nearly the same height as Rob, before he died. Good genes meant the boys had that "All American" look. There was a picture of the family, Jeff with his arm around Rob's shoulder, on par with his son in height, and Tommy with his arm around his mother's shoulder, much taller already, but still a wee bit to go before he caught up with his brother and father. *They looked so happy.*

Then she pulled out photographs without Rob. Sadness appeared on every frame. *How hard it must be to lose a child.* No funeral photographs were included in the collection. It appeared that no photographs had been taken for some time, because in the next packet Tommy was taller than his father.

Then she found the large packet with high school photos tucked inside. She could hardly contain her curiosity. She cleared a large space on the sheet and upended the contents.

There was Tommy, in all his glory, and in full colour. Joy radiated from every image. His dark hair cut short, his suit jacket buttoned, his tie a little crooked, wearing an imitation jewel-encrusted gold crown, with his arm around Maggie Cuthbert's waist. Heat spread up her neck to her cheeks and jealously stung her heart, witnessing how happy he looked. *What did you expect? He was popular back then. Anyone would have been thrilled to be crowned Prom King.*

She spread out the many photographs taken on that night. Grouped them into locations, trying to get a picture of the flow of the evening and of the comings and goings in the hall. She spotted teachers she recognised, and parents who had volunteered to be chaperones. Helen stood in the corner of the buffet near the punchbowl, unwittingly ladling out cups of fruit punch, which probably had been laced with vodka or gin, or both if she remembered correctly. It had tasted disgusting whatever it was. She only had one cup. Maggie, on the other hand, had a few cups, and she had produced a hip flask in the toilets, which she passed around to her friends. *She didn't offer any to me though. Not that I would've taken it.*

She needed a magnifying glass. And thanks to her clean up last week she knew where she could find one. She locked the cottage behind her and made her way down the alley to the garage. Don was under the hood, working on a car engine. Tommy's legs could be seen poking out from under a truck. The volume was turned up high on the local radio station, and the noise of machinery under the car meant Tommy wouldn't have heard her approach. She kicked his feet. He slid out on a flat trolley.

"Hey. Just going up to the office to get a magnifying glass I found under the paperwork the other day. I found the photos. And some good ones of you. Boy you were cute when you were little."

"I'm cute now. Everyone says so. They say, 'Hey, there goes Tommy Slater, isn't he cute.' Isn't that right Don?"

Don grunted and kept on working.

"I won't be long. I'll call Sarah while I'm in the office."

Lauren found the magnifying glass in the top drawer, right where she left it. The office didn't look too untidy, so her hard work labelling everything had paid off. She sat behind the desk and pulled the phone towards her. It was answered on the third ring, and went to a pre-recorded message. She spoke after the beep.

"Sarah, it's me. I thought I'd call and see if you're you busy tonight, Tommy and I . . ."

Sarah came on the line, sounding a little out of breath. "Hey, Lauren, sorry. Didn't get to the phone in time before the answering machine cut in."

"Tommy suggested we bring some pizza, and come for a visit tonight if you're up for it?"

"That would be lovely. I was wondering how you're getting on. And if you had any news."

"No official news. But I do have news to share. I was invited to Tommy's folks for dinner last night."

"Wow, things are moving fast. Why did his folks ask you around? Hey, they didn't give you a hard time, did they?"

"Nope. I had a good time, I really did. They couldn't have been nicer to me. His mother was especially sweet. I had the feeling she was checking me out. You know. As a future daughter-in-law."

"Did you make the grade?"

"She gave me recipes of a few of Tommy's favourite meals, so I guess I must have."

"Well, they're not getting any younger, and now with Jeff's heart attack. She would probably like to see some grandchildren since Tommy is the only son left."

"Thanks, Sarah, you'd have me married off and popping out a couple of kids soon . . . good work." Lauren laughed along with her friend at the suggestion. But the laughter was hollow. A sliver of fear had had always accompanied any talk of children. She couldn't imagine herself being a mother. She had no positive reference point to use. *Tommy said he loves me and wants me to stay with him. But he didn't say anything about marriage. Did he?*

"Come about seven. I'll feed the kids early and the adults can have some time to talk."

Lauren hung up the phone, picked up the magnifying glass and rearranged the paperwork on the desk, filing away what she could. *Every little bit helps.* She couldn't stand clutter.

Don and Tommy hadn't moved from their previous positions. Lauren nudged Tommy's foot again. "Sarah's happy if we come around seven. The kids will be fed already, so it will only be the adults eating tonight."

Tommy slid out from under the car. "I'll go clean up after work and come back and pick you up at six-thirty. We can call in the pizza order and collect it on the way."

Lauren went back to the cottage and her task of sorting through the photographs. There were faces she didn't recognise. She named the ones she knew with strips of pink sticky notes.

Her mobile phone rang, jolting her out of her task. Sarah's name appeared on the screen.

"Lauren have you seen the paper this morning?"

"No. Why? What's in the paper?"

"There's a picture of you and an article about Brett. They're saying you are the number one suspect. It's on the front page."

Lauren's heart hammered in her chest. "I'll go get a newspaper and call you back."

WHEN SHE REACHED THE STORE, THERE WERE A FEW CUSTOMERS pouring over a copy of the local paper spread out on the counter. They stopped talking when the door opened and glanced at her, wariness and guilt written all over their faces. She picked up a copy from the stand, paid for her purchase, left the gossips to resume their chatter, and hurried back to the cottage before opening it up. The picture had been taken as she was leaving the cottage the other morning to get the flowers for Tommy's mother. She recognised the clothes. And an article on the fourth page. Someone must have snapped it from a car at the end of the alley. It wasn't a very good picture, but it was shocking to see her face with the caption *Suspect questioned by police*. Then the article stating she was the last person to have been seen with Brett, who mysteriously disappeared from town on prom night fifteen years ago. The same night she disappeared.

Lauren's hands were shaking. The details that flowed in print could only have been collected from people who knew her back then, classmates and teachers who had access to information long forgotten. It was a local paper, but news travels fast, and with social media these days it would not be long before her friends and past colleagues in the city would be calling her. *Shit!*

She walked back into the garage. Tommy had finished working under the truck, and was about to road test his handiwork. He saw her face, the paper in her hand, and motioned for her to climb aboard. They drove onto the street and made their way out of town.

"You saw this already, didn't you? Why didn't you tell me my picture was plastered all over the front page?"

"I thought I'd wait until after work." Tommy pulled over to the side of the road. "I knew you would be upset. I thought talking it over with Sarah and Sam would be a good idea."

"Someone's been busy. I shouldn't be surprised. This was what I used to do in my previous working life. I guess it's still a shock when it happens to you, seeing your face splashed over the front page. I'm guilty until I can prove otherwise, not the other way around."

"We have to find something to turn this in our favour. Maybe it's time for us to start asking questions. See what we can find out ourselves."

"I don't know what the chief will say about that."

"He doesn't seem to be doing anything, as far as I can see, to investigate what actually happened."

"I'll start making my own enquiries. I'll start with the people I've identified in the photographs. I'll talk with Sarah and Sam tonight. We'll make a list."

"We can split it up and share the load."

"Can you drop me back? I'd like to get started."

Tommy turned the truck around and headed back to town. He dropped her off at the end of the alley and took off again.

Lauren inserted the key in the lock, and turned to watch a car approach. Sarah jumped out, her face concerned.

"You didn't call me back and I was worried."

"Sorry, Sarah. I'm okay. I should have expected the press would pick up the story at some stage. I was going to call you. Where are the kids?"

"Jake is at school and I dropped Milly at Sam's mum's house." Sarah hugged her friend. Concern written all over her face.

"Come in and I'll make coffee. I want you to see these photographs. Maybe you can help me put names to the images."

They got to work sorting through the remainder of the photographs, identifying other parents and friends who were chaperones. Lauren made a paper grid with timelines, and they placed the photographs into three piles of before the crowning, during the crowning and after the crowning.

"There are a few people on this list I don't recognise. And who is this woman in the corner of the hall near the door? I can just make her out, but I cannot see all of her face in the shadows." Lauren passed the photograph to Sarah.

"I don't recognise her at all. Maybe she was a caterer."

"She's wearing a coat. I don't think she is part of the catering team. Here she is again in this one after I left the hall. See, Brett is following me out here, and then this one is taken afterwards. She is heading out the door. You can see the time on the clock above the door. Maybe she saw something?" Lauren peered at the image through the magnifying glass, hoping it might answer some of her questions.

"Here's Maybelline, over on the food table earlier. See, she's wearing black and white. All the catering staff are wearing black skirts or pants with white shirts." Sarah held out a photograph for Lauren to view.

"Who's this guy here?" Lauren passed a photograph and the magnifying glass to Sarah.

"Another mystery man. I have no idea. Put a question mark against him. Maybe Tommy will recognise him." Sarah stood up and stretched her back. "I have to go. School's out soon and I have to pick up the kids. I'll see you about seven tonight."

"Thanks for your help, Sarah. We've narrowed down the list of people who were still there." Lauren gave her friend a hug and opened the door. Chief Bailey was standing on the porch with his hand raised, obviously about to knock.

"Ladies." He glanced past Lauren to the patchwork quilt of images on the floor. "I saw the article in the paper. Thought I would drop by. It looks like you've found the other photographs from that night."

"Yes. Jeff Slater took the photos. I was going through them trying to work out who was at the prom that night."

"You've started to do our work for us. That's a great help. Now, if you could pack all of this up, with your notes, I'll take it down to the station." He attempted to enter the cottage.

Lauren took a step in front of him to block his path. "I promised Jeff and Helen I would take care of their photographs."

"You can rest assured I will record each photograph and give Jeff a receipt for them. This is official business, not a job for amateur investigators." He pulled out his radio and called for his deputy, never taking his eyes off Lauren.

Sarah left to pick up the kids, but not before giving Lauren a reassuring hug.

The deputy arrived, accompanied by a female officer carrying a large archive box to transport the photographic evidence and Lauren's notes. When they had left, Lauren shut the door and flopped down on the couch, deflated. She had managed to keep all of the family photographs aside. They were only interested in prom night.

She wanted to do something constructive for Jeff and Helen. Anything to keep her fingers busy and her mind from going crazy. She headed out to the dollar store and picked up some cheap photo albums, and stick-on labels. Arranging the photographs in chronological order, she captioned any she could identify with a cute little message. When she finished, she had a quick shower and was pulling her hair into a ponytail when Tommy arrived at six-thirty to take her to Sarah and Sam's. While they drove to pick up the pizza, she recounted what had occurred earlier.

"I was going to give the information to the chief. I hadn't expected him to take all the photographs *and* my notes."

"Yeah, that's a shame. Can you reconstruct any of the information?"

"Probably. Sarah saw what I had put together. We could map it out tonight."

They pulled into the curb to pick up the pizza.

"Oh my God . . . the negatives. I remembered there was a packet with the negatives in the box. We can have more copies made."

"Let me talk to my old man. He has a darkroom at the back of the garage."

"I feel there are clues in those photographs, Tommy. We just have to find them."

WHEN SAM OPENED THE DOOR, SARAH WAS RUSHING BY, HUSTLING the kids upstairs to watch a movie so that the adults could have dinner together without disruption. Jake and Milly yelled goodnight and whooped up the stairs, excited by the prospect of watching a movie in their parents' bed.

"Hey guys, that pizza smells good. Come on in." Sam gave Lauren a peck on the cheek and shook Tommy's free hand.

"Did Sarah tell you what happened today? Such a shame, when we were making progress." Lauren sat at the dining room table, and accepted a glass of wine from Sam. "We had an idea though. I think there are negatives in the box of family photos. Jeff has a darkroom at his place, and we are going to ask him to make copies." Lauren flipped opened the pizza boxes and passed around the plates.

"Or you could just look at the pictures I took." Sarah appeared and placed her mobile phone on the table.

"You what?" Tommy stopped the progress of a slice of pizza, midway to his mouth.

"I didn't see you take them." Lauren pulled the phone towards her, dinner momentarily forgotten.

"The images are upside down and at a bit of an angle, but I am sure I got everything. You were busy talking to the chief. I grabbed the chance when he wasn't watching me."

"You are wonderful, Sarah. I can even read my notes when I zoom in. Amazing work." Lauren flipped through the images.

"We'll write them out again after dinner. Maybe Tommy can help identify those people we couldn't name."

"Let's raise our glasses to Sarah. The heroine of the day." Lauren clinked her glass against all the others.

Maybe we can solve this mystery ourselves.

TOMMY HAD COME TO THE REALISATION THAT SOME OF HIS happiest moments were when Lauren was snuggled against him after they had made love. Her warm body pressed against his, her hands tucked under her chin as she drifted off to sleep. She looked like an angel. Nothing could compare to this. The love he felt for her was matched by the appreciation he had for her intelligence and humour. He knew that this situation she found herself in was dire, but she seemed to find a positive in everything. Their evening had been fun, with friends who had enjoyed their company. Like it or not, they were a couple in a few people's eyes. That fact alone made him smile. He tucked her in closer and whispered into her ear. "I love you."

"Mmmmm. I love you too."

"Then stay with me."

"I'm afraid. Afraid of being the one everyone points to and whispers about."

"Then let's give them something to talk about. Marry me."

"What!" Lauren sat up and stared at him.

"I said marry me. Let's show them we don't care what they say. Let's show them you have nothing to fear. We know you had nothing to do with Brett's death. Let them prove you did.

In the meantime, let's get married. We'll elope. Come and live in my house, write your book. We would be happy, Lauren. What do you say?"

"You're crazy. We've only been together a few days."

"I've known you all my life." Tommy pulled her back down beside him.

"Married. To Tommy Slater. In my teenage life that was all I wanted. That was my dream."

"It could be your reality."

"I want to say yes. I really do."

"Then say yes. It's simple."

"No, it's complicated. I had a life I was proud of in the city. No one looked at me like I was a loser. I lost my job because I was good at what I did and I pissed people off. I need to prove to everyone that I did not do this, and I am not the loser everyone *in this town* thinks I am. Maybe then I will be worthy to be Mrs Tommy Slater in their eyes."

"You are the crazy one, you know that, don't you? You are so very worthy already. Why do you care what everyone in this town thinks? But we'll play this your way. Just don't expect me to stop asking you."

"Mmmmm. Spoken by someone who was always the cool kid, always the popular boy. You have no idea what it was like for me growing up, do you? If you want to keep asking, that's your prerogative, I guess. G'night." Lauren snuggled back into his embrace.

Tommy was only mildly upset by her rejection of his proposal. He would wear her down. After all, she didn't say no.

CHAPTER SIXTEEN

MAYBELLINE PINNED THE "HELP WANTED" SIGN ON THE DOOR OF the diner. Jake had finally agreed they needed an extra pair of hands on a weekday, especially on the breakfast shift. Although the hours and the pay offered were not fantastic, maybe it would suit someone who just needed a few extra dollars to get by. It certainly wouldn't suit a mother with school-age kids, as the shift started at six am, unless she had an understanding partner prepared to do the school run. She doubted many would be beating down the door to stand on their feet for hours, clean up everyone's dirty dishes, and receive meagre tips. But you never knew.

The sounds and smell of bacon and sausage sizzling on the grill, coffee percolating on the counter and the deliciously wicked aroma of spiced apple cake just taken out of the oven, greeted customers as they walked in the door a little after six am.

This was the part of the day Maybelline enjoyed the most. Setting everything up just as she liked it. Freshly baked muffins and pastries displayed in shining glass domes on the counter, condiment bottles filled and lined up ready to be placed on the tables, and paper napkins neatly wrapped around knives and forks. Cream formica tables shining from extra elbow grease, stools lined up like soldiers standing to attention at the counter.

Working with Mario, the new breakfast chef, who arrived early each day to prepare the rolls and baked goods for the morning trade, was pure heaven for Maybelline. His rotund body testified to his appreciation for cakes and pastries, and his sunny personality and fondness for bursting into song delighted Maybelline. She didn't have any idea what he was singing most of the time, but as Italian songs go, she found them happy and uplifting. His voice was like velvet. Rich and melodic, it stirred things inside Maybelline that she had long forgotten. When her husband had died twenty years ago, looking after her daughter had become her focus. She counted her blessings when her daughter finally married, producing three grandchildren for her to spoil. However, as Maybelline was fast approaching her sixtieth year, loneliness had crept into the equation, and she found herself thinking of her husband and what she was missing in her life. Work was her life since her daughter and family had moved away. These days she worried about the future, and what lay ahead for her when she would be forced to retire and leave Jake's.

Mario jolted her out of her reverie. "Bella, do you wanna try ma apple spice cake? I made special for you." He forked up a piece of cake and held it out to her. His twinkling blue eyes held mischief.

"Mario, you know I love your cakes. My waistline has not improved since you came to work here." Maybelline happily took the forkful, licking the sugar and cinnamon from her lips. "Lovely, as always."

"Just like you, Bella."

Maybelline smiled. "Put aside a piece for later, Mario, please."

"I 'ave made a special one for you, *cara mia*. With extra spice." Mario winked at her.

Maybelline folded her arms across her bosom and sighed.

Mario brought the extra spice into her life every day with his beaming smile, and cheeky winks. What a pity he was eleven years younger. She was not about to flaunt convention. The whole town would be talking about her if she took Mario seriously with his flirting ways. Even although they were both single, and free to live their lives as they pleased, she was too old for a forty-eight year old "toy boy".

LAUREN AND TOMMY ARRIVED, JUST AFTER THE EARLY MORNING rush. Maybelline was wiping down a table and setting it up for the next customer.

"Hello my lovelies. What can I get for you two lovebirds this morning?" Maybelline handed each of them a menu.

"I'll have the special please, May. And an orange juice."

"Same, May, but with coffee thanks."

Lauren pointed to the sign on the door. "I see you need some help."

"Yes, just a couple of hours in the early shift."

"I'd like to help till you find someone permanent. I sure could use the cash, and the distraction. Who do I have to talk to?" Lauren handed back the menu.

"Are you sure, Lauren? It doesn't pay much."

"It's more than I'm making sitting on my butt at the moment. So yeah, I'm sure."

"Well . . . Jake left the hiring to me. So I guess the obvious question is when can you start?"

"As easy as that, eh?"

"It helps to know the person who's going to work for you from the time she was a child. So yes, as easy as that."

"I can start straight away."

"Okay, Monday it is. Five hours from Monday to Friday. Five forty-five am to ten forty-five am. We have someone who covers the weekend shifts. I'll tell Jake we have a temporary staff member. I'm going to leave the sign on the door."

Maybelline retreated to the kitchen to place their orders. "Are you sure?" Tommy said.

"I need the money, and as I said I need to be doing something. Besides, it'll get me out of your hair for a few hours."

"I'm getting used to you hanging around the garage."

"Look at it this way. I'll eat breakfast for free, and I can still write my book in the afternoon."

Plates of bacon, sausage and sunny-side up eggs appeared on the table, with a basket of fresh rolls and butter. They watched the local news channel on the TV, which was mounted on the wall. There was no mention of the case. Maybe she was yesterday's news.

"Do you have the pictures you wanted to show May?"

"Yeah, Sarah sent them to me." Lauren used the napkin to wipe her hands and pulled out her phone.

"What pictures?" May appeared with a fresh pot of coffee. She added some to Tommy's cup.

"I have some pictures here of prom night. I don't recognise a few of the chaperones. Maybe you can?" Lauren brought up the photographs on her phone.

"I don't recognise that man. Nope. I haven't seen him before. That guy looks like Johnny Willis, Blake's dad. But . . ." Maybelline peered at the image.

"What is it?"

"I can't make out the woman's face, as she's turned away. I can't be sure."

"Do you recognise her? Is she a local?"

"Lauren, I can't be sure."

"Spit it out, May . . . who do you think it is?"

"Looks like Alice . . . your mother."

"My mother! At the prom? You're crazy. She was long gone by that time."

"You asked me who I think it is. It looks like your mother." Lauren pushed away her plate. Feeling sick.

"I'm sorry, honey. I didn't mean to upset you. I thought you must have guessed." Maybelline laid a hand on Lauren's shoulder.

"Why would my mother be at the prom? It doesn't make sense."

"Maybe she came to see you."

"Then why didn't she talk to me, May? I tried to find her. All these years she hasn't wanted to be found."

"Lauren, you have to talk to the chief. If she was there, maybe he can find her. Maybe she saw something? Looks like she's heading out the door in this one." Tommy pointed to one of the pictures.

"I don't hold out much hope of the police finding anything. I think we should look into this ourselves."

LAUREN HEADED FOR THE WALMART STORE TO MAKE A FEW COPIES. When she returned to the garage, Tommy and his father were drinking coffee at the table in the corner. She showed Jeff the photographs.

"It could be Alice. It's not a very good photograph. I can only see one side of her face. It looks a bit like her, only a bit fuller in the face. I certainly didn't notice her that night." Jeff handed back the prints.

"See. In this one she is standing at the back of the hall in the shadows. With the dark coat she's not very noticeable. And here, she's nearly out the door. She's only come forward when Brett started to follow me out."

"What are you going to do with these prints?"

"I'm going to pin them up in the supermarket, and in the diner if they let me. Maybe someone knows who this is."

ON MONDAY MORNING SHE WAS UP AND DRESSED BRIGHT AND early, ready for her first day at the diner. The pink and white uniform didn't fit very well on her slim frame, but as it was only temporary, what did it matter. She fastened a belt round the waist and pulled it in tight. She took the price tag off a pair of cheap but comfortable flat shoes she'd bought at Walmart and slipped them on.

She arrived at five forty-five, the same time as Maybelline, who was unlocking the front door. Mario was already singing along to the radio in the kitchen, with the volume turned up high. Lauren bent down to retrieve the tied bundle of newspapers left outside the door.

Lauren wasn't prepared for the shock of seeing herself on the front of the local newspaper again in such a short time. This time they had caught her when she was leaving the police station.

She marched into the diner with a newspaper scrunched up in her fist. "Have you seen this? When are they going to stop following me around?"

"You're the biggest news story in town. Why would they give up the chance to sell papers?" Maybelline took the crumpled newspaper, examined the photograph and read the article beneath. "They are rehashing the story. They've got nothing new."

"Is this going to be a problem, me working here today?"

"Not from my point of view. If anyone gives you a hard time, let me know."

"I'd better get started. Show me what you want me to do first."

Lauren was given an apron with the diner's logo emblazed on the bib, and a quick run-down of the morning shift. After checking with Maybelline, she pinned the photographs to the community noticeboard, and within a few minutes the early risers had trickled in and she was off and running. The morning flew by, with only the occasional inquisitive look, and a few whispered conversations as she approached the tables. No one had actually broached the subject of the article in the newspaper this morning with her. She was cleaning a table when a woman approached her with a small child in tow.

"There's a photograph on the noticeboard, asking if anyone knows this woman. I think I know who that is."

"You do? Who is it?" Lauren tried hard to keep her face impartial. "It looks like John Norris's widow. He lived over in the next county." The woman tucked the child onto her hip. "I'm a nurse at the local hospital in Drewdale. He was a regular there for cancer treatment. I was on nightshift when he passed away. Such a shame, he was a real charmer. That was the last time I saw her. Keeps to herself since he died, I heard."

"And you think this woman lives locally?"

"As I said, I haven't seen her since he passed away, but I think they lived on a farm in Drewdale. I hope you find who you are looking for."

"Thanks for your help."

The woman put the child down, took her hand and left the diner. "Someone recognised her?" Maybelline inclined her head towards the woman and the little girl leaving the diner.

"Said she looked like someone's widow. A guy called John Norris. Do you know anyone by that name?" Lauren watched as she got into her car.

"Nope. Doesn't ring any bells. Not from around here to my knowledge."

"She said he was from the next county. From Drewdale. Maybe I'll look him up later in the White Pages."

CHAPTER SEVENTEEN

TOMMY'S MORNING HAD BEEN A ROLLER-COASTER OF EMOTIONS. HE had seen the picture in the paper, and knew that Lauren would be upset, but he fought the urge to call her. She would be working, her first day on the job, and he didn't want to cause any issues. Coupled with that, the local radio station had contacted him, and he knew the story had made the papers in other counties.

He heard her drive up to the cottage. "I'm gonna have a break, Don. Be back in ten."

Lauren was unloading groceries from the car, and she smiled when she caught sight of him.

"Hey. How was your first morning?" He gave her a quick kiss and a proprietary pat on the butt.

"Busier than I expected. But the time flew by. I have some cake here from Maybelline. You coming in for coffee?"

"I saw the article and your picture in the local paper. How're you feeling?"

"Pissed off. But I guess I'm still news, and they want to sell papers. Maybelline says it's the most excitement they have had here in town for a while."

"Yeah, I can't remember when they last had a murder in Clearwater. Petty crime, yeah. Bodies buried in the school grounds, no. Not in my lifetime."

"I pinned the pictures on the noticeboard and someone thought the woman in the photo was the widow of a guy in Drewdale. A guy called John Norris. I looked him up. There is a John Norris listed. I thought I might drive up there and talk to his widow."

"I have to take the car I'm working on for a test drive later. We could go together."

"Sure. I'd like some company."

"I'd better get back to it then. Should be ready about four o'clock."

TOMMY TURNED OFF THE MAIN HIGHWAY AND DROVE SLOWLY UP the winding, untarred country roads. A billowing cloud of grey dust followed in their wake. Picturesque farmlands stretched out around them, rolling hills, trees and orchards spread out for miles in any direction. When they arrived at the property indicated on the GPS, Lauren was surprised at how quaint the neat farmhouse looked sitting on top of the hill, surrounded by flower gardens. A verandah ran along the front of the house, and two wooden chairs sat to the right of the front door. A deeply rutted track wound up from the fence, forked off in one direction to the double-storey barn behind the house, and in the other direction to the front of the house. The nameplate on the padlocked gate said "Norris". There was a large metal bucket inside the fence, beside the letterbox, with bags of groceries inside.

"Looks like she gets groceries delivered. Do you think she's home?" Lauren wound down her window. The temperature in the car was rising.

"No way to tell. Can't see a car. Did you find a phone

number? Try calling." Tommy copied Lauren and opened his window to let a soft breeze flow through the car.

The phone rang for a few seconds and then switched to the answering machine. What Lauren imagined to be John Norris's recorded voice asked callers to leave a message and phone number, and he would call them back. *That's never going to happen now.*

She ended the call. "No one's picking up."

"The gate's padlocked and I have to get this car back. Maybe you could try another day. Leave a message on the phone next time and let her know you're coming."

"I didn't want to let her know I was looking for her. It might not be her in the photograph, and she's lost her husband. It would be a bit pushy."

"And turning up on her doorstep unannounced isn't pushy?" Tommy wound up the windows in preparation for the return journey on the dusty road.

Disappointed but resigned to the fact they would have to return, Lauren pocketed her phone. Tommy turned the car around in the small space and they headed back to Clearwater.

No one noticed the curtain twitch in the window of the farmhouse.

CHAPTER EIGHTEEN

SARAH PULLED HERSELF UP ONTO THE STOOL AT THE DINER AND dropped her purse on the seat next to her. Lauren appeared from the kitchen carrying a pot of coffee and some pancakes.

"Hey there. This is a lovely surprise." She leant over and kissed Sarah on the cheek. "I'll be back."

Sarah pulled the menu in front of her, ready to order. "You're out and about early."

"I had a doctor's appointment. My regular check-up. I thought I would drop by and see how you're going."

"It's only my second day here, but it's good so far. I've made a few dollars in tips." Lauren jingled the change in her pockets. "Seems I'm a bit of a celebrity. People are coming in to see the prime suspect, so the diner is making a killing. I'm thinking of asking for an appearance fee."

"Tommy told Sam you think you might know who the woman is in the picture."

"No. There have been a couple of different opinions. Maybelline thinks that it may be my mother . . ."

"Your *mother!*"

"Yeah, you sound as shocked as I was. Even Jeff, Tommy's

dad, thinks it could be her. Then a woman came in yesterday and said it looked like a widow from Drewdale. I looked up the guy's address and Tommy and I drove out there, but no one was home."

"So what are you going to do now?"

"I'm going back. Tommy wants me to call and let the widow know I'm coming over, but I don't think that's a very good idea."

"Do you want me to come with you?"

"I've got another half an hour and my shift is over. We could go then. I take it Milly is with her grandmother?"

"Yes, I dropped Jake at school and took her over this morning. My mother is picking up the kids after school to give me a break. Sam and I are going out for dinner. A date night. To celebrate getting another six months all clear from my oncologist."

"That's great, Sarah. Maybe you should go home and put your feet up. Get ready for your big date."

"No, I'd rather come with you. I'd like to help solve this mystery. Be in the thick of it, you know."

"It wasn't very exciting yesterday when the gate was locked and the house looked closed up."

"I'll take my chances. I'll have a coffee and some apple pie while you finish your shift."

"Comin' up."

THE SUN SHONE IN A PRISTINE BLUE SKY, NO CLOUDS TO STOP THE heat beating down on them as they made their way along the same dusty roads to the Norris farmhouse. The gate was still padlocked. The groceries had been removed from the metal box.

"I'll try the phone again." Lauren hung up as soon as she heard the recorded message. "No one picked up."

"What are you going to do? Shall we wait a while?" Sarah pulled a notebook from her purse and fanned her face.

"No, I'm going up to the door. Do you want to come, or are you staying here?"

"I'll come."

"We're going to have to climb over that gate."

"Isn't that trespassing?"

"I don't want to go back without at least trying the doorbell."

They helped each other clamber over the small gate and made their way towards the front of the house. Lauren watched the windows. The curtain moved slightly.

"See that? The curtain moved. I'm sure someone's in there."

Lauren rang the doorbell. Apart from the echoing bell, not a sound could be heard, in or out of the house. She rang it again. Then she cupped her hands around her eyes and peered into the front window. The room was sparsely furnished with what looked like antique furniture. There were bookcases lining the walls, and a rocking chair next to the fireplace.

"Come on let's go. Nobody's here. Or if they are here they don't want to answer the door."

"Okay, let's go back to the car." Lauren took Sarah by the hand, motioned for her to be quiet. As they descended the steps she dashed off to the right, and around the side of the house to the back door. The woman standing at the open kitchen door was startled as Lauren sprinted around the side of the house. She turned away quickly to go back inside.

"Please don't go. I just want to ask you a couple of questions." Lauren tried to catch her breath.

The woman turned back around. One side of her face was puckered and drawn, the skin folding in on itself, pulling her eye downwards and the edge of her mouth upwards into a grimace. The other side was perfect. A little fuller in the face, a little wrinkled, a lot older.

But definitely her mother.

"OH MY GOD, IT IS YOU. WHAT HAPPENED TO YOU? WHERE HAVE you been all these years? Why didn't you contact me? Do you know how much I wanted to find you! And you are here—*here* —in the next county!" Lauren's voice finally broke and she dissolved into tears.

Sarah appeared around the side of the house and rushed over to her friend.

Alice took a few steps across the porch. Lauren held up her hand to stop her. She sat down on the top step; her hands clasped together on her lap as silently, tears fell.

Sarah drew Lauren over to the bottom step and sat her down. She hugged Lauren to her chest and looked up at the older woman. "You must have had a terrible time. I can see by the look in your eyes that you are in just as much pain as Lauren. Can you tell us what happened, and why you're living here? And if you were at the prom when Lauren graduated. That's why we're here. She's a suspect you see . . . in a crime . . . being blamed for something she didn't do."

"I was afraid the day would come that I would have to face you, Lauren. I'm so sorry." Alice spoke very softly, her voice cracking.

"Why did you leave me?"

"Your father was . . . he . . . he was an abuser. I couldn't take it anymore. He did this to me." She touched her ruined face. "He nearly killed me. I had to leave."

"You left me with him! You ran away and left me there." Lauren sobbed.

"I always intended to come back for you. All I wanted to do was get away while I still could. You were at camp that week. I would have gone back for you. But I was unwell for a long time. Then I was too scared to go back."

"What happened to your face?" Sarah asked.

"Greg . . . Lauren's father, had been particularly nasty all week because of problems at work. He kept his wild temper hidden most of the time because of Lauren. Wouldn't have wanted it to get out that he wasn't Mr Perfect. But she was away that week. He was angry about his dinner not being ready when he got home and he picked up a pot from the stove and threw it across the room. It hit my head and knocked me out. It was full of hot oil. He probably thought he had killed me. He left the house, took off in his car. When I came to, I got in my old Ford and drove. Until I ran out of petrol. John found me unconscious at the wheel and brought me here. He looked after me. I had concussion. He tended to my face. But the damage was done. I begged John not to tell anyone I was here. I was afraid if Greg found me he would kill me. I was worried for John too. He would have killed him, knowing I was staying with John. So John hid my car in the barn. I helped him with the farm accounts, and running the house. I stayed indoors so no one knew I was here."

"If you had gone and got help, they could have looked after your face." Lauren said.

"Your father would have found me. He would have dragged me back and one day, he would have finally managed to do what he threatened to do every time he flew into a rage. And now I was worried not only for myself but for John. He was a kind man. He had lived here alone for many years since his first wife died. I could not bring that upon him."

"Can I get her some water? It's all bit of a shock." Sarah pulled a clean tissue from her pocket and offered it to Lauren.

"Come in. I'll get something to drink." Alice rose and opened the back door.

The kitchen had been painted a soft yellow, and the white cotton curtains were tied back with yellow ribbons of the same shade. The cabinets and benches were polished oak. There was a matching dresser against one wall stacked with pretty blue patterned cups and plates. A scrubbed wooden table and six chairs dominated the space. Everything was clean and tidy. Not a thing out of place. It was a picture-perfect country kitchen.

But Lauren shivered as the weight of unhappiness hung in the air and settled over her.

"I have some fresh lemonade. Would you like some? Or just water?"

"Just water." Lauren said.

"I'll have some lemonade please." Sarah pulled out a chair for herself and Lauren, and motioned to her to sit down at the table.

"Tell me about prom night. Why did you come to the school that night?" Lauren asked Alice.

"John heard about the prom and said he would take me to see you, all dressed up in your prom dress. He said I should talk to you, tell you where I was living, but I was too afraid once I got there. So I watched from the back of the hall. It was dark there, and no one paid any attention to me. It's like that when you're disfigured. People avoid looking at you. Being invisible is not as hard as you think."

"So you watched, and followed me when I left the hall?" Lauren asked.

"I thought that maybe I could summon up the courage to approach you at first. But you looked upset. Then I saw the boy follow you. I thought he was going to comfort you. When I realised he wasn't, I went back to find John." Alice took a sip of water. Her hands shook as she replaced the glass on the kitchen bench. She came to sit at the table opposite Lauren.

"Go on." Sarah said, encouragingly.

"John pulled the boy off you, he was furious, and there were punches thrown. I knew that type of anger. I had lived with it for many years. John was stronger, and he began to drag the boy towards the hall. We were going to turn him in to the chaperones. He had been drinking. You could smell it. He threw a punch at John, then knocked him to the ground, pushed me over and took off into the darkness."

"And what about me. Did you even care about me?"

Alice reached out to touch Lauren, but she flinched and pulled her hand away. "Of course. John helped me up, and we went back over to see if you were okay. But an officer was standing over you. He helped you into his car. I had missed my chance to talk to you. I was still worried. Didn't want to be recognised by anyone else, in case someone told your father. So we came home to the farm."

"So you don't know what happened to Brett after you left?" Sarah asked.

"Not until I saw the article in the local paper."

"You have to talk to Chief Bailey. We have to work out what happened that night. Someone else must know something." Sarah said.

"So you just went back to your life on the farm with this man, John, and you never tried to contact me again?" Lauren's voice rose.

"John did go back. He found out you had left town. I thought it best we left things as they were. After all, you hadn't had me around for a long time. You were grown up. Making your own way."

"In other words, you chickened out again." Lauren spat out the words.

"Lauren!" Sarah exclaimed.

"What. Are you trying to say what she did was acceptable?" Lauren yelled.

"There is no point in yelling. It won't change what happened." Sarah finished her lemonade and carried the empty glass over to the sink. She laid her hand on Alice's shoulder. "You do have to talk to the police. Would you like us to go with you? Or would you like them to come here? You don't go out much, do you?"

"Not since John died. I'm used to being at the farm. I think I would rather they came here."

"Someone in town said you were John Norris's widow? Is that right?" Lauren asked.

"John made sure we got the local papers delivered. I saw the notice about your father's death. John got cancer a couple of years later. He wanted to make sure I was taken care of, so we got married. He sold the surrounding farmland to pay for treatment, but kept this house. It's in my name. As I said he was a good man. A kind man. He loved me."

"We'd better get back," Sarah said.

"We'll call the chief and ask him to get in touch." Lauren stood and walked to the door. "Isn't there anything they can do . . . I mean, have you looked into treatment?"

"For my face? No, I haven't. It is my punishment, you see."

"Your punishment?"

Alice looked up at Lauren, with tears in her eyes. "For leaving you. For not going back and taking you away from that man. I have to live with that every day when I look in the mirror."

You could have heard a pin drop. All three were locked into their own thoughts of how things may have turned out differently in the last few years.

If only they could have turned back the clock.

CHAPTER NINETEEN

"**A**RE YOU ALRIGHT? THAT MUST HAVE BEEN A HUGE SHOCK." Sarah reached over and squeezed her friend's hand as she drove.

"I think there was a part of me that didn't want to believe it was her."

"What are you going to do now?"

"We should talk to the chief. But we're still no further, are we? She was there. But we don't know what happened to Brett after he ran off."

"She can corroborate your story. Maybe something will come up when she's interviewed."

"I have a feeling someone else was out there that night. Watching us. But if that was the case, why wouldn't they have spoken up to help solve this?"

Lauren dropped Sarah off to collect her car, and returned to the garage. As she drove by, Tommy was signing for a delivery by the roller door. She lowered her car window.

"Can you take a break? I've got some news."

"I'll let Don know and be right there."

Lauren entered the cottage and pulled a bottle of wine from the fridge. She filled a glass and took a big mouthful.

Tommy appeared at the door. "Bad news, I take it?"

"Close the door and take a seat. Do you want a drink?" She flopped onto the couch. The wine sloshed over the rim onto her jeans.

Tommy joined her on the couch. He looked concerned. "It's a bit early for me. What's up?"

"I found my mother. She's living at that farmhouse. She's been there since she left Clearwater."

"You're kidding me. Are you okay? What did she say? Why didn't she come back?"

"My father abused her. She has some horrific scars on her face. Terrible burns. She said she was afraid to come back. I think she's agoraphobic now."

"Was she at the prom that night? Did she see anything?"

"Yes, it was her, and the man she was living with. They got married a few years ago so she is John Norris's widow, like that woman said. They saw Brett and pulled him off me. They tried to turn him over to the chaperones but he ran off. When they went back, they saw the chief helping me off the grass. She said she was too scared to show herself in case someone recognised her and my father found her."

"It blows my mind to think she was in the next county all these years."

Lauren finished her wine, got up and poured another glass. "I don't know what to feel. I'm relieved to know she isn't dead. But I'm horrified to know she left me with someone capable of that kind of abuse. And I still hate her for leaving me."

"It's going to take time. Drinking that entire bottle isn't going to help."

"It will help to take the edge off. I want to scream. I want to go back to when I was a kid and change all this." She sat back down beside Tommy.

"Let me go and finish one job, and we'll close up early today. I'll take you out to dinner."

"No. Thank you. I'm going to stay here and drown my sorrows. It's all been too much. I just want to sleep. Maybe when I wake up it will have been a bad dream."

"I'm here for you. Let me help."

"I won't be much fun tonight. Please, Tommy. I want to be on my own."

"Call me if you change your mind." Tommy dropped a kiss on her forehead and went back to work.

Lauren threw back her head and drank the glass of wine, and poured another glass. It had been a while since she had drunk to forget. Her liver was forever grateful for her change in diet in recent years and a healthier lifestyle. But tonight she was determined to quieten the demons in her head. She had another bottle on standby.

She would shut them up one way or another.

THE FREEZING SHOWER SHOOK LOOSE SOME OF THE COBWEBS FROM her brain. In the cold light of morning, she could appreciate she was on a mission last night. A destructive mission. Going to bed instead of opening that second bottle had been the best idea. She had a responsibility to Maybelline to turn up for work. And a responsibility to herself to not slip down that rocky road again. Drowning her sorrows in alcohol had resulted in self-loathing. It would've been cheaper to see a shrink.

Lauren packed the photo albums onto the back seat of her car, intending to drop them off to Jeff and Helen on the way home from her breakfast shift. She shivered and pulled her jacket around her. There was that feeling again, that someone was watching her. At this time of the morning, the shadows held a multitude of secrets.

As she climbed behind the wheel, she saw movement near the rear of the garage. The sensor light illuminated cardboard cartons piled beside the dumpster. In the middle of the cardboard fort, a man sat up, rearranging an old blanket over a sleeping bag.

Lauren turned on her headlights, and he shielded his eyes. *Marty James, sleeping rough again.* She turned off the motor and got out.

"Marty, what are you doing out here? Why aren't you back at the mission?" The nearer she got to the dumpster the more overpowering the stench of alcohol became. "Ah, I see. They won't take you if you're drinking, will they? Why are you doing this to yourself?"

"Leave me alone. You don't understand."

"I understand more than most Marty. The drink is killing you. Is that what you want? I'm sure there are places you could go that would help you dry out."

"If I wanted your help I would've asked for it. Now leave me alone."

"When did you last eat? Huh? Look, I have to go to work. If you're still here when I get back, I'll bring you something to eat."

"Why do you care?"

"I've been in your shoes, believe it or not. I've been so low that I had no respect for myself. I finally woke up to the fact that if I didn't care, why should anyone else. It was tough but I made it through to the other side. I'll be back in a few hours."

Lauren climbed back in the car, more resigned to not use a bottle to quieten the voices in future. Look where it got Marty.

She had Tommy now. He said he was there for her. She had to give him a chance to prove it.

※ ※

SHE RETURNED A FEW HOURS LATER WITH A COOKED BREAKFAST, paid for out of her tips.

"Marty." Lauren nudged his foot. "Come on. Wake up."

"I told you I didn't want your charity."

"Well I don't want a dead body on my doorstep. Didn't anyone tell you they blame me for another body they dug up?"

"Yeah I heard. They don't know what they are talking about."

"What do you mean?"

"The newspapers. I read the story."

"Yeah, I'm the number one suspect alright."

"What about that bloke? The one that was dragging the kid across the schoolyard."

"You're kidding me. You saw that?"

"I was a chaperone that night. Colin was at the prom too."

"What did you see?"

"Just that. The man dragging him, trying to get him into the hall, and the kid throwing a punch, knocking him and a woman over and taking off round the back of the school."

"Why didn't you come forward before?"

"They would have found a way to blame me for something. I don't get involved. Best that way." Marty tore open the paper sack. He obviously couldn't resist the smell of the bacon and hash browns. He picked a sausage out of the polystyrene container with his grubby fingers and finished it in two bites. There was a plastic fork inside the bag. He shovelled the food into his mouth, wiping the back of his hand over the dribble of grease running down his chin. He licked his hand. Lauren squirmed. He looked like he hadn't washed in days.

"Look. I don't want to be pushy, but do you want to have a shower? And maybe Tommy has something you could fit into, and then you could wash your clothes."

"No. Just leave me alone." Marty pushed aside the empty container, picked up the sleeping bag and rolled it up with the blanket. He knocked over an empty bourbon bottle in his haste. "Thanks for the food."

"Will you talk to the chief about what you saw?"

"It won't do no good. No one's gonna believe me. I'm a drunk, remember."

He secured the bedding with an old belt, slung it over his shoulder and took off down the alley without another word.

Lauren gathered up the rubbish, put it in the dumpster, and returned to the cottage. *There's no helping some people. He's got to want to help himself.*

TOMMY STUCK HIS HEAD IN THE OFFICE, WHERE LAUREN WAS working at her computer. "You look better today. I thought we might go back to my house tonight and I'll cook something?"

"You can cook?"

"I can make a mean barbeque."

"What time should I come over?"

"We can go together when I finish in about an hour. You can relax while I have a shower, then I'll light up the grill."

Lauren worked on adding more words to her manuscript. *Who am I kidding?* She couldn't concentrate now. Not with the prospect of a visit to Tommy's. *This should be interesting.* She couldn't deny the fact she was curious about where he lived. She gave up, packed away her notes and picked up her laptop.

The next hour passed very slowly. She made another cup of coffee and changed clothes a couple of times from her meagre wardrobe, and still had time to kill.

Excitement bubbled inside her. She tried to imagine what his house would look like. He was used to living in a lovely home, having a certain lifestyle. He had grown up in the better part of town with acreage around the houses, while she had lived in an area where the gardens were not always neat and tidy, the garbage was not always tucked away behind gates and you could hear the neighbours yelling at their kids to go to sleep.

THE CUTE RANCH-STYLE HOME SAT SEDATELY IN THE MIDDLE OF

half an acre of well-maintained lawn, a few minutes drive out of town, and within walking distance of Tommy's parents' house. The late afternoon sun had cast a warm glow over the appealing property, turning the picture-windows rose gold. When they pulled up in the driveway, Lauren didn't try to hide her delight.

Tommy climbed out, and Lauren followed him up onto the wide verandah, which flowed around the house on all sides. He kicked off his workboots at the door, and held it open for Lauren to enter. Following his example, she slipped off her shoes and carried them inside.

Polished hardwood floors ran the length of the hall, into the open-plan room at the rear of the house.

"Go on back. Make yourself at home. I'll get cleaned up." Tommy disappeared into the bedroom to the right of the front door.

Lauren took her time walking down the hall, glancing through open doors to her left and right. Every room appeared set up, sparsely furnished but shipshape and tidy. *Tommy sure is a surprise*. She could hear the water running in the bathroom behind her. She entered the large family and kitchen area, and walked to the rear glass-doors to take a look at the yard. The barbeque, table and chairs took pride of place on the rear verandah. A huge tree at the bottom of the garden had a rope swing attached, and a homemade tree house perched on its massively thick branches. *It's a family home*.

In her mind's eye, a lanky dark-haired boy of about eight or ten, wearing a plaid short-sleeved shirt and denim shorts ran around the tree chasing a much smaller girl, with pink ribbons in her hair, a pink T-shirt, and cut-off jeans. He caught her around the middle, and they tumbled onto the grass laughing. The giggling pair rolled around for a few minutes until someone called them in for dinner. A dog bounded forward, barking joyfully, to join the children in their game. A picture-perfect family scene. Perversely, when she tried to picture herself in this scene, it brought anxiety, not pleasure. She shivered.

"I bought it from a family who had to move to Canada. They needed a quick sale. I got a bargain." Tommy had come up behind her when she was daydreaming. He placed his arms around her from behind, snuggling in and resting his cheek against hers. She could smell soap and warm male skin, toothpaste and his spicy deodorant. She turned in his arms and his whiskered chin scraped her cheek. *Didn't take time to shave.* He was wearing jeans and a soft faded blue T-shirt. His feet were bare. Water droplets clung to his tousled dark hair. He smiled, his eyes searching her face, finally resting on her mouth.

"It's a lovely house. A beautiful home for a young family, complete with tree house."

He kissed her then. Softly. His lips taking time to reassure her how much he wanted her, how happy he was to have her here in his home. Kisses such as these induced the butterflies in her stomach. More kisses dropped along her jawline, and up under her ear, brought about the goosebumps. She rose up on tiptoe to accommodate him. His teeth grazed her earlobe and her breathing became shallow. She gripped his shoulders as a wave of longing swept through her. His hands slipped around her waist, stroking her lower back, enticing her further into his embrace. Her nipples brushed his chest, peaked, a delicious quiver of excitement running through her at his touch. His mouth was now on her neck, and a moan of appreciation escaped her lips.

"No one has ever kissed me like you do," she whispered.

His mouth closed over hers and words became futile. Demanding kisses cut off all thought other than pleasure. He lifted her, carried her to the kitchen bench, and sat her on the edge. They were now almost the same height. He unfastened the row of buttons all the way down the front of her dress and smiled when he saw she wasn't wearing a bra. Her nipples puckered and tingled as his eyes swept greedily over them. He cupped her face in his hands, turning his head for better access. His tongue delved deeper into her mouth, drawing from her, pulling the very essence of her longing from her mouth to his. Kisses like this could not be explained in any literature she had ever read. It was as if he had taken control of the frightened hesitant girl of her youth and replaced her with a confident passionate woman who knew what she wanted, what she desired and what made her more than willing to do anything he demanded of her.

He pushed forward, easing her shoulders down, until she was lying back, her arms wide and her dress spread out along the bench. His eyes roamed over her, the heat in his stare making her bold. She cupped her breasts, offering up the soft pliant orbs with nipples peaked and awaiting the wet suck of his mouth. They tightened, demanding his touch. He gave it without hesitation.

Each nipple in turn enjoyed his administrations. From licking and sucking, to squeezing and tugging at their sensitive peaks, every touch accentuated Lauren's desire to have Tommy inside her. She arched her back, drawing his attention downward to where she wanted him to concentrate on next. He looked up at her and grinned. "In a hurry, are we?"

"I need you inside me. Filling me. I need my arms and legs wrapped around you, so I can take as much of you inside as possible."

"Be patient. Lie back and enjoy it." And with that he pushed her legs wide and buried his head between her thighs. Longing tugged at her core. He hooked his fingers into the waistband of her panties and pulled them off.

"Ohhhhhhh." Lauren's head cleared of all thoughts other than the delicious sensation of his tongue sweeping through the soft folds of her flesh and dancing over her clit.

His tongue lathed her with long slow strokes. Her body quivered as the tip of his tongue found the sensitive nub and circled it over and over again, drawing her closer and closer to her peak. He pulled her forwards to the edge of the bench, unzipped his jeans and eased himself out, teasing her with the tip of his cock.

She inched forwards until he was firmly inside, her bottom balanced on the very edge, and rocked her hips while he stroked into her.

"No condom!" He tried to pull out.

"No, no, no. Stay right there. Pleeeeease!" Her climax broke and her body welcomed each thrust, tightening around him, pulling him deeper in his release.

They embraced and held each other tight. The kiss that passed between them was an unspoken pact.

Each aware of the risk they had just taken.

LAUREN PULLED TOMMY'S ARMS AROUND HER, SO THAT SHE WAS tucked into his embrace in the middle of his comfortable bed. His chin rested in the curve of her neck, his thighs warming the backs of hers.

"I want to talk about what just happened. You don't have to worry about me getting pregnant. I'm on the pill. No, before you ask, it's not because I sleep around. It's because I need to regulate my cycle. And I have been checked out, just last year. After the last guy I was dating had a fling with a co-worker."

"I should have been more prepared. But you don't have to worry about me either. I'm clean. Squeaky clean really; I've been going solo, enjoying a deep and abiding love with my shower stall. I haven't been with anyone since I got back. I had regular tests in New York. All good."

"So we're going to save a bundle on condoms then. Good to know." Lauren squirmed in his arms and turned to face him. "Changing the subject, I spoke to the chief today, and told him what Marty said. They're going to bring him in to talk to him, get some more information. I feel as if some of the pieces are starting to fall into place."

"You haven't talked about your mother. I haven't wanted to

push you, but don't you think you need to go back and see her?" Tommy said quietly.

"I don't want to talk about it. Especially not now."

"I know she wasn't there when you were growing up, but from all you've told me, she's had a hard life. Maybe it's time to—"

"I said I don't want to talk about it! I'm still trying to clear my name. Then I'll be able to sort out how I feel about my mother."

"You said she's housebound. She's probably wondering what's going on."

"Give. It. A. Rest. Please." Lauren pushed out of the circle of his arms, slid out of bed and began to get dressed. "You're spoiling *what was* a lovely evening."

"Where are you going? I thought you'd stay tonight."

"If I stay you'll have to take me home for the early shift at the diner."

"That's okay. I'm sure I'll be awake at the crack of dawn with you tucked in my bed. Or maybe I won't go to sleep at all." Tommy stood up, unbuttoned her dress, slipped it off and threw it onto the chair by the window. He pulled her back down into the warm bed and tucked the covers around them. The goosebumps on her skin subsided in the cocoon of his arms. Her pounding heart slowed a fraction. She turned her face into his neck and breathed in the scent of him. Suddenly and irrationally afraid to jeopardise whatever this was between them with an argument.

She closed her eyes and clung on tight to the notion that they could weather any storm. She had to believe that.

CHAPTER TWENTY

MAYBELLINE WAS IN THE KITCHEN CHATTING WITH MARIO WHEN Lauren arrived at the diner. It hadn't gone unnoticed that whenever Mario was in the vicinity, Maybelline lit up. Mario's smile and singsong Italian accent had May blushing like a sixteen-year-old.

"Hey, you two lovebirds. How are you this morning?"

"Hush, child. Lovebirds indeed. Tsk, Tsk. You don't know what you're talking about. Mario and I are friends. Isn't that right, Mario?"

"You know I no look at another woman, same as I look at *Ma Bella. Allora.* You 'ave my heart."

"*Ma Bella?*" Lauren asked.

"Mabella is his nickname for me. It's short for Maybelline, you see."

"Ah huh. Sounds a bit more than that to me. In Italian it means 'my beautiful', May." Lauren nodded at Maybelline. "He's sweet on you."

Maybelline pushed Lauren out of the kitchen ahead of her, and into the restaurant. "Nonsense. He's much younger than me."

"Only a few years. What are you so worried about? You're adults, and both free to do whatever you want."

"He's eleven years younger than me. I'm a grandmother for goodness sake. The last thing I need is to give the gossips any more ammunition."

"Ohhhh. Maybelline has a 'toy boy'." Lauren folded her arms and smiled. "Come on! Surely having a toy boy would spice up your life. You're a long time dead, May. Besides. The gossips might leave me alone then."

"Ah-ha. Now I see. You have an ulterior motive." Maybelline paired the knives and forks and proceeded to wrap them in napkins. "And talking about motives, have you any more information about Brett Hagar?"

"Marty James told me he saw a man, who we know now was John Norris, taking Brett back into the hall, but he got away from him and ran off. I called the chief. He was going to pick up Marty for questioning."

"Why didn't he come forward before?"

"Says no one would believe a drunk."

"He has a point. Even back then he was a heavy drinker. I know for a fact that he had a flask of whiskey in his hip pocket that night, and he kept going outside to take a swig. If the principal had caught him he would have been in big trouble. It wouldn't surprise me if he provided some of the kids with some alcohol. There were a few lads that night who behaved like they had been drinking."

"Brett had for sure. I could smell it on him, even before he grabbed me."

The door opened as the first customers arrived, and with them, a chilly blast of air swirled around the room. The early risers made their way to the stools or the booths. Before long, the diner was filled with the aroma of bacon and eggs and fragrant coffee, sweet sugary cinnamon donuts, pancakes and maple syrup. The noise level had increased due to the companionable chatter of friends and co-workers, and the drone of the television mounted on the wall. Maybelline and

Lauren didn't have a chance for more discussion. The office workers wanted to be fed and on their way lickity-split, the truck drivers wanted takeaway to eat on the road, and the two elderly pensioners nursing a pot of coffee between them just wanted to feel a part of the bustling world while they read the free morning papers in the booths by the window.

Lauren loved the mornings in the diner. She had started to recognise regulars, and once they got over the shock of seeing "the prime suspect", as she had become known, working and talking and laughing with Maybelline, they relaxed a little and accepted her.

Half an hour before the end of her shift, a young woman approached Lauren, clutching the "Help Wanted" sign.

"Who do I see about this job?"

"Go and talk to Maybelline over there." Lauren nodded in the direction of the kitchen, and unloaded her tray onto a customer's table.

Maybelline gave the young woman a form to fill out, invited her to sit at an empty booth, and sat opposite her.

After about fifteen minutes, the young woman left. Maybelline went back behind the counter.

"What happened? No good?"

"She's the first applicant and she's had no experience. I'm hoping someone with some experience will apply. I don't want to have to babysit someone. She was young. And a bit shy, to be honest. She'd run at the first abuse from a customer if she messed up an order."

"So my job's safe for another day."

"If you put it like that, yes, it is."

"Cos I'm planning on buying a condo at the end of the month. The pay is so good here."

"You *are* a cheeky little minx this morning, aren't you." Maybelline caught sight of a woman getting out of a car. "Helen's just pulled up."

"Good morning, Maybelline. Good morning, Lauren." Helen unbuttoned her jacket, hung it on the back of a chair and sat down. "No need for a menu. I'll have a cinnamon roll and coffee please."

"You're looking exceptionally happy this morning, Helen." Maybelline brought the cinnamon roll to the table. Lauren poured the coffee.

"I dropped in on Tommy. His father and I are very proud of how the business is coming along. He tells me you visited his house last night, Lauren."

"I did. He has a beautiful place."

"He got a bargain when that couple had to sell up and leave so quickly. His father and I were shocked at how well he did. He's made some improvements. But there's still so much you could do with that place."

"Oh, that reminds me, I have the photos in the car. I could get them in fifteen minutes when I my shift is over."

"Don't worry about that now. Why don't you bring them around tonight, with Tommy? I'll make dinner. It would be lovely to see you both again so soon."

"Are you sure?"

"I love to cook, and it makes a difference when I'm cooking for more than just me and Jeff. It will be a pleasure. How about six o'clock? Jeff gets tired if we eat too late."

"Six sounds perfect."

Helen finished her coffee and sweet roll, paid her bill and left.

Lauren watched her getting into the car.

"She sure thinks a lot of you. Two dinners in less than two weeks." Maybelline cleared the table. The breakfast rush was over, and they were alone in the diner except for Mario.

"It's starting to get real, May."

"What do you mean?"

"Tommy wants me to stay. And he took me to his house last night. He cooked for me. His parents couldn't be nicer to me. His mother is treating me like I'm daughter-in-law material. And all I want to do is prove I didn't have anything to do with Brett's death and get out of town."

"Are you really going to leave Tommy?"

"I have an apartment in the city. I have a life there, with friends, and I *had* a job. I'm hoping to get another one. A good job, with decent money and a future."

"Some people don't see what's in front of their face!"

"What do you mean by that?"

"Tommy loves you. You won't find a man like Tommy in the city. You may never find a family as accepting as his family has been. They want the best for their son and yet they have opened their home for you, *knowing* you are under suspicion for a murder."

"I know about all that. But this town still gives me nightmares."

"And what about your mother? Sarah told me she's in the next county."

"Oh, don't look shocked that we've been discussing it. Sarah's concerned about you too. She told me your mother's badly scarred, and spends her time alone on that farm. After all these years, don't you want to try to get to know one another again?"

"Don't *you* go on about my mother, *please!* Tommy and I already argued about this last night."

"Seems to me you are running away from more than just this town, missy. You seem to be running away from the truth. You have a man who loves you and wants another go at making things work. You have a chance to know your mother, who disappeared when you were young. She's had a terrible life. Surely you can bury the past and work out a better future. If you go back to the city now you may never get another chance. What are you afraid of?"

"I can't talk about this now. My shift is over. I'll see you tomorrow."

"There you go. Running off again. Face your fear, Lauren. Whatever it is, or you will be running forever."

Lauren took off her apron, grabbed her purse and left the diner as quick as her legs could carry her. Her heart was beating fast, and her chest felt tight. *A panic attack.* She hadn't had one for years. It took a few seconds to get the car started, and then she took off out of the car park as if the devil was after her. *Running off again. Running off again. Running off again.* It played over in her head, like a broken record, until she reached the cottage.

She unlocked the door, threw her jacket and purse down and flopped on the couch. She sat back with her eyes closed.

Face your fear, she said. What the hell am I so afraid of? Staying in this town feels as if I am being buried alive. "But my heart belongs to Tommy and he is in this town. He wants to marry me, which means I'll be expected to stay here." Lauren shook her head. "Failure. I'm afraid I won't live up to being a good wife. He'll want children and I don't know if I can ever give him children. And now I'm talking to myself. Another sign I'm going crazy. A shrink would have a field day with this behaviour."

She glanced at the floor near the front door and noticed some dirt, and more dirt on the way into the bedroom. There was no way she had left dirty footprints on the floor. She followed them into the bedroom and it was obvious someone had been in the cottage, searching through her things. Being such an organised neat freak, there was no way she would leave drawers open a crack, or books not squared with the corners on her bedside table. What was someone looking for? And more importantly, who had a key to the cottage? She phoned Tommy.

"Have you been in the cottage today?"

"No, I've been here all morning. Why, what's wrong?"

"Someone's been in here, and they've been going through my things. Who has a key?"

"Me. My folks. That's it. And you, of course. Is anything missing?"

"No, nothing is missing that I can see. But I haven't looked properly yet."

"Don's out in the tow truck picking up a car. Are you okay?

You sound stressed. I can't leave the garage unattended to take a look. I'm expecting a parts delivery."

"I'm okay. I had an argument with Maybelline at the diner. I'll come over there shortly. I want to take a look around first."

She swept the dirt off the floor, and went through room by room, trying to work out what had been touched or moved. It gave her the creeps to think someone had been touching her things. Her suitcase was in the bottom of the closet, zipped and padlocked, and tucked in behind a set of drawers. She always locked it when she left anything of value in it. The few dollars she had saved and the jewellery she had brought with her was still safely inside, with her laptop. It did not look like it had been moved. She opened the suitcase and pulled out her laptop.

She checked all the windows, to make sure they were firmly closed. Lauren changed out of her uniform, tucked her laptop under her arm, pocketed her keys and made her way to the garage. Tommy was at the roller door, signing an invoice for his spare parts delivery. He winked at her as she passed, heading for the office. He caught up to her halfway up the stairs and stole a quick kiss.

"Did you notice if anything was missing?"

"Nope. Doesn't appear to be anything missing. Wonder what they were looking for?"

"And you're sure someone was in there."

"I'm sure."

"My offer still stands. Come and stay with me. I'll advertise the cottage for rent. It's closer to the diner." Tommy's smiled deepened the laugh lines around his eyes. He pulled her in for another kiss.

Lauren put up her hand to stop him. "You have a point. And to be honest, the place is giving me the creeps. But—"

"There's always a but."

"If I move in with you—"

"Yeah, I get it. You're not ready to make that commitment." Tommy let her go, and took a step down.

"Can we leave things as they are for the moment? Please."

"Seems like I don't have much choice." Tommy turned around to head back down the stairs. But not before she saw his smile disappear and his shoulders slump down.

There was nothing she could say. If she moved in with him, and then left him to go back to the city he was going to be hurt. She was going to hurt him no matter what.

She grabbed his arm to stop him. "Oh, by the way. Your mother came in to the diner this morning. She suggested we go over to your folks for dinner later. Have you made other plans?"

"Nope, no other plans. Did she tell you what she's cooking? Maybe I'll call and drop some hints for chicken schnitzel."

"I'm sure she'll make it for you. I think you could ask for pretty much anything you like and she'd cook it for you. Spoiled isn't the word."

"Can I help it if I'm the adorable one in the family?"

"Spoiled *and* full of yourself." Lauren patted him on the cheek. "Oh, I have something for them too. I put the family photos into albums. They're not expensive albums but I think they look pretty good."

"Are you working on your book today?"

"I sure am. I'm getting to an interesting part."

"Are you ready to share?"

"Nope. Not until I've finished it, and revised it."

"I'll leave you to it then."

THE PHONE RANG IN THE OFFICE, AND LAUREN AUTOMATICALLY picked it up.

"Slater & Son. Can I help you?"

"Lauren?"

"Yes?"

"Lauren, it's your mother."

"Why are you calling here?"

"I didn't know where else to call to contact you. The newspaper said you were working at the garage."

"And that was another thing they got wrong. I'm not working here, just helping out. What did you call for?"

"I thought you might come back to the farmhouse. I think we should talk."

"I don't know if I'm ready to talk to you yet."

"Well, I'll come to you."

"No! I don't want you here." Lauren recognised the panic in her voice.

"There are some things I think you need to know."

"You're going to have to give me some time. Then I'll come to you."

LAUREN HUNG UP. SHE CLOSED THE LAPTOP, SAT BACK AND STARED unseeing at the ceiling. For years she had tried to find her mother. Now she was living a short drive away, she didn't know what to say to her. Numbness had invaded her heart. Hate had bubbled under the surface during all the years she had felt abandoned, unloved, uncared for in a town where they made a point of labelling her a loser from a dysfunctional family. She was the teenage kid who more often than not had clothes from Goodwill, and didn't have money to spend on movies and the normal things teenagers craved. Until an after-school job at the mini-mart bought her a reprieve from the worst of the bullying. Knowing her mother had been abused should have made it easier for Lauren to forgive her now for leaving. But it only made it worse. *She left me in that environment. With that monster. How did she know he wouldn't abuse me?*

She flipped open the laptop. The cursor blinked at her.

Who am I kidding. I can't go back to writing a book today. Better to concentrate on the prom night photographs. She packed up her laptop and returned to the cottage.

"There has to be something here I'm missing." Lauren spread out the images she had printed from the negatives, and picked up the magnifying glass again.

She ran the glass over every person in the photographs. She had almost committed each one to memory. The dresses the girls wore, the suits and ties the boys wore . . . or didn't wear. A lot of guys had removed their ties by the time the Crowning photos were taken.

She had a sudden flashback of Brett, lassoing her, wrapping his tie around her neck, pulling her in for a kiss she didn't want to give, pulling her tight against him. His erection pressed hard against her stomach had disgusted her and she tried to push him away. The more she struggled, the more determined he had been to kiss her. She tried to fight him and they had stumbled back onto the grass. The image of his face looming over hers, spittle flying from his lips as he yelled abuse at her, suddenly made her flinch. He told her she was filthy trash and it didn't matter how hard she struggled, he was going to show her what she was missing and tell everyone what a lousy fuck she was anyway. She had raised her hand to push his mouth away and tried to turn her head. His silver medallion hung in between them, and she grabbed it, wrenched his head away and screamed. . .

. . . *that must have been when he punched me.*

The next memory was of the sergeant helping her to her feet, feeling dazed and bruised and being helped into the back of the patrol car.

The memory of that night suddenly as clear as crystal, she could almost smell the damp grass beneath her, could almost feel his spittle on her face, and the chain from the medallion digging into her hand.

Bastard!

She got up to have a glass of water. She couldn't let those memories crush her now.

She picked up the magnifying glass and got back to work.

LAUREN RANG SARAH'S DOORBELL, KEEPING HER FINGERS CROSSED that Sarah would be home at that time of day.

"Lauren, what a lovely surprise!" Sarah hugged her friend.

"Sarah, I need your opinion on something."

"Sure, come in." Sarah headed for the kitchen. Milly was sitting at the bench. "I have half an hour before I have to pick up Jake from school." Sarah handed her daughter a plate of apple slices. "Milly and I are having a snack. I'll make some coffee."

"Hi, Milly. You're looking very pretty today." Lauren ruffled the little girl's curls.

"Hi, Lauren. I'm having a snack with Teddy." Milly slipped off the stool, tucked her teddy bear under her arm and carried her plate of apple slices into the backyard.

Lauren spread out the photos on the table. "I want you to look at these. In every one of these school photographs, Don is standing either behind or beside Brett. Have a look at the expression on his face in this one. What do you see?"

"He looks happy."

"That's all you see?"

"Yes, what more is there to see. He's smiling, he has his arm around Brett's shoulder, Brett is laughing. What do you see?"

"I see a young man in love! Look at all these images. He's never more than a foot away from him, he's watching his every move. If that isn't infatuation, I don't know what is. I remember what it was like for me. I wanted to be near Tommy at every opportunity. Look at this photo of me and Tommy. You can see I love him by the expression on my face. Now look at this one of Don and Brett. The exact same expression is on Don's face. It's more than hero worship. I think Don's gay."

"Really?"

"Have you ever seen him with a woman?"

"I thought he was just shy."

"There is shy, and there is not interested in females at all."

"That's a big jump."

"It's not just that. For some reason he is very cagey around me. He is so neat and tidy. Have you seen that kitchen in the garage? Oh. My. God. I thought I was organised. He won't look me in the eye. He follows Tommy around like he is his shadow. He's very loyal to Tommy, would do anything for him."

"What are you saying? That he's in love with Tommy now?"

"Yes. That is exactly what I am saying."

"That is a pretty big assumption, Lauren."

"I don't think he likes me being with Tommy. I can feel his hostility whenever Tommy touches me or kisses me in public."

"What does Tommy think?"

"We haven't discussed it. I'm not going to say anything at the moment."

"Why are you focusing on this? What difference does it make if Don is gay or not."

"It makes no difference to me. But if Don was interested in Brett, and Brett was not aware of it, and he followed Brett around, he might have seen Brett follow me out of the hall that night."

"God, this is getting complicated."

"It was always complicated. We have to work out how to simplify all the facts. No one was going to stand up and say, 'I did it. Take me in, Chief.'"

"So you think Don followed you and Brett outside."

"The pictures of Tommy and Maggie show their gang around them on the stage. Brett and Don are missing."

"You're right. They are nowhere to be seen." She pulled the photographs closer.

"I need to ask Marty if he saw Don outside that night too. He remembers seeing Brett being dragged back."

"Good luck. He's not a very reliable witness. From what you've told me, prepare to get your head bitten off."

"It is worth the chance. What do I have to lose?"

Helen opened the door when Lauren and Tommy arrived for dinner. "Come in, you two. Jeff is downstairs in the basement picking out some wine."

"I brought your photographs back. Well, most of them. The chief has the prom night ones." Lauren accepted the arm Helen linked through hers. They proceeded down the hall.

"I guess he needs to see them to work out what happened. They sure are taking their time." Helen patted the couch for Lauren to sit beside her.

Tommy carried the box and placed it on the coffee table.

Helen pulled the box closer, surprise written all over her face. "Lauren, what a wonderful thing to do." She selected an album and flipped through, noting the funny and cute captions Lauren had added to the pages. "Oh, these are such a trip back in time. Look, Jeff."

Jeff appeared in the dining room, with a tray of glasses and a bottle of wine. He added the glasses to the table already set for dinner. "Hang on, Helen. What are you so excited about?"

"Look at what Lauren has put together for us." She leant over and hugged Lauren. "Family photographs are such fun. We can keep these albums on the coffee table, and look at them later, after dinner."

"Riveting entertainment." Tommy mumbled. Lauren elbowed him in the ribs.

"Maybelline tells me you've found your mother, Lauren." Helen leant over and placed her hand over Lauren's. "I imagine that was a big shock."

"It was. I really don't want to talk about it."

"And Maybelline said she had remarried but she's now a widow." Lauren turned beseeching eyes towards Tommy.

The atmosphere in the room turned from friendly banter to awkward silence in an instant. Tommy took Lauren's hand between his.

"Mom, Lauren is not comfortable talking about this. If you cannot respect that, we'll have to go." He stood up and Lauren followed.

"No, no, no. I'm sorry. I didn't mean to upset you. We'll talk about something else. Sit down. Please. How is the garage going, Tommy? Jeff said you got some new business from the post office and supermarket, servicing their delivery vans."

Tommy kept a hold on Lauren's hand. His reassurance conveyed with every stroke of his thumb on the back of her fingers. "Yeah, their service contract ran out with Lawson's so I was able to make them an offer. Every little bit helps."

"I'll just check how the chicken is coming along." Helen hurried off to the kitchen.

"Helen didn't mean to upset you. She really has your best interests at heart. We won't talk about it now, but if you do need someone to talk to, we want you to know we are here for you." Jeff handed each of them a glass of wine.

"Thank you." Lauren took the wine and smiled, but the smile did not reach her eyes.

THEY DROVE THE SHORT DISTANCE WITHOUT CONVERSATION.

"That dinner could not have been more awkward if I'd tried. I'm sorry. I imagine you are getting sick of sticking up for me."

"It's only natural people will be curious. You have to admit they probably think meeting up with your mother after all this time would be a happy occasion."

"Therein lies the problem. Most people have no idea what it's like to come home and find their mother has just up and left, and their father is like a bear with a sore head most of the time. You're trying, but even you don't really understand. You came from a loving family home. Even after tragedy, with your brother's accident, your mother never stopped showing you she loved you."

"I guess you're right. I have no idea. But I do know that the more you bottle up your feelings the more it builds inside you. Why don't you just go and talk to her. Tell her how angry and how hurt you've been. The bitterness will not go away until you forgive her."

"Maybe I don't want it to go. It drove me forwards. I have carried that bitterness . . . no, that hatred . . . with me for years. Holding everyone at arm's length. Keeping my heart safely locked away. It has motivated me to be an independent woman in a man's world. It has made me stronger when other reporters jockeying for position in my office cut me down. When I lost my job, I did not fall to pieces. I got out there and started looking for something else." Lauren drew in a ragged breath. "But now there's you. You've have crept below my defences, reminding me of why I loved you when we were kids. Maybe you're the one person that can heal that broken part of me."

"I'd sure like to try."

They pulled up in the alley in front of the cottage. The sensor lights illuminated the porch. Lauren turned to Tommy.

"You know, the last place I imagined I would be this year was in Clearwater Springs. I was afraid to come back here. Afraid of the memories. Of how I would feel. Yet you have done everything you can to show me things can be different now. You show me you care every single day. You gave me a place to stay. I just needed to tell you I was afraid and you put the sensor light in the cottage. You're a good man, Tommy Slater."

"And because I care about you, I encourage you to open up to your mother. There are wounds that only you two can heal. Now let's go inside so I can kiss that sad face and turn it into a happy one."

CHAPTER TWENTY-ONE

As she drove up the alley after her shift, Lauren spotted a woman sitting on her doorstep with her face turned up towards the sun.

It took a second before she recognised her ex-work colleague Tiffany Ward behind the oversized designer sunglasses.

"Tiffany. To what do I owe the pleasure?" Lauren got out of the car and hoisted a bag of groceries onto her hip. She searched her key ring for the key to the cottage.

"Hey, Lauren." Tiffany scrambled to her feet and pushed the shades onto the top of her head. "I heard about the 'Body in the Hole' reunion weekend. I thought I would come and get an interview straight from the *prime suspect*. Considering we're friends an' all."

"We were never friends, Tiffany. And you showed your hand by jumping into my office chair as soon as I left the building. Or maybe you already had it before I left. They just forgot to tell me."

"Now, now, don't be bitter and twisted, Lauren. You know

you stepped on many toes while writing your column. I couldn't help it if they decided I was a good fit."

"And since I refused to sleep with the boss to keep my job . . . oh yeah, that was *your* job. Tell me, has his wife found out yet?"

"Ohhh, bitchy."

"No. But here's a little titbit you probably don't know. His wife's family money and connections got him that position, and he will throw you to the wolves if she ever finds out. Her family have been in the publishing business for decades. Her family knows where the bodies are buried. Probably helped put some in the ground. You'll be a liability. Good luck finding a job then."

"Look. I had nothing to do with you getting fired, or you losing your office. I came here to get your side of the story. I'm sure there will be others soon, knocking on your door. We can give the public the facts. You can veto anything I write."

"Why am I finding that hard to believe? Why should you care?"

"Okay, here's the truth. I need a good story. Something to get my teeth into, to make them notice me. I've been given fluff pieces since you left."

"That's because the only good investigative reporter is a male reporter, in their eyes. Go back to the city, Tiffany. I've got nothing for you."

Tommy chose that moment to come out the side door of the garage carrying a crate of mangled car parts, destined for the dumpster. Muscles rippled across his chest, his biceps bulged and his corded forearms holding the crate were smudged with grease. The navy singlet he wore beneath his bib-coveralls did little to hide all that action going on, and by the look on Tiffany's face, his body had gone into "slow motion" in front of her eyes. Lauren could hear the soundtrack, and the "Oh yeah" as he strode towards them. *Fuck.*

"Hey babe." He hoisted the crate higher and tipped it into

the dumpster, giving Tiffany a good look at his mighty fine rear view.

"Introduce me to your friend." Tiffany straightened the navy pencil skirt she wore, smoothing it over her hips. She deftly adjusted the opening of her white blouse, which allowed a bit more cleavage to be on show, and licked her scarlet lips.

You've got to be kidding me. "Tommy, this is Tiffany. She works in my old office. Literally!"

"Hey." Tommy smiled at Tiffany. "Visiting or just passing through?" He turned his cheeky lopsided grin towards Lauren and leant over to kiss her cheek.

"I'd like to write a piece about the body they found, but Lauren is being less than cooperative."

"That's an understatement," Lauren mumbled.

"I'm trying to help." Tiffany propped her fists on her hips, pulled back her shoulders and pushed out her breasts in Tommy's direction.

Did she just pout at him?

"Help who. Me? Or you?" Lauren asked.

Tommy looked uncomfortable under the hot gaze of "Tiffany the seductress".

"Better get back to it. I'll leave you to it. Nice to meet you, Tiffany." He all but ran back into the garage.

"Was it something I said?" Tiffany feigned innocence, and turned her wide-eyed baby blues on Lauren.

"You're full of it. He knows a predator when he sees one. Go back to the city." Lauren walked passed her and unlocked the cottage door. "I can't help you." Lauren began to close the door.

Tiffany stuck the toe of her red patent-leather pump into the space, just before it closed. "Can't or won't? Look, I know you think I'm not worth your time, but I am begging you."

"Begging me? Come on, Tiff. What's really going on?" She opened the door wider.

"I . . . well I promised, you see. I told them I would get an inside scoop. I told them we had talked and you'd agreed."

"You dug yourself into a nice hole, didn't you. How ironic." Lauren looked at the young woman standing before her. A seriously attractive twenty-five-year-old, and not afraid to use her womanly ways to get ahead. But Lauren knew that in the end, if you didn't have any talent to back that up, you didn't last long in the publishing industry. "Okay. Come in and we'll talk. But only because you are in a position to help me as much as I can help you."

"Thanks. I know you don't have any reason to trust me right now. But I would like to help. As long as I get an exclusive."

Lauren placed the bag of groceries on the bench. She washed her hands and pulled out bread, salami and cheese. "I'm making lunch. Take a seat. Do you want a sandwich?"

"That would be great, thanks. I left early this morning and didn't eat breakfast. I picked up a coffee on the way." Tiffany perched on the edge of couch and crossed her legs.

"Where are you staying?"

"I haven't booked in yet. I was going to stay at the Holiday Inn."

"It's clean and cheap. Central too. How long are you planning on being in town?"

"Maybe two or three days. That should give me enough time to talk to a few people and get a draft started at least. I can work on it back in the city."

"Here you go. Do you want ketchup?" Lauren handed Tiffany a sandwich cut into four triangles, and a glass of orange juice.

"Awwww. Cut up like my mama used to do. You do love me after all. No ketchup, thanks." She balanced the plate on her knee, polished off half of the sandwich in record time, and washed it down with some juice. "So you used to live here? How does it feel to be back in town?"

"Strange. It's hard to step back in time. I've been used to living in the city where everything is larger than life, the pace there is fast and frenetic. Here, it's slow and there's always tomorrow."

"Who's the hottie from the garage?"

"That's Tommy Slater. His family owns the garage. Owns this cottage too."

"He's your boyfriend?"

"Yeah, I guess you could call him that. We were pretty tight in high school. We've become reacquainted since I came back."

"He looked familiar."

"He played baseball for a few years in the Southern Pacific League, in New York State."

"Ah-ha. Maybe I *have* seen him before. My brother was a mad- keen baseball fan. Watched all the games."

"He's not long back in town. About a year. He was injured."

"Ah, now I remember where I've seen him. There was a promo video for his team. They ran a piece in the sports section. He had a nickname. Sir Galahad, I think. He was quite a hit with the ladies, from memory."

"He's always been popular with the ladies. Now, if you've finished I have work to do." Lauren stood and opened the door. "Don't you have interviews to get to?"

"Sure. Thanks for the sandwich. Can I start with Tommy? If he was your boyfriend back in the day, he can give me some background information."

"Knock yourself out. He's working, so don't expect to get too much information from him."

"I'm sure he'll have time for me." Tiffany stood up and straightened her skirt over her hips. "Don't worry. I won't try to steal your guy."

"If he falls for your charms, he's not worth keeping."

"No, you're not jealous. You're not jealous at all, are you?"

"Don't let the door hit you on the way out, Tiff." Lauren opened the door.

"I need to know who you think I should talk to. Can you email me a list to get me started?"

"Sure." Lauren closed the door and leant her forehead against the solid surface.

She had to get out of the cottage. The idea of that man-eater with Tommy was making her anxious. She got in her car and drove out of town. Maybe she should take Tommy's advice.

She called her mother.

CHAPTER TWENTY-TWO

As she drove to the farmhouse, Lauren thought long and hard about Tommy's advice. It was time to build bridges and let her mother talk through her years of separation. By refusing to go and see her mother, she had been avoiding facing up to the truth.

The gate was standing open. Lauren drove up to the back of the house. Alice was sitting on the back porch. She put down her glass of iced tea and approached the car.

"I'm so happy to see you. I want to show you something. Come with me."

They entered the barn through a side door, and climbed the wooden staircase to the second floor. Alice unlocked the door to the loft and stood back for Lauren to enter her studio.

The room had white plastered walls, a vaulted ceiling and huge skylights, flooding the room with sunshine.

Canvases were hung on every available wall, some were stacked two or three deep against crates, some mounted on easels. Hundreds of images in black and white and in colour, in charcoal and in oils. Some were hard and fast sketches, appearing forlorn and obviously unfinished. Some were delicate, intricately detailed portraits in soft hues. All showed a talented artist, albeit in different stages of development.

Lauren gaped in amazement. Multiple images of her face stared back at her.

YOU ACCUSED ME OF LEAVING YOU BEHIND AND NEVER GIVING YOU a second thought. That could not have been further from the truth.

I thought of you every day. And when I was able, I came in here and tried to record a memory I had of you when you were growing up. You were a beautiful child. You have grown into a beautiful woman. But the last image I painted before you left town was this one."

Alice uncovered a portrait of Lauren in her pale blue prom dress. Memories came flooding back to Lauren of how she had loved that dress. This was the dress she had scrimped and saved to buy. She had convinced herself that Tommy would take one look at her and announce his undying love to the world. But that never happened.

Lauren moved forward until she was only a few inches from the canvas. She ran her fingers over the gentle sweep of her cheek, the full lips and sparkling eyes. There was a small photograph pinned to the corner of the canvas. Her mother must have captured her at the moment she had watched Tommy receive his crown. The happiness on her face was apparent, and on show for the entire world to see.

"I don't know what to say. These are so good. You are very talented." Lauren turned to face her mother "You didn't forget about me." Tears ran down her cheeks.

"Not for one single moment. But I was so ashamed. I didn't think I could ever go back. Who would want this?" Alice gestured to her ruined face.

"I've held hate in my heart all these years, it was my armour.

Because of you I've never let anyone get close to me for a long, long time. Now I'm back here, and with Tommy Slater, the boy I loved in high school. But I'm afraid of opening myself up to be hurt again."

"I'm so sorry. I'm ashamed that because of me you've missed out on so much. But it needs to end, for your sake, Lauren. It's too late for me. But it's not too late for you to live a life filled with love." Alice reached out and touched Lauren's shoulder. She held open her arms. For a few seconds they just looked at each other. Then Lauren took the hardest two steps of her life and walked into Alice's embrace.

LAUREN SAT AT THE FRONT DOOR OF THE COTTAGE, WATCHING THE sun go down, nursing a cup of coffee. A car pulled up in the alley.

Tommy got out and meandered towards her holding a small pink bakery box, with a cheeky grin on his face.

"How'd it go with your mother?" Tommy followed her inside the cottage.

"Pretty good, actually. We talked about the past, and we talked about the future. We've come to an agreement. We're going to try and move forward and give each other time to get used to this new situation."

"I'm happy you've taken the first step. I know it was hard for you."

"I'm still not able to let it all go, but I'm trying to see things from her point of view."

"There are always two sides to every story. Walk a mile in my shoes as they say."

"And I've learned something about her today. She's an artist. She has a studio filled with sketches and canvases." Lauren perched on the edge of the couch.

"Any good?" Tommy put down the box, leant up against the kitchen bench, and crossed his arms.

"They're all of me. At different stages of me growing up. It was strange to see so many images of my face."

"Wow. That says a lot. Don't you think?"

"I have to admit it does. And yet I still cannot understand why she didn't come and find me . . ."

"You told me she'd explained that. Who knows what happens when you're the constant recipient of abuse. And from someone who's supposed to take care of you, love you, support you."

"You know, he never laid a hand on me growing up. Until my mother left he was a normal father. Not overly affectionate, always working, but he never hit me. When she left he just shut me off, like I was a burden, like he didn't want anything to do with me. He didn't want to spend time with me, or any money on me. Not even for school stuff, that was obvious. He had money for booze though. I'm not even sure if he ever loved me. You know I wrote to him, after I left. He never answered my letters. That was why I didn't come back for the funeral."

"I knew he didn't like me spending time with you. Even though everyone thought we were just friends. The looks he would give me if I saw him in town would have skinned a wild animal. Maybe he guessed."

"Not that it stopped you."

"No. Nothing would have stopped me from being with you. Laughing with you, just hanging out. Watching that light in your eyes when I kissed you. Holding you in my arms."

Lauren got up and crossed to Tommy. "You were my world back then, my only happiness." She cupped his cheek with her palm.

"I wish I'd known what had happened that night. I wish I could have stopped you from being hurt. From leaving. Things might have been different for us."

Lauren shook her head. "I'm not sure if things would have worked out for us if I had stayed. Your folks wanted someone better for you. And you had ambition to play pro-baseball. It would have been wrong to hold you back, even if I could've stayed. We were young then. Foolish and in love, but very young."

"Yes, I was young. I agree things might not have played out back then." Tommy tucked a strand of hair behind her ear, and tipped up her chin. "Now I know what I want. I've had a taste of life outside of Clearwater, and it's just the same shit, in a different town. You make your own happiness, Lauren, and I want to make mine with you."

"You said you wouldn't pressure me."

"Just stating a fact."

Lauren watched his face. The serious expression belied the twinkle in his eyes. *He is such a good man. What the hell are you waiting for?*

"What's in the box?" Lauren tapped the pink cardboard.

"Chocolate éclairs. Sweets for my sweet girl."

"Bullshit. *You* are the one with the sweet tooth."

"Well, sweets to sweeten you up. Some chocolate icing to lick off your lips, and other parts of you, after dinner. Before I make mad passionate love to you." Tommy placed his hands on the swell of her hips, tugging her closer.

Lauren's core muscles contracted thinking about Tommy's deep kisses, and the power of his tongue all over her body. The tingling those provocative words produced had her clamping her thighs together.

"Do you think by distracting me, I will give you what you want." Lauren smiled and looked into eyes.

"Oh I know you'll give me what I want. Eventually. I want Miss Lauren Taylor to be Mrs Lauren Slater. You need some time to get used to the idea. That's all."

"Always so sure of yourself."

"Someone has to be the glass half-full person in this relationship."

"It's a relationship, is it?"

"Hell yes. Are you the only one who doesn't see that? Everyone in town knows we're a couple."

"Maybe it's time for you to take a shower . . . a cold shower . . . and we can go get something to eat."

"Sounds like a great idea. I think you should join me."

Tommy picked her up in a fireman's hold, marched to the bathroom and turned on the water. He stood her back on her feet and miraculously stripped off her clothes, as well as his, in a few seconds. Lauren squealed when he backed her into the shower, and up against the tiled wall.

"Oh. Don't like cold water? Maybe this will heat it up for you." His hand snaked around the back of her neck and he captured her mouth in a wet slippery kiss.

Lauren squealed as jets of cold water sluiced over their entwined bodies, pebbling her nipples and diminishing Tommy's erection. His hand reached out and turned off the flow as he concentrated on turning her goosebumps into tingles of pleasure. His mouth captured hers once more, his tongue dancing around hers, and delving deeper. The shiver coursing through her body now was one of need. She grabbed handfuls of his tight firm buttocks and pulled him against her stomach. His renewed arousal became evident, nudging against her mound, growing harder more persistent with each sweep of her tongue on his.

She lifted her leg and he slid against her wetness, the friction delicious and teasing, nudging her and moving away, nudging again and moving away, until she couldn't stand it anymore and she tilted her hips and applied some more pressure to his tight buttocks, inviting him in, encouraging him. He eased into her, slowly, sliding against her clit with each stroke, building the pleasure. The moan she heard came from her own lips. The satisfied sighs she heard against her ear came from his. As the tiny sparks of desire became a torrent of pleasure and she clenched around him, the guttural moan from his throat pushed her over the edge and her climax followed his.

CHAPTER TWENTY-THREE

Understandably, there had always been a dark lingering cloud in her memory over the day the lawyer had called to inform her of her father's death. As the executor, he was bound to notify her she was her father's sole beneficiary, and that he had left an envelope for her with Colby & Colby. She told him she wanted nothing from her father. She hung up, cutting him off before he could finish. She had been at work, and she had tried to continue with the article she was writing about kickbacks to the local council. It came as a complete surprise when someone walked past her office to say goodnight and she realised an hour had elapsed. She had been lost in the past. It shocked her to think that she cared enough to be upset by the news. Resolutely, she had decided it was time to cut all thoughts of him from her mind. After all, he had caused her enough anguish. Time to move on.

She had never returned to Clearwater Springs. After she had a job and a place of her own, she had written to her father a few times, but he had never replied to her letters. Or called. She wasn't sure what she had expected, but had faced up to the fact he didn't care. He knew where she was and yet had made no effort to contact her. After the lawyer called, Sarah had been the one to make contact and inform her of the service being held at the local church. She wondered why her father had chosen a church service. There had been little respect for religion demonstrated in their house when she was a child. She had flatly refused to go back for the funeral. He had shown no interest in her when she was living there, or in finding her when she first left town. He didn't deserve her tears. She was on her own now, and she would make the best of her life. Alone.

Given the fact that she was now back in town, and had found her mother, she decided perhaps a visit to the lawyer's office was something she should finally get out of the way.

She strode purposefully down the main street and stopped in front of the lawyer's office. The renovated building looked impressive, with a dark brick facade, a heavy oak door and a brass nameplate announcing "Colby & Colby, Attorneys at Law". The door creaked a little as it swung open.

The receptionist looked up from her task. "Can I help you?"

"I don't have an appointment but I was wondering if Jason Colby could see me. I had been asked to come and see him some time ago and this is the first time I've been back in town."

"I will buzz him. And your name is?"

"Lauren Taylor. It's about my father, Paul Taylor."

"Take a seat please."

Lauren moved away to let the receptionist make her call. When she glanced back, the receptionist was replacing the handset. "He'll be out in a few minutes. Would you care for a coffee, or a tea?"

"No thank you, I'm fine."

Lauren pulled a financial magazine from the coffee table and sat back to wait.

The silver-haired gentleman who opened the door and approached her was not at all the picture she had in her mind of Jason Colby. Thinking back, his voice had been soft and quiet on the phone, but the bear of a man standing before her surprised her. Not to mention his firm, bone-crushing handshake.

"Lauren. Please come in." He stood back and allowed her to enter his office. Bookcases full to capacity lined two walls. The only window, hung with velvet curtains, overlooked a lush green courtyard.

A table lamp cast a soft amber glow over an armchair in one corner, the décor muted and calming. There were two tobacco-coloured leather armchairs facing the mahogany partners desk, which took up a substantial amount of the space in the room. *A big desk for a big man.* "Take a seat." Jason resumed his position behind the desk, clasped his hands together over his padded waistline, and settled back in his chair. "How can I help you?"

Lauren sank into the soft comforting leather, which yielded under her weight. *This client's chair has seen many summers in this office, and probably borne witness to many sad stories.* "You called a few years ago to tell me my father had left something with you. My father was Paul Taylor. It's all a bit vague. I haven't been back to town until now. Do you still have it? Whatever it was."

"Ah yes. One moment." Jason typed something into his laptop, and took a minute to read what had appeared on the screen. He got up, unlocked a filing cabinet and pulled out a large manila envelope. "As I tried to explain on the phone, your father came to me after his diagnosis, to tidy up his affairs. He instructed me to give this envelope to you after his death."

"To be honest, I don't remember exactly what you said that day. It was a bit of a shock. My father and I didn't keep in touch. Well, I had tried at first, but he never answered my letters."

Lauren broke the notarised legal wax seal and opened the large envelope. She tipped the contents onto the desk. Her letters tumbled out. The letters she had written to him. The torn crumpled envelopes left her in no doubt they had been opened.

"Your father also set up a trust fund for you."

"What?" Lauren's hand stopped midair. Her letters sat in a small jumbled pile on the desk. She stared down at her own handwriting; as if it would give her a clue to what she was hearing. "I don't understand. A trust fund? Why would he do that? He didn't even answer my letters."

"Maybe he was trying to make amends? He sold his house and set up a trust fund in your name. He knew he didn't have long. The doctors had given him six months but he passed away quite quickly after the operation."

Lauren stuffed her letters back into the manila envelope. Confusion, anger and disbelief fought an internal battle with her composure. Trying to process why he would refuse contact with her yet want to set up a fund in her name resulted in bitter tears. She rubbed her fingers over her eyes, pushing them back. *I will not cry for you. Not now. Not ever.*

"If this is the money from the sale of the house, then I think my mother should have it. It was her house too."

"We were never able to find your mother."

"I have. She's been living over near Drewdale. From what she tells me it was not a good marriage. I think she deserves any money he left."

"What you do with the money is entirely up to you. But for the purpose of this meeting, I must follow my client's instructions and have you sign this paperwork so that we can get the ball rolling."

Lauren read the document placed before her, and happily signed on the dotted line. She wanted nothing to do with the money, but an idea had popped into her head about what her mother could do to get her life back.

Lauren handed him a slip of paper. "Here's my phone number, and the address where I am living at the moment, as well as my mother's address. I would like something drafted up to say I am signing over any money to her."

"I'll have something for you in a day or so. I'll call you."

Lauren stood to leave. "Thank you. I'm sorry it has taken me so long to come and see you. But I had no idea he had left me money. To be honest, I wasn't even going to come today. But something made me do it. Thank you for your help." She shook his hand.

"My pleasure, Lauren. My secretary will call you to make an appointment. You were lucky today. I had a cancellation. Don't forget your envelope." He came around the desk to show her out.

"Oh yes, my letters." Lauren folded the manila envelope and shoved it into her carry bag.

LAUREN PULLED OFF THE ROAD OUTSIDE THE FARMHOUSE AND called her mother.

"I've just pulled up outside. I have some news we need to talk about."

"Oh Lauren, how lovely to hear from you. I'm in the studio. The gate's unlocked. Come on up to the farmhouse. I'll be right down."

Lauren could hear the excitement in her mother's voice, and it made her smile. Maybe they could find a way back to one another. *Baby steps.* She unlatched the gate and drove up to the back of the house. Her mother appeared from the barn, wearing a paint-stained shirt over her clothes, and wiping her hands on a rag. She hurried towards the car.

"Come on in. I'll make some morning tea." Alice reached out and tentatively squeezed Lauren's hand. She climbed the steps and unlocked the back door to the farmhouse. Then bustled about, pulling cups from cupboards, heating water and cutting up cake.

Lauren pulled out a chair at the kitchen table and sat down. "I've been to see a lawyer in Clearwater. Colby & Colby, have you heard of them? Jason Colby contacted me years ago when Dad died, but I didn't want anything to do with him or a lawyer back then, so I didn't pursue it until today. It appears he left some money from the sale of the house. I want you to have it. It was your house too."

"I had wondered what had happened. I knew the house had been sold. But Lauren, he left you the money. I think you should keep it. John left me this house and enough in the bank. I'm fine." Alice put a cup of tea in front of Lauren, and placed a plate of lemon cake in the centre of the table.

"I don't want it. I wanted his love and attention, and he couldn't give me that. I don't want this money. But I know what you could do with the money to perhaps change your life, and stop living like a recluse." She took a sip of her coffee.

"I'm used to being here. I don't know any other way now." Alice collected her own cup and sat opposite.

"What would you say if I told you I know a plastic surgeon who might be able to restore your face? Maybe not perfectly, but they can do wonderful things these days."

"I don't know."

"The money from the sale of the house could be used to pay for the treatment. I made a call today. The specialist has agreed to see you if you want this. You would have to go to a hospital in the city."

"I'm afraid."

Lauren reached out and took her mother's hand. "I know. But I will be there with you. Cheering you on. You deserve this, after what he did to you. You deserve to have a normal life, not hidden away here, locked inside this farmhouse."

"You . . . you would come with me?"

"Yes. As soon as they let me leave town. In fact, I'll talk to the chief to see if I can take you to the specialist's appointment."

"I'll think about it. I will."

"Good, that's a start. And while I'm here, I wondered if I could have one of your sketches to show Tommy. I've told him about the studio, and your work."

"Yes. Wait here. Have some cake. I made it this morning. I know just the one you can take." Alice hurried off to her studio.

Lauren took a good look around the room as she ate her cake. Everything was clean, bright and perfect. All the appliances shone. But the air of sadness in this room was overwhelming. How could she be happy here? A picture of a man sat in a frame on the dresser. Lauren picked it up and stared at the man she assumed was John. He had a kind face, and an easy grace in front of the camera. His hand was resting on the neck of a horse, his wide brimmed hat tilted back as he looked up at the sky. His beaming smile had caused the weathered skin around his eyes to crinkle. *A man who laughed a lot.*

Her mother appeared at the screen door carrying a covered canvas, which she placed on the table.

"You would've liked John. He was a very kind man. A happy soul, even after all the tragedy in his life. A lesser man would have crumpled. Not John."

"He looks contented."

"We were happy. In a strange kind of way, quite contented to be here in each other's company. Farming is a tough mistress. Up at the crack of dawn, working till the sun went down most days. If he hadn't got sick, he would still be managing all the farmland around here. It had been his father's before him. He sold it to a neighbour who wanted to increase his farming property. He needed the money for his cancer treatment, you see. And he couldn't work anymore."

"You must miss him."

"More than I had ever imagined. He saved me in more ways than rescuing me that night. He saved my sanity. And restored my faith that there are good, kind-hearted people in this world. He encouraged me to draw and to paint. He saw the potential in my sketches, and he knew it was good for me. Helped me to process things I had gone through." Alice wiped a tear away with the back of her hand. "Now let me show you the painting I thought you'd like." She removed the cotton cover.

"Wow, this is very good. Although it's strange saying that about my own face. I meant it's very detailed. Such fine brushstrokes." Lauren held the painting up to the light. "I will be very careful with it."

"No, it's yours, dear. Let me know what Tommy thinks."

"That's . . . em . . . really kind. Thank you." On impulse, she leant over and kissed her mother's scarred cheek.

Her mother flinched. "You're very welcome."

"Is it painful?"

"No. I'm just not used to anyone touching me. Except John."

"I've been reading up about the new procedures for skin grafts. They can do wonderful things now."

"I'm sure they can."

"I'd like to think something could be done to help you."

"Having you here, seeing you, talking with you is the best gift you could give me."

An uncomfortable silence stretched out the seconds. The clock ticking on the wall seemed deafening.

"I'd better get back to town. Thanks for the tea. I'll let you know what Tommy says about the painting. Please think about what I proposed."

Lauren backed down the driveway with the image in her head of her mother's shocked expression at being kissed on her scarred cheek. It was an automatic gesture, something she had not thought about. Given time, maybe old wounds could heal. Both the mental and the physical ones.

Maybe my father's money can do some good.

CHAPTER TWENTY-FOUR

TOMMY FINALLY SAT DOWN BESIDE LAUREN ON THE COUCH IN THE cottage. He had listened to her revelations of all that had gone on that day while standing by the bench, arms crossed, without comment.

"I'm shocked. Why would he treat you like he did and then leave you money? It makes no sense."

"I know. I'm just as confused as you are. But at least I can do something with it to help my mother. It was her house too. She should have the money. It's not mine to keep."

"I agree. She should have it. If the surgery can help, your father will have helped your mother. In a roundabout way."

"The plastic surgeon needs to see her to determine if he can do anything to restore her face. He told me there was no guarantee."

"It's worth a shot. If she takes you up on your offer."

"She said she'd think about it. I can't push her to do this. Oh, by the way, I brought a painting to show you. She gave it to me as a gift." Lauren lifted the painting from beside the couch and handed it over.

Tommy unwrapped the canvas carefully and propped it up on the table.

"It's amazing. It could be a photograph." He stood back to get a better view.

"You would be totally blown away if you saw what she has in that studio."

"Did you know she could draw or paint? Did she do this when you were a child?"

"Nope, not to my knowledge. There were some that were very sketchy, and I would say those were the ones she did in the beginning. The latest ones are much better."

"Has she drawn or painted anything else?"

"No, there were only images of me the day she took me up to the studio. But she may have others. There were a lot of canvases stacked against the walls." Lauren got up and wrapped her arm around Tommy's waist, and leant her head against his shoulder. "She does beautiful work. But it makes me sad to look at it. That farmhouse is full of sadness. It must be so very lonely out there without John. Although she says she's used to it."

"So what's the next move?"

"I'm going to talk to the chief."

LAUREN APPROACHED THE EMPTY FRONT DESK AND RANG THE BELL. A sergeant appeared from the back room.

"I'm here to see Chief Bailey. Tell him Lauren Taylor would like a few minutes of his time. Please."

"Have a seat."

Lauren pulled out her phone and noticed Tiffany had left her a text message to call her back.

"Hey, Tiff. What's up?"

"I'd like to see you today if you have time. Can we meet for dinner? Kill two birds."

"I don't know if that's a good idea . . ."

"I've found out something you might find interesting. I think it's worth your while to meet me." Tiffany announced emphatically.

"Okay then. Dinner at Pizza Delight, it's over near the . . ."

"Yeah, I know where it is. I've eaten there. I'll see you at seven?" The sergeant opened the connecting door. "You can go in."

"Hi Lauren. What can I do for you?" Chief Bailey pushed away the file he was working on and motioned for her to take a seat.

"I want to take my mother into the city for an appointment with a plastic surgeon. I know you told me not to leave town, but I don't think she'll go if I don't take her."

"It was a request to stay in town. I can't officially hold you. But it's better if you stick around until we piece together what happened."

"Funny, I thought it was more a directive than a suggestion. I'll make arrangements as soon as my mother agrees to go. Since I haven't heard from you, maybe you could get me up to speed on what you've found out?"

"I'm not at liberty to discuss the case with you at the moment."

"Since I was the one who found my mother, and she was a witness to what happened to me, and I notified you of Marty James backing up her story, I would think you could tell me if you've found out anything else. I cannot produce the truck driver who stopped to give me a lift into the city that night. Or the homeless old man who protected me, and let me sleep under the bridge with him. The restaurant that gave me a job washing dishes for a few bucks a day so I could find a shitty room to rent has changed hands. I don't know what else I can give you. Now it's your turn."

"You are one pissed off, sarcastic young woman, aren't you? Yes we've interviewed your mother and Marty James, and they do verify what you've told us. We've also interviewed a few other folks who were chaperoning at the prom that night.

Pretty much backing up what you said. There was alcohol being handed around, no doubt about it. The actions of some of the graduates that night were questionable. But I'm no nearer to finding out who put Brett in the ground, I'm afraid. There was nothing in the gravesite other than his identification."

"It's not easy for people to remember a night that long ago."

"There are a lot of crimes that remain unsolved. There wasn't the same digital technology fifteen years ago. No apps to find missing persons."

"I want to find out what happened just as much as you do. I'd like to clear my name from any suspicion in this case."

"Believe me, I want to close this case too. We're still hoping someone will come forward. Someone must have seen something that night. The place was swarming with people."

"I hope you're right. If there's no problem with me leaving town, I'll set up a meeting with the surgeon. Just so you know, I have no plans to move back into the city at the moment. I'm trying to decide what to do. Tommy wants me to stay."

"I heard you two were tight. Just like old times, hey, Lauren?"

"No. Not like old times. We've grown up now, and have a better idea of what we want. I'm just not sure if I want to stay in Clearwater."

Chief Bailey stood up and opened the door. "Let me know when you plan on leaving. If I hear any more I'll be in touch."

Lauren doubted she would hear from him. So far she was the only person uncovering leads.

TIFFANY WAS ALREADY SEATED IN A BOOTH IN THE CORNER WITH A glass of wine in front of her when Lauren walked into Pizza Delight. She was impeccably dressed in a dark suit and white shirt. Lauren wondered if she ever relaxed, let her hair down and wore jeans and sneakers. Her red-lacquered nails tapped impatiently on the wooden table as she perused the menu. She glanced up and smiled when Lauren reached the table.

"Hey Lauren, right on time. I'm so glad. I'm starving. Can you take a look at the menu so we can order and get that out of the way first?"

"I don't need to look. I'll have the Capricciosa with extra anchovies. And a glass of wine."

"Sounds perfect. Okay if we share?"

"Works for me. Make it a large. And garlic bread on the side, hey?" A waitress passed by their table and Tiffany pounced on her, rattling off their order, swiftly handing her the menus and turning her attention back to Lauren as the cue to leave them alone. Lauren noticed the waitress raising one eyebrow before she turned to walk away.

She wondered if Tiffany knew how rattled people were around her. She spoke her mind, barked orders and generally pissed people off. Customer service was *not* her forte.

"Has anyone ever told you you're direct, bordering on rude?"

"Sure, plenty of times."

"And it doesn't bother you?"

"No, not really. I have a thick skin. And I usually get what I want. Part of being a soldier's brat I suppose."

"Your father was in the forces?"

"Both my father and my mother, actually. We travelled all over the world when I was a kid. Never lived in one place very long."

"I guess your folks taught you to defend yourself. What classes did you take?"

"My father taught martial arts. My mother was a weapons instructor. I had all the bases covered."

"Wow. Remind me never to take you on."

Lauren had just worked out why she had never seen Tiffany hanging around the other girls in the office, or joining the team for drinks on a Friday night. It must be tough moving constantly and never being able to keep friends. *You would eventually just give up trying.* No wonder she had latched onto the boss, had an affair to land a good position, and didn't care who she burned along the way.

"So what was so important you had to meet me tonight?" Lauren smiled up at the waitress who had just placed her glass of wine on the table. She mouthed her thanks and received a smile in return.

"I've been making enquiries at your old school. Did you now the same groundsman is still working at the school, and he was the one who dug the hole? The hole where they discovered the body?"

"I had no idea."

"I had a long chat to him about the time capsule that your class buried that year. It was the day before the prom. He remembers it specifically because as he was filling in the hole his wife had been rushed to hospital to have their third child, and he had left the job incomplete. The time capsule had never been fully covered over, and he knew that he was in trouble if they found out. But when he came back the *day after the prom,* the soil was in the hole and the grass had been replaced. He thought that someone from the school had done it, and he never questioned it."

"What's so important about this fact?"

"Whoever buried the body couldn't have known that there was a time capsule buried there. Otherwise they would've known that time capsules get dug up eventually. And the body would be discovered."

"You're right. It had to be someone unaware. So you could rule out the kids in the class, and you could rule out the teachers. That leaves the caterers, possibly the chaperones and the band."

"I've spoken to the catering company. They're still in business, remarkably. They always make it a point to finish by eleven pm because they don't get paid after that. They would've left and packed up before the Prom King and Queen were crowned, judging by the time in the photos. So we can most likely rule them out, too, from witnessing anything."

"The few chaperones who were not teachers were mostly parents or relatives."

"I have five names left who have not been interviewed. Two of them have passed away. One of them is hospitalised with dementia and the last two are Jeff and Helen Slater." Tiffany sat back to allow the waitress to place the steaming hot pizza on the table.

"Tommy's parents? I know they were there that night, but they haven't told me anything. I doubt they are withholding information."

"I'm going to interview them all the same. They may open up more to me, since I am not in bed with their son. Not that I wouldn't go there if he had shown the slightest interest. Don't look at me like that. Sheesh. I'm winding you up." Tiffany extracted two large slices onto her plate. "I wanted you to know before I approached Jeff and Helen Slater."

"Maybe I should come with you. Jeff hasn't been well." Lauren helped herself to a slice, balanced it on her hand, folded the tip and took a huge bite. "Mmmm, heaven," she mumbled.

"I don't think that's a good idea. You being there may hinder them talking to me." Tiffany extracted a knife and fork from the cutlery basket provided and cut up her pizza.

"Come on, Tiff, get your hands into it. It tastes better this way."

"I don't think so. And I prefer not to get grease or tomato paste on my clothes."

"I think you're wasting your time. They haven't alluded to seeing anything unusual that night."

"Did you interview them directly? No? I didn't think so." Tiffany chewed a piece of pizza. "Mmmmm, this is good. Maybe they saw something and are unaware. Until we connect the dots, often innocent actions can add pieces to the puzzle."

"At least let me take you over there and introduce you. They

181

might talk to you if they know we worked together, and you're are writing a story with my blessing."

A warm breath on the back of Lauren's neck generated goosebumps, which ran up her arms. She didn't need to turn around to know who was leaning down to kiss her ear.

"Hey ladies. I didn't get an invite to the party, but I thought I'd crash it anyhow. And my favourite pizza's on the table. Thanks, don't mind if I do." Tommy pulled up a chair, sat down and shovelled a slice of spicy Capricciosa into his mouth and still managed to give them a big grin.

"You're all class, Tommy Slater." Lauren reached over and playfully clipped him behind the ear.

"I'll order another." Tiffany raised her hand and ushered a waitress to their table. She lifted the now empty plate. "Same again. And a beer, Tommy? Yes?" Her eyes devoured Tommy as if he was going to be the next course.

"Tiffany was just explaining that the only two chaperones remaining who we can question about prom night happen to be your mom and dad. I told her your father wasn't a well man. I'm not sure that it's a good idea. What do you think?"

"Dad won't talk to a reporter. He had enough of reporters when Rob was killed. He was full of pain and anger and they pursued him relentlessly for a comment. They twisted his words and printed an inflammatory story in the paper. It caused a lot of grief when the court case came around. That idiot kid was arrested for driving under the influence, but he nearly got off scot-free because of a smart lawyer. So no, I don't think it's a good idea."

"Maybe you should come along?" Tiffany suggested.

"Hey. I said I would come and you shot me down." Lauren frowned, and took a sip of her wine.

"You are not their child. Tommy might be able to help them see this is better than talking to the chief."

"They've already talked to the chief. He interviewed all the chaperones, teachers and parents." Tommy lifted the glass of beer from the waitress's tray.

"Really? You didn't tell me that." Lauren extracted a piece of the newly delivered pizza.

"I only found out about it today. We were discussing the fact that nothing new has come up, and he told me the chief had called them both in to the station for a statement." Tommy said.

"It's still worth a try. Don't you think? Call them." Tiffany picked up Tommy's phone from the table and handed it to him.

TOMMY, LAUREN AND TIFFANY WALKED FROM THE CAR TO THE front door. "I explained I was bringing over a friend of Lauren's to ask some questions. They weren't very keen when I told them you were investigating for a story. But they have agreed to answer some questions." Tommy stopped a few feet away from the door. He pointed a finger at Tiffany. "I promise you, if you fuck this up, and write something they did *not* say, you will have me to deal with. Got it?"

"Got it. I promise I will not misquote them. But I will record everything they say, so you can be sure what I write is factual."

Tommy and Tiffany stared each other down. Lauren wasn't sure who was going to come out on top with this one. The protective son or the bossy, insufferable reporter.

Jeff opened the door with a guarded expression on his face. "Evening, folks. Come in." Tiffany entered first, and as Lauren passed by, Jeff winked at her. *Good, he doesn't appear to be thrown by this impromptu visit.* Tommy gave his father's shoulder an affectionate squeeze as he closed the door.

"Go on through. Take a seat." Jeff sat in his favourite chair by the fireplace. "Tommy explained on the phone why you're here. Although I don't know what I can tell you. I didn't see anything out of the usual. I was inside the hall most of the night. I didn't see Lauren get attacked. I didn't see Brett after the ceremony. I was the official photographer, taking pictures of the Prom King and Queen. I had my tripod set up, and I took a few pictures around the room, but I can't remember leaving the hall after that until Helen and I went home. Isn't that right, Helen?"

Helen Slater appeared from the kitchen and sat in the armchair opposite to her husband. "That's right. Hello, Lauren, Tommy. And Tiffany, isn't it? Can I get anyone some coffee?"

"No, we're fine, Mom." Tommy leant over and gave his mother a reassuring kiss on the cheek.

"Mr and Mrs Slater, do you agree to let me record this? That way no one can deny what was said and what wasn't."

"Yes, fire away."

"Can you tell me if you saw Lauren in the hall when the crowning was happening? And did you see Brett?"

"Yes, I took pictures of both of them in the hall at that time." Jeff said.

"Why do you remember that so clearly?"

"Because the chief showed me the pictures he had collected from Lauren. I remember seeing both of them in the hall not far from the stage. Curiosity had me looking for Brett, given he is the reason we are all being questioned."

"Did you see anyone in the hall that you didn't know?" Tiffany scribbled some notes on a pad in her lap.

"At the time I didn't notice anyone. The chief showed me some photographs, believed to be of Alice, Lauren's mother. But I told him I didn't see her."

"What about the grounds. You may have had to walk past where the body was buried at the back of the administration building on the way to the car park. Did you notice anything then? Did you notice if there were garden tools lying around?"

"Nope. We didn't go that way. I didn't notice anything out of the usual. Helen and I and another couple of chaperones and a teacher were probably the last folks to leave the building. We locked up, set the alarm and walked to our cars. I had to get some help with my camera gear and tripod. Everyone got in and we drove away. The teacher and chaperones were behind us. There were three cars in the parking lot when we left."

"Why are you so clear about the cars in the parking lot?" Tiffany enquired.

"Cars are my business. I might forget a face, but I won't forget the car my customers drive."

"So you locked up, left, and went home."

"Yes, Jeff was responsible for the keys. We were both on the committee, you see. We nearly didn't make it home that night though, when that car came around the bend and nearly hit us head on." Helen announced.

"Yes, some idiot joyriding around late at night." Jeff said.

"What did you do with the keys for the hall?" Tiffany asked.

"We held onto them until Monday morning. No one needed them before then." Jeff said.

TOMMY DROVE THEM BACK TO THE CAR PARK AT PIZZA DELIGHT.

"I told you they had nothing new to contribute." Lauren turned in her seat to talk to Tiffany. "What's next?"

"I'm heading back to the city tomorrow. I'll write up what I've got, but it's still a mystery." Tiffany climbed out. "Thanks for tonight. I'll email you."

They watched her drive away.

"I told her your folks would have nothing to contribute."

"I guess we have to be grateful that someone is poking around trying to dig up something. The police haven't found anything." Tommy reached over and squeezed Lauren's hand. Her phone buzzed in her pocket. She pulled it out to check the screen.

"My mother has agreed to see the plastic surgeon."

"Good news. When did he say he could see her?"

"I'll send him a text. He said he would fit us in. Hopefully soon."

"You coming back to my place tonight?"

"No, I'll head back to the cottage. I've got an early start

tomorrow, and I want to write a few more pages of my book. I'm trying to finish it and get it to an editor."

"Maybe I'll get a good night sleep tonight then, with no one hogging the sheets."

"Keep talking like that and you'll have the sheets all to yourself from now on."

CHAPTER TWENTY-FIVE

ALICE WAS IN PART TERRIFIED, HOPEFUL AND EXCITED, ALL AT THE same time. The appointment with the plastic surgeon had come quicker than she had expected. But she couldn't look a gift horse in the mouth. Her daughter . . . she had to take a few minutes to just breathe and let those words linger and sink in . . . *her daughter*, had arranged an appointment with a renowned plastic surgeon. And now they were in Lauren's car, on their way to the city, and she couldn't believe it was happening.

Just sitting in the passenger seat watching Lauren's facial expressions gave Alice joy. Listening to Lauren talking about her life, her apartment in the city, the many people she had encountered in her line of work. Even when Lauren had enough of talking, and switched on the radio, she didn't mind. Alice enjoyed listening to Lauren's choice of music. She hungered to learn any tiny detail of Lauren's life, now that fate had brought them back together. Each piece of information added to the puzzle that was now her grown-up daughter.

They pulled up outside Lauren's ground floor apartment at noon. The midday sun slanted through the tree-lined streets onto the windows and render, which had baked to a pale biscuit colour. The charming neighbourhood, with pretty parks and boutique shops they had passed on the way, had delighted Alice.

After being shut up for a couple of weeks, the apartment was a little stuffy. Lauren pulled up the blinds and opened up the front window and rear bedroom window, to allow a warm breeze to flow through the space. There was only one bedroom, which Lauren insisted her mother use, and a couch in the living room, which converted to a double bed. The furnishings and fabrics in pastel colours appealed to the artist in Alice. Framed prints on the walls, and an assortment of books highlighted Lauren's taste in art and literature.

The kitchen, which opened off the living room, through an arch, had enough space in the corner for a small table and two chairs. The window overlooked the same leafy courtyard as the bedroom. Alice sank into an armchair and watched her daughter unpack and fill the refrigerator with the basic supplies they had purchased on their way into the city.

"How about some lunch? And a cold drink? I make a mean omelette."

"Would you like me to make lunch while you do something else?"

"Sure. Thanks. I need to pack some more clothes to take back. I didn't take much with me before."

"I guess you weren't expecting to be there so long."

"I certainly wasn't expecting to be in Clearwater Springs weeks later."

"What are you going to do? Are you planning to come back here? Or are you thinking of staying with Tommy?"

Lauren shook her head.

"You can tell me to mind my own business."

"I honestly don't know. I want to stay with Tommy. Especially now I've found you. But . . ."

"It's a different life back there, isn't it. You can be anonymous in the city."

188

"Yes, but it is lonely too. It wasn't so bad before because I had my job, and I was busy, travelling and working long hours."

"I can understand what it's like to be lonely. Can you see yourself back in the same job? Is journalism what you want to go back to?" Alice took the eggs and cheese out of the fridge and looked around for a bowl. Lauren pulled a whisk from a drawer and a frypan from a cupboard. They dodged around each other in the small space and laughed. It had triggered a memory of when they cooked together at home when she was learning as a child.

"Takes me back to a time when I was just a normal happy kid."

"I wish things had turned out differently. I really do."

"This trip is about the future. Your future. Let's not talk about sad things, okay. We have an hour to eat and then get to your appointment. I'd better get a move on." Lauren set out plates and cutlery and left her mother to prepare lunch.

IN THE WAITING ROOM, THERE WAS A MAN WHO LOOKED TO BE IN his thirties, and a little girl of about six years of age sitting beside him. The girl, with short black hair, dressed in a pink long-sleeved shirt, blue jeans and sneakers, had a book balanced on her knee. She looked up when Alice sat opposite to her, and stared, her eyes as wide as saucers.

"I guess it can be difficult when you're out in public." Lauren whispered to Alice.

The man tried to distract the little girl, but she wouldn't take her eyes off Alice. After a few minutes, she put the book down, slipped off her chair and came to stand in front of Alice. She pulled up the sleeve of her shirt. Her arm was scarred, red and angry.

"Bonnie, come and sit over here with me. Leave the ladies

alone." The man got up and took her hand, but the child refused to move.

"She's fine, really. Leave her." Alice watched the child collect the book from the chair, and realised it was a sketchpad. She showed the page to Alice, and placed it on her knee. She had drawn a car with what looked like flames shooting out of the windows. There was a figure on the ground, clearly female and wearing a dress. A smaller figure knelt beside the woman.

"This drawing is very good, Bonnie. Is this you? Here?" Alice indicated the small figure. The child nodded. "Who is this?"

"She can't answer you. My daughter hasn't been able to speak since the accident," the man said. "Bonnie normally won't interact with anyone. She hasn't done this before." He frowned, his head tilted to one side, perplexed.

"We have something in common. Don't we, Bonnie?" Alice nodded her head.

The child never took her eyes off Alice. She slowly reached out her hand and gently touched Alice's ruined cheek. You could have heard a pin drop.

The door opened suddenly, breaking the spell. Bonnie snatched her hand away, grabbed the book and ran over to her father, who put his arm around her shoulder. Dr Bergin called Lauren and Alice into his office. Alice reluctantly left the waiting room and the little girl who was obviously very traumatised by her accident.

* * *

"COME IN, LAUREN. NICE TO SEE YOU AGAIN." DR BERGIN SHOOK Lauren's hand, and then took Alice's hand between both of his.

"Hello, Alice. Lovely to meet you. Please take a seat. Lauren has explained a little, but I would like you to tell me what happened to you that night."

"It happened a long time ago, twenty years this summer. My

husband had anger issues. He often pushed me or struck me. Usually not anywhere that could be seen to leave a mark. He was an upstanding citizen, you see. He wouldn't have handled people knowing. He came home from work very angry one day when Lauren was at a school camp, and his evening meal wasn't ready. He'd had a bad day at work. Been overlooked for promotion. Again. That was the story of his life. He started yelling at me. On those days I couldn't do anything right. He'd been drinking, and he kept on drinking. He got angrier and angrier and he grabbed the handle of a pot from the stove and threw it at me. It hit me on the head and knocked me out. It had boiling hot oil in it, which splashed onto my face and clothes. When I came to, he was gone. I got in my car somehow and I drove. I drove until the car ran out of petrol. A kind man found me beside the road, and took me in. He cared for me. I was concussed. When I was able to talk, I told him what had happened. I was so afraid. He hid my car, and protected me from my husband. I was sure if he had found me he was going to kill me. He wouldn't have wanted anyone to know what he had done."

"So you never sought any help for your burns?"

"No, I was afraid my husband would find me. And I was afraid for John."

"And John has passed away now, Lauren tells me." Dr Bergin sat back in his chair. "This procedure will take some time. You will be in hospital for a week or so. But you will need care. Who will look after you?"

"I will." Lauren said.

"I'd like to examine your face a little closer. Would you slip off your shoes and hop up onto the bed over here, behind the curtain."

While Dr Bergin washed and dried his hands, and put on some sterile gloves, Alice did as she was asked. She tried not to shake, but her body would not respond. The doctor gently and carefully examined Alice's face. Then he examined areas to harvest skin for the graft. When he had completed his examination, he helped her to sit up and asked her to take her seat at the desk.

"I believe I can help you. You will regain a more normal profile, but I cannot guarantee that side of your face will ever be the same as it was. I will do my best. I can guarantee that. What do you say?"

"Yes. I would like you to try. When?"

"I'll have to speak to my secretary, she has my surgery calendar. She will email Lauren so that we can get your medical history and blood group, etc. I have a colleague visiting from overseas who will be very interested in this procedure. I would like to start soon, within the next week or so. Does that work for you?" Dr Bergin came around to perch on the edge of his desk.

"Yes, the sooner the better. So I can't get cold feet." Alice shook his hand. "Thank you for seeing me so soon."

"Thank Lauren. She can be very persuasive. I'll be in touch." Dr Bergin opened the door for them to leave, and called in his next patient.

"Good luck, Bonnie." Alice said to the little girl as she passed by, holding her father's hand.

"How'd things go with the specialist?" Tommy asked.

"He thinks he can help. He wants to start soon, and I think that would be a great idea, before she changes her mind. We just finished filling in her medical history and emailing it back." Lauren lay back against the pillow on the couch, the phone cradled against her ear. "We'll head back in the morning. How are you doing?"

"I'm okay. We've been busy. I bumped into Deputy Morgan at the diner. I found out that they arrested a guy for breaking and entering near the garage. That must have been why you felt you were being watched. He was probably casing the joint."

"I don't think it's the same guy. The door was locked, and there was dirt on the floor. Unless he picked the lock."

"I guess you're right. It makes me happier to know they've picked him up though. I don't want anything taken from the garage. The insurance on the place is high enough."

"I'm going to make myself a cup of tea, and get some more words down, before I turn in."

"How's the book coming along?"

"It won't win a literary award, but it's shaping up to be interesting. I might sell a few copies."

"I guess I'll see you tomorrow then. I miss you. Goodnight."

"I miss you too. Night." Lauren disconnected the call, and noticed she had a text message from Dr Bergin's secretary. She shot up from the couch and knocked on the bedroom door.

"Mom, are you awake?"

Alice opened the door dressed for bed. "What's wrong? You look upset."

"How do you feel about going into hospital tomorrow. They have a slot for you, a cancellation in Dr Bergin's surgery schedules."

"That soon? I hadn't expected . . . I guess if I'm going to do it, best to do it now. Before I have second thoughts. Don't you think?" Alice sat down on the end of the bed, concern etched on her face.

Lauren sat down beside her. "You don't have to do this, if you need more time. But if it were up to me, I'd take the chance. The stars seem to be in alignment at the moment. Don't you think?"

"Text them back and say yes. We'll be there."

"So no more food or drink now." Lauren got up. "I was going to offer you a cup of tea, but you have to fast. We have to be at the hospital first thing in the morning."

"I'd better get a good night's sleep then. Thank you." Alice put her arm around Lauren's shoulder and hugged her.

"You don't need to thank me. I think it is serendipitous that we are here at this point in time, when Dr Bergin had a cancellation and a surgery procedure he wants to show off to an international colleague. Now get some rest. I'll turn in too."

Lauren settled on the couch, called Tommy to tell him of the change in plans, and set her alarm for five am. Tomorrow was shaping up to be an exciting day.

CHAPTER TWENTY-SIX

THE SURGERY HAD GONE WELL. DR BERGIN WAS HOPEFUL THAT THE skin grafts would take, and there would be no cause for concern or complications arising from the old scar tissue. He had some compression facemasks fitted and designed for her, to aid in the healing and minimise movement of the graft.

Lauren had stayed in the city since the operation to be able to visit her mother every day. It had given her an added bonus of time to write more of her novel. Now she was out of the woods and clearly improving, Lauren headed back to Clearwater for the weekend. She was missing Tommy. No denying it, he had charmed his way into the number one spot in her heart.

When she pulled up in front of the cottage, the car door was yanked open and Tommy drew her into a firm embrace. The deep, knee-trembling kiss he gave her left her in no doubt of his feelings.

"I've missed you like crazy." Tommy murmured, and rained kisses on her lips, her ears, and her neck.

"Now that's a welcome I don't get every day." Lauren chuckled. "I like it."

"Tonight we're going to celebrate with some wine or perhaps champagne, a beautiful dinner prepared by me, and maybe a massage if you're lucky." Tommy drew her to his side and they walked together to the cottage. "I'll get back to work and let you unpack."

"Could you bring my cases into the cottage, please?"

"Cases? Plural? Does that mean what I think it means?"

"That I brought more clothes so I could pick and choose . . . yes."

"You think you're so smart. I've a good mind to put you over my knee. But that might come later."

"Now that's a promise I might make you keep. A bit of sexy spanking is worth looking forward to." Warmth flowed to the apex of her thighs. She unlocked the door with a smile on her lips, and a mental bookmark to investigate that scenario later.

Tommy lifted the cases as if they weighed nothing at all. His biceps bulged and his shoulders took the strain as he carried them into the cottage. Lauren stood back to appreciate how fit he was and marvelled at how much she enjoyed admiring his physique and knowing he was all hers.

"You really are a sight for sore eyes. All those muscles at my disposal." She ran her fingers over his broad shoulders.

"I'll see you later, and we can discuss what else is at your disposal. Be ready at five on the dot. I'm locking up on time tonight."

⁂

As she drove, Lauren was considering what she could do to make things easier for Alice when she came back home. If she stayed at the farm with her mother, they were far away from everything. Besides, she didn't want to be so far away from Tommy. The most practical option would be for her mother to come and stay in town for a while. But the cottage was too small. A couple of weeks ago Tommy had asked her to move into his house. She had refused because of all the wagging tongues in town. But this would be an excellent way to kill two birds with one stone. She could look after her mother, still do her morning shifts at the diner, work on her book in the afternoon and be there when Tommy got home from work. It seemed like a perfect solution to tie up all the loose ends.

When Lauren arrived at the diner, Maybelline was at the coffee machine, frothing up a cappuccino and talking to Helen sitting at the counter.

"Hello, ladies." Lauren hopped up onto a stool.

"Welcome back, honey. How's your mother doing?" Maybelline asked.

"She's doing really well, thanks. She's still in hospital but she's doing so well, I had to come back here for a few days. Have you given away my job, May?"

"No, I managed, honey. I haven't taken the job advertisement down, but no one's been interested."

"I'll be back on deck at five forty-five am Monday. When they release my mother, I'll have to go back into the city to pick her up, but I'll only be gone for a day."

"I'm happy things are improving for you. I bet Tommy is happy you're back for the weekend." Maybelline said. "He dropped in a few days ago and brought us up to speed with your mother's surgery."

"Did you hear they had arrested a man for breaking into local businesses in town? Tommy thinks he's not doing this alone. He suggested that we increase the security around the garage. Perhaps put in some cameras," Helen said.

"I think it would be a good idea. You can't be too careful these days. You're not only worried about them stealing, but also the damage they can do. I was working on piece for a car dealership last year. The damage these local louts did to the luxury cars inside the showroom was phenomenal. The insurance claim was in the millions. It was alleged a rival had orchestrated the break-in through an underworld criminal connection. I heard drugs were involved too. They're probably still fighting about it in court."

"You had a pretty exciting life as a journalist, didn't you? You must miss it," Helen said.

"I do miss some things. But I don't miss the stress. And I have other things to keep me occupied these days. Which is my cue to go. Tommy is making dinner tonight, and I have to unpack and get ready. Nice to see you, Helen. Say hi to Jeff, will you?" Lauren slid off the stool. "See you on Monday, May."

AFTER DINNER, TOMMY LAID OUT A BLANKET UNDER THE TREE IN his backyard. They took their wine in an ice bucket, a platter of cheese and biscuits to nibble on, and settled back on some pillows to watch the stars pop out on the ink-black sky overhead. "The stars seem closer out here, away from the city."

"There is something to be said for living in the country."

"Do you miss New York?" Lauren asked.

"Sometimes I do. It was hard to come back here and give up baseball. But if I have to be honest, I think I was imagining that fame and fortune would make me happy. That once I had money in the bank, and maybe a sponsorship or two, everything would fall into place."

"Fall into place?"

"Yeah, you know. Meet a nice girl, buy a house, and have some kids." Tommy took her hand in his.

"Oh."

"But no matter where I looked, no matter who I dated, I couldn't imagine settling down with them to have a family."

"You couldn't picture having a family?"

"No, I couldn't picture having a family with anyone but you. You were the only one who seemed to come to mind whenever I tried to visualise that picture. Me playing baseball with a son with dark brown hair. Me bouncing a little girl on my knee, with a cheeky smile and a turned-up nose."

"I don't know what to say."

"Did you ever think about having a family?"

"Not really. No."

"No? No kids. Why?"

"After the childhood I had, I didn't want to bring kids into the world. I wouldn't know how to look after them."

"Of course you would. You'd be a great mother *because* of those things that happened to you. You'd make sure that your kids were brought up right. With love."

"I don't know about that." Cold, hard fear had formed a knot in the pit of her stomach.

"I reckon you'd be a great mother, and I know I'd love to have a family with you. I've asked you this before but I'm asking you again. Move in with me. Let's see what living together means." Tommy sat up and pulled her up too. He took her hands in his. "I love you. I know that more now than I did a week ago, because I felt as if I was missing a limb all week, with you so far away. I know you're scared of commitment, but I'd like to make this relationship official."

"Are you proposing?"

"You want me on one knee? Hang on." Tommy knelt before her on the blanket. "Lauren Taylor, will you do me the honour of becoming Mrs Tommy Slater. I have no ring to give you now. But we can pick one out together. What do you say?"

"I do love you. But I'm scared."

"So we take it one step at a time. You love me, yes? You want to live with me, yes? You want the gossips to back off, yes? Then if we're engaged to be married, they will have to keep their opinions to themselves."

"If it doesn't work out . . ."

"There you go again being a glass half-empty kinda girl. You need to be like me, a glass half-full kinda guy. It will work out. Trust me."

"It's funny you should bring this up tonight, because I was going to ask you if I could move in . . ."

"Perfect."

"Wait! With my mother. To look after her, for a little while. It would be easier all round. And I was quite excited by the idea of being here when you came home. Of staying here with you."

"I'm happy we're on the same wavelength then. I think it is a great idea. Bring your mother. Sure. But you haven't answered my other question. And that one is the most important one of all. Will. You. Marry. Me?"

"Yes."

"Yes? You said yes?" Tommy rose to his feet and pulled her into his arms. He kissed her with such enthusiasm, and lifted her off her feet as he spun around. "I don't believe it. I thought I was going to have to work harder to convince you."

"I've come to realise, in the last week since I was gone, that I've never been happier in my life than the time I've spent with you. Even with all the drama and stress, the love I felt for you shone through. I want to feel that love every day. It scares me, but I want to be *with you* every day."

"Let's open that bottle of champagne now. Better still I think we should share with my folks."

"It's too late."

"It's not too late for good news. They'll be happy for us. Something for them to look forward to. I know my mom will love having a wedding to plan for. Since the old man had his health scare, they haven't had happy news."

Lauren sank into Tommy's embrace, and tried to imagine the idea of children with Tommy. But no matter how hard she tried to picture it, the thought of children, of her being a mother, frightened her. She couldn't be responsible for a small person's welfare. Or their happiness.

TOMMY TUCKED THE ICE BUCKET CONTAINING THE CHAMPAGNE IN the crook of one arm, and pressed the bell. He took Lauren's hand to wait.

Jeff answered the door. "It's Tommy and Lauren, Helen.

Come on in, kids. What have we got here? Champagne." He ushered the couple before him into the sitting room.

"Tommy, you should've called. I would have made some supper." Helen stood up to greet them. She was shorter tonight, in her fluffy slippers.

"No need for supper. Get some glasses, Mom. We have some good news to share. Lauren and I are engaged."

"Oh, I am thrilled. For both of you." Helen pulled a tissue from her pocket and dabbed her eyes. She stood on tiptoe and hugged Lauren and then Tommy.

Jeff shook Tommy's hand, and kissed Lauren's cheek. "Congratulations. When did this happen?" He went in search of champagne glasses.

"About half an hour ago."

Helen's eyes darted to Lauren's hand. "Can I see your ring?"

"We don't have a ring. It was a bit of a spur of the moment thing. We'll pick something together." Tommy said.

"And you came right over to tell us. We are honoured you shared your news with us first. What about your mother, Lauren?" Helen asked.

"I'll call her in the morning. It's a bit late. She may be asleep."

"A wedding in our family. When?" Helen asked excitedly.

"Mom, we haven't decided about that yet. Just the engagement part." Tommy said.

Jeff handed out glasses, filled nearly to the top with bubbles. "Yes. Let them enjoy being engaged, Helen. Let's toast the happy couple. To Lauren and Tommy. Congratulations. We're thrilled for you."

"Congratulations. Such happy news." Helen said, dabbing her eyes once more.

CHAPTER TWENTY-SEVEN

LAUREN CALLED HER MOTHER WHEN SHE HAD HER BREAK AT THE diner. She hadn't wanted to call too early and disturb her, but couldn't wait any longer to hear her reaction.

"Good morning. I wanted to give you some good news. Tommy and I are engaged."

"Oh, I'm so pleased for you both. I don't know him very well, but Tommy seems like a nice young man. If he is anything like his father, he'll look after you, Lauren."

"We'll look after each other, I think. I love him and he loves me, so we'll work out the rest together."

"That means you'll stay in Clearwater. Oh, I'm so happy. When is the wedding? Have you made plans?"

"No, no plans for a wedding yet. One step at a time. I'm engaged and staying in Clearwater. That was a big step for me. I'll have to let my apartment go. Hopefully they can get another tenant in soon."

"It's a great apartment, in a nice area."

"I'm sure it'll get snapped up. I'll be paying rent in the meantime." "I have some good news too. I can leave the hospital in a day or so. I have to arrange home care."

"That was something else I wanted to talk to you about. I'm moving into Tommy's. And Tommy would like you to come and stay in his house too. There's plenty of room. I thought it would be better if you were in town so that I could make sure you're being taken care of. It won't be so lonely either. Just till you get back on your feet? What do you say?"

"I don't want to be a burden to anyone. I thought I could have a nurse visit me at the farmhouse. Although the idea of spending time with you is very appealing."

"You won't be a burden. It will save me driving back and forth to the farmhouse. You'll get to know Tommy better. He's looking forward to getting to know you too."

"Well, if you're both sure. Just for a few weeks."

"I'll tell Tommy. I'll make enquiries about a visiting nurse. Let me know when I can come and pick you up from hospital."

THE JEWELLERS' SHOP IN THE CITY WAS TUCKED AWAY ON A SIDE street. A tiny shopfront with an impressive display of gold and silver, of glittering diamonds and precious stones encased in intricate designs, all protected behind thick, shatterproof glass. A bell and an intercom on the doorframe alerted the staff to the arrival of approved customers. Tommy pressed the bell, gave them his name and waited in the frame of the camera until the door buzzed open. Tight security for a small business, but this store was the front for a manufacturer, and they took no chances with strangers wandering in off the streets.

"Wow. This security is impressive." Lauren said.

"Yes. The owner and the old man went to school together. He gets all his jewellery from Mike for my mother. He will give you what you pay for. And when it comes to diamonds, you never can be too careful." Tommy took her hand and they pushed open the heavy front door.

A clerk greeted them and showed them to a table with a display cabinet embedded in the top. "Do you see anything here that you like? Or did you want something made for you?" The clerk asked.

"I like the shape of this square-cut diamond ring. Can I try it on? And this one here with the small diamond in the band. Oh, and this one. So many beautiful rings."

The clerk unlocked the case and removed a tray of rings for Lauren to try.

"This is stunning. What do you think?" Lauren held up her hand for Tommy's opinion.

"It looks beautiful. Try on some more. I want you to pick the right one."

"I keep going back to this one. And it fits me. It's perfect. How much is this one?" Lauren asked the clerk. The square-cut princess diamond, nestled in an 18K white gold band, looked as if it was made for her.

"I don't want you to worry about the cost. Mike and I have already made a deal. I take the ring and we hand over our firstborn when he's ten, to work in the shop. Seems like a sweet deal to me."

"Very funny. How much is this one?" Lauren asked the clerk again. "That's for me to find out and you to mind your own business. Keep trying them on. Make sure you know what you want. I'm going to talk to Mike."

A gentleman had appeared from the rear of the shop. Tommy shook his hand and they discussed prices in low voices. Lauren strained her ears but couldn't make out what they said.

"Lauren, I'd like you to meet the owner of this fine establishment. Mike, this is my fiancée, Lauren."

"Very pleased to meet you, Lauren. I see you have selected a few lovely rings. You have excellent taste."

"Very nice to meet you too. I really love this one. And it fits me. Look how it sparkles in the light."

"An excellent choice for the shape of your hand. If this is the one you like, we can have it cleaned and ready in a few minutes."

"If this is the one Lauren loves, let's do a deal. Lauren isn't happy with handing over our firstborn, so I guess it will have to be cash."

Mike laughed. "Money talks. Come on over to the register and we'll discuss it while Jenny cleans your fiancée's ring."

They left the shop hand in hand. Lauren couldn't stop extending her arm to examine the ring. No matter which way she turned, the sun reflected off all the facets of the diamond, throwing out a rainbow of colourful sparkles. Just the sight of it sent tingles of happiness through her.

"I love it. I can't stop looking at it. Thank you." Lauren kissed him on the lips.

"You're welcome. And since you are going to be wearing it every day, I wanted you to have something you love and can't stop looking at."

"Are you going to pull that macho trick with me every time I ask about the price of something? I didn't want to choose something out of your price range."

"I wasn't trying to be macho. I had some money put away from my days in baseball. It's worth every dollar to see the smile on your face. Believe me. The tray they brought out to show you was within my price range."

"I love it. And I love you, Tommy Slater. Now let's go pick up my mother so I can show this beauty off to all the hospital staff."

***

SETTLING INTO TOMMY'S HOUSE HAD BEEN FAR EASIER THAN Lauren had imagined. Not that she had much to transport from the cottage.

The big move had been when she brought all her worldly goods from the city apartment. They had found a new tenant to rent it out almost straight away, and he had been happy to buy most of her bulky furniture, which was a blessing. It wasn't as if the furniture meant a great deal to her. She wasn't sentimental about most of her possessions, besides a few trinkets she had collected over the years.

Her mother had brought her easel and sketchpads with her for her stay at Tommy's house. For a few hours every day she kept herself busy reading, sitting under the shade of the tree in the backyard, or sketching or doing some light cooking. They ate together in the evening and then her mother would often retire to her room to watch television. But Lauren suspected she was giving the engaged couple space to spend time together. She didn't leave the house other than to attend her medical appointments with Lauren. She was accustomed to people staring, but she never felt comfortable. Now, with the facemask protecting her grafts, she was more of a curiosity.

Lauren still worked the early shift in the diner, and spent the afternoon working on her novel. It was at the critical stage, where she hated every word she wrote. But she had to push through that feeling. In every craft book she read, they stated that this was a common problem with writers. Just grin and bear it, and get the words down. She had found an editor online, and had booked some time in her busy schedule. So now she had no choice. *Just finish the bloody book.* She was nervous about handing over her first manuscript. It both thrilled and terrified her.

LAUREN'S MOTHER HAD MADE THEM BOTH A LIGHT LUNCH AND retired to her room for a rest. Lauren made a pot of coffee and gathered her snacks and pens and reference material onto the dining table. Procrastination at its finest, and she knew it.

She had a sip of her coffee and opened her laptop to check her word count from yesterday. This afternoon she needed to get at least another thousand words written to keep on track with the goal she had set herself. *Now, where are the notes I made this morning?* She hoisted her bag onto her knee.

Rummaging around in the depth of the tote bag was getting

her nowhere fast. Her fingers encountered objects, but not the scrap of paper she desired. She upended the bag onto the table and spread out the contents. Success! Whew. There were a couple of good quotes jotted down that she could use.

She loaded all the bric-a-brac back into the bag. Pens, notepads, key rings, lipstick, a novel and a hair tie, tissues, a comb, a brochure for Walmart. Then she saw the folded envelope she had picked up from the lawyer that day. She sat on the bed and opened it up. Why would he keep my letters and return them to me? Why didn't he write back? She extracted the envelopes, noting the torn edges. He had obviously opened them. Didn't he realise she wanted to reach out one last time? Appeal to whatever he had once felt for her.

Five envelopes all opened. Hang on. Six envelopes in the bag. One was addressed to her. She recognised the handwriting. Why hadn't she noticed this before? She tore open the seal with shaking hands.

My Dear Lauren,

If you are reading this I will already be dead and buried. It seems strange to me to write these words, but there it is. My time is up.

You are probably wondering why Jason Colby has been holding your letters to return to you. I know you will find this hard to believe, but I kept them because they were precious to me. I wanted you to see that I didn't throw them away, that they meant a great deal.

Let me explain why I didn't answer you, why I didn't write back, or contact you. I knew you would be better off forgetting about me and getting on with your life.

Too many things had happened in my lifetime to make me the man you knew. But one thing I know for sure. I was an angry man, a violent man, and a man who didn't appreciate what he had until it was gone.

I know you were very upset when your mother left us. You blamed her, I could see it in your eyes. I want to set the record straight. Your mother left ME because I took my anger and bitterness out on her. Lord knows why she didn't leave me sooner. One night the rage erupted in me and I threw something at her. I knocked her out and I thought I had killed her. I ran. She wasn't there when I returned, so I guess she survived but I never knew what happened to her or where she is now. I don't blame her for being scared of me. When the red haze of anger overtook me, I wasn't in control.

Every time I looked at you, I was reminded of what I had done. I couldn't wait until you were old enough to leave home. I felt useless, and no good for anybody. That was why I stayed out of your way, and drank so much. I guess I was drinking myself into an early grave, and I won.

The night you came home and told me Brett Hagar had attacked you, you thought I was angry with you. No. I was angry with the boy who had done this to you. No one was going to do this to my daughter. Crazy, isn't it. I was furious at someone who had treated you badly after I had done the same and treated you with indifference for years.

I got in my car and went to the school, determined to find Brett and make him pay for what he had done.

I found him hiding in the shadows behind the buildings, sulking and drinking from a flask. Probably waiting until most of the people had gone home. He tried to run. He begged me not to hurt him, and I reminded him he didn't take no for an answer where you were concerned. My intention had been to give him a good hiding. Rough him up a bit. I didn't mean to hit him so hard. He fell to the concrete and didn't move. I felt for a pulse but I knew he was dead. I panicked. I hid him until everyone had gone home.

You need to know that Brett is buried on the school grounds out behind the administration building. There was a hole dug in a cordoned-off garden bed. I threw him in and covered him up. All these years I have expected someone to come knocking on my door to say they had discovered the secret I had buried.

It's up to you what you do with this information. I know there was talk in town that you had left with Brett.

I am telling you this to clear my conscience. I took a life. Killing that boy had a profound effect on me. As I said, I pretty much drank

myself into my grave. If you had stayed I don't know if I would ever
have told you. I was a coward, you see. I know that now.

I know you will never forgive me for what I have done. Only the
Lord can do that. Yes, I have been attending church since that night.

Jason has formed a trust for you with money leftover after my
treatment, from the sale of the house. It will never make up for what
happened, and you can choose to give it to charity if you wish.

Goodbye Lauren. I know you won't believe me but I do love you. I
just wasn't man enough to change my ways and show you.

Greg Taylor

Lauren sat in stunned silence, staring at his signature. Her
father had killed Brett. *Her father.* She couldn't believe it. He
had stood up for her that night. But this time his temper had
been way out of control.

She finally had the key to the mystery. And she had carried
this envelope around for weeks, completely oblivious to its
importance.

She had to tell the chief. But first she had to tell Tommy and
her mother.

She called Tommy to come home right away.

"YOU'RE NOT GOING TO BELIEVE WHAT I'M ABOUT TO TELL YOU.
Mom, you had better sit down." Lauren pulled out a chair and
sat opposite her mother at the table. "You too, Tommy."

"What's going on? Why wouldn't you tell me on the
phone?" Tommy asked.

"I've carried this packet of envelopes around in my bag for
weeks. Since I went to the lawyer's office and he told me about
the trust. I thought the packet only contained my letters. But I
was wrong. There was a letter in here addressed to me from my
father. It's a confession. My father killed Brett. He went back to
the school that night, and fought with him. He must have hit
his head on the concrete. Then he buried him in the hole

conveniently dug for the time capsule. That was why he didn't contact me when I wrote to him. He was afraid someone would discover his secret. He said I was better off without him. I think he was afraid to face me after what he had done." Lauren handed the letter to her mother.

Alice read the letter in silence. She covered her mouth with trembling fingers, tears welling in her eyes. "He had a vicious temper. I knew one day someone was going to die from his hands. I always thought it would be me."

Lauren reached over and squeezed some reassurance into her mother's hand. Alice passed the letter to Tommy.

Tommy finished reading the letter, and shook his head. "Unbelievable. And you carried this around and didn't open it?"

"I had no idea it was in the packet with my letters. I tipped the envelope onto the table that day, but I only saw letters in my handwriting. The shock of the trust fund threw me. I stuffed them back in and didn't look through them until today."

"How do you feel about this? Are you okay?" Tommy asked. "It must have been quite a shock."

"I guess I am in shock. This was not what I was expecting. Not at all. I was even beginning to think that Don had something to do with it. You know he never looks me in the eye. And I was sure he was in love with Brett, and he's in love with you now. That somehow he was involved."

"Not Don. He wouldn't hurt a fly. He's not gay. He's just protective of me. You left town once. He probably thinks you'll leave me again," Tommy said.

"What are you going to do now?" Alice asked.

"I'm going to go and see the chief. Will you come with me? He's going to want to verify my father's signature. If he needs another opinion, I guess the lawyer will have it on file."

"Yes, I'll come with you." Alice dabbed her eyes with a tissue. "Oh dear, now I've started I can't stop."

"I'll come with you too." Tommy pulled Lauren to her feet

and gave her a hug. "I know this is very upsetting for you. At least now they can close the case. You won't have this hanging over your head."

"I should feel relieved, yet I feel sick to my stomach. Someone died because of me."

Tommy placed a finger under her chin and tipped up her head. He looked into her eyes. "You can't blame yourself for this. Brett didn't deserve to die, but he put this turn of events into motion, not you. If he hadn't attacked you that night, none of this would have happened."

"That's right Lauren. You can't live with 'what ifs'. I did that for many years and it doesn't change anything." Alice said.

"Well, let's take this confession to the chief, and see what he says." Lauren folded up the letter, replaced it in the envelope, and tucked it safely in her bag.

"AND YOU FOUND THIS WHEN?" CHIEF BAILEY ASKED. FURROWS appeared in his forehead.

"Today. I haven't been keeping it, holding on to evidence, if that's what you're asking me. I wasn't protecting anyone. My father's dead. You can see the original date on the envelope, stamped and sealed by Jason Colby. You can ask him when I picked it up. I can assure you I hadn't noticed this white envelope, along with all the other white envelopes in the packet, until today."

Chief Bailey sat back in his chair. "I guess this clears up the mystery."

"Can I have a photocopy of it? I know you have to keep the original as evidence."

"I'll have the deputy make one for you on the way out."

"Thanks. Is there anything else you need from me? I can come and go from town without reporting in, I presume?"

"Nope, nothing more I need. If I think of something I will be sure to let you know. You'll receive some official paperwork in due course. Take care, Lauren. Are you planning on going back to the city?" Chief Bailey looked from Lauren to Tommy.

"I'm staying in town. We're engaged." Lauren held up her left hand to show off her ring.

"Congratulations. To all of you." Chief Bailey smiled, and nodded his head. He appeared genuinely happy for them. "I think you could all use some happiness in your lives about now."

LAUREN CALLED TIFFANY AND TOLD HER ABOUT THE LATEST developments. "So now you can finish your article and put this to bed."

"We need to talk a bit more about your father's letter. Obviously I won't print anything directly from it, but would it be okay if I have a look at it? So I can phrase my comments appropriately?"

"Sure. I'm bringing my mother into the city tomorrow morning for a check-up. Why don't we meet at the hospital café while she's seeing the plastic surgeon? Bring what you've already written and we can talk."

"I really appreciate it, Lauren. I can write a serious piece, you know. This might make them take more notice. Maybe they'll give me more meaty stuff to write about and not just fashion shows and fluff pieces."

ALICE WAS DRESSED AND READY TO GO, DRINKING COFFEE AT THE kitchen table, when Lauren appeared for breakfast. They left town just after dawn, when the sun was peeping over the hills in the distance and the traffic was light. They arrived at the hospital in plenty of time for her appointment.

Bonnie and her father were sitting in the hospital corridor waiting for a dressing change. Bonnie hopped off her chair and ran up to Alice and Lauren. She clutched a knitted doll which had a bandage wrapped around its arm.

"Hello, Bonnie. Lovely to see you again." Alice sat down beside Bonnie's father. "Peter, this is my daughter Lauren."

"Yes, I remember. Nice to meet you, Lauren. Bonnie has been making leaps and bounds since we saw you in the hospital, Alice. She's even said a few words. Haven't you?" Peter placed his arm around Bonnie's shoulder. "I think I have you to thank for that. She seems to like spending time with you."

"And I love spending time with her too. She is doing so well. Maybe we'll have another drawing session soon. What do you think, Bonnie?"

Bonnie nodded, and fussed with her doll on her knee, while casting shy glances at Lauren.

The nurse appeared and called Bonnie and Peter into the examination room.

Bonnie walked ahead and took the nurse's hand. Alice stood up and spoke quietly to Peter. "It gave me great pleasure to help the children express themselves, and try and rid themselves of some of the anguish and trauma on paper. I know what it's like to hold all that emotion inside." Peter patted her shoulder, and followed his daughter into the other room.

"I didn't know you visited Bonnie." Lauren said.

"Yes, Bonnie had an operation right after mine. Dr Bergin told me she was in the children's ward. You were back in Clearwater, so they wheeled me down. It kept me occupied for part of the day. Her mother died in a car accident, and Bonnie was burnt when the car caught fire. It has been very traumatic for the child. She wasn't speaking then. It's lovely to think she's making progress."

Lauren's phone buzzed in her pocket. "Mom, that will be Tiffany. I'm helping her with the article. She's meeting me in the hospital café while you have your appointment. Text me when you are done and I'll come back."

TIFFANY HAD TWO CUPS OF COFFEE, HER LAPTOP AND A CLEAR plastic folder of photographs spread out on the table. "I ordered you a cappuccino. Hope that's okay? Or did you want a tea?"

"Relax, a coffee is great. Thanks. Here's the letter. Let me see what you've written already."

They exchanged paperwork. Tiffany handed over a printed copy of her article, entitled "The Truth behind the Body in the Hole Mystery".

"It's good. No, I'm not saying that to flatter you. But you need more detail in here about how they searched for clues and the lack of witnesses. I guess the letter will help fill in the blanks."

"Really? You think so. I want to tell the truth, so that people know what had transpired. But I don't want to hurt your family."

"You've stuck to the facts. I can't ask for more. Even if they are painful. My father was responsible. He's dead, Tiffany. We need to move on and put this behind us. What are these photographs?"

"Those are the ones I took when I was in town. I like this one of you, outside the garage. It's casual enough. There's Tommy in the background. Oh, congratulations on your engagement by the way."

"News travels fast."

"No, I can see the rock on your finger. You kept that quiet, didn't you. When's the big day?"

"We haven't set a date yet. I'm just getting used to being engaged and living with Tommy. Actually, my mother is living there too. She needs a bit of care for a while."

"Things are turning around for you, Lauren. That's really good to hear. I mean it. I'm not the bitch everyone seems to think I am. I don't make friends easily. But I think we're edging towards a friendship here. Or am I wrong?"

"Edging towards a friendship is a pretty accurate description. Let's leave it there for now."

"I'll finish the piece today and email it to you. If you have any objections get back to me asap. I am hoping they might run this in the paper soon." Tiffany reached out her hand. "I want to thank you for sticking to your part of the deal."

Lauren shook her outstretched hand. "You owe me. You do realise that, don't you?"

"I certainly do. Maybe one day we could work together again?"

"I have no plans to return to journalism at the moment. No plans other than trying to slip back into the slow lane in Clearwater Springs and completing my novel." Lauren's phone buzzed. "Time to go pick up my mother. Take care, Tiffany. I'll look out for that email."

She couldn't help but think if she had written the article she would have handled it differently. Not that she lied to Tiffany. The article was well written. But it lacked a bit of cutting-edge journalism, a bit of pizzazz she knew in her heart she could have provided. Lauren made her way through the hospital corridors sublimating a sudden longing to be back at the forefront of one of the countries' popular newspapers. *Face it, you miss the excitement of a deadline.*

THE ARTICLE APPEARED IN THE PAPER THE FOLLOWING DAY, complete with pictures. Tiffany had used the one of Lauren standing outside Slater & Son. Tommy had complained that it wasn't a good representation of him in the background. Lauren was prepared for the onslaught of questions and strange looks from the locals. What she didn't expect was the flurry of other reporters and media arriving on her doorstep trying to dig up more dirt. After a few days of being told "no comment", they finally relented and left her alone. They printed their stories anyway, without verification. She couldn't blame them.

She was one of them a lifetime ago.

Life settled into a steady routine. Lauren was resigned to losing her apartment in the city. Tommy rented the cottage to a young couple starting out. Alice was healing well, and yearning to return to her farmhouse. Lauren had become comfortable having her mother around, and wouldn't hear of it. She was trying to make up for lost time.

"I don't think it would be a good idea to go back to the farmhouse yet. Don't you like it here? Aren't you happy?"

"Of course I'm happy. Though I'd like to get back to my studio. Sleep in my own bed. It has been wonderful spending time here with you. Getting to know Tommy. But I miss my home. My things."

"If the doctor says you can go back home, and I can arrange for someone to come in to do light housework, maybe cook a meal or two?"

"Someone to help with the housework, yes. But I can cook for myself. I've been cooking here."

"I'm fussing. Sorry. Yes, you have been cooking here. I guess you're bored now you're feeling better."

"I'm not bored exactly. I'm restless here. It's like I'm on holiday. I want to go home now. It's time. I'm going back tomorrow."

"I can't stop you. I've enjoyed the time we have spent together. And I'll still take you to your appointments in the city. Until they let you drive by yourself."

"You'll visit me at the farmhouse, and I'll visit you here. The time we've spent together has meant the world to me. When I can drive, I'm going to start a class at the hospital for the children in the burns ward. Dr Bergin is very hopeful that it might make a difference. If I can help those poor children, it will give me a purpose."

"That sounds wonderful. It's a long drive to the city for a class."

"We are going to have Skype classes too. I believe they are all the rage these days. I'll have to get a computer and step up to the internet age. Can you believe it? Learning computers at my age."

"You're never too old to learn a skill. Good for you. And if you have Skype, we can talk too. I can keep an eye on you from here."

A<small>LICE HAD GONE TO HER ROOM FOR A REST BEFORE DINNER.</small> To avoid tackling a difficult scene in her book, Lauren opened her laptop and procrastinated on the internet. A "ping" alerted her to the arrival of an email. She opened it to waste a few more minutes, and sat back in shock at the content. Although it shouldn't have surprised her. Life, as she knew it, had been turned upside down in the last couple of months. She sat staring at the words *Exciting Opportunity* until they blurred before her eyes, and two fat teardrops hit the keyboard. *Why now?* She dashed them away with the back of her hand. *Don't be silly.*

Perhaps her career had been too easily dismissed. Perhaps when all was said and done, writing for the newspaper healed something in her, which had been broken for a long time. It appeared she missed it more than she had been willing to admit.

She scanned the website and brought up the job description of the new position. She had all the skills. A thrill ran through her thinking that she could actually apply for this position, and she might get it.

Tommy's car pulled up in the drive. He was home early. She hurried to meet him at the front door.

"Shhhh. Mom is resting. You're early. I haven't even started preparing dinner yet."

"My folks called and asked us over later. They want to put on a small party soon. To mark our engagement."

"That's kind of them. Do you want a beer, or a glass of wine?"

He pulled out a chair and sat at the kitchen table. "A beer sounds great." He moved the laptop over on the table and the screen came to life. "What's this?"

"Ah . . . Nothing. I was just looking at what was out there."

"You were looking at vacant positions? Why? Are you thinking of another role on the newspaper?"

"I got an email from Garry. My old boss. They have an opening." "But we talked about this. You said you're happy here, working on your book."

"Just because I'm looking at what the job entails doesn't mean I'm going to take it."

"You told me about the long hours, the research, the travelling, and the deadlines."

"I'm not sure I'm cut out for being the little woman. Sitting patiently waiting for the big strong man to come home. Or looking after the two point two kids. It scares the crap out of me."

"How have we come from accepting a job to not sure if you can have kids?"

"I've told you that I wouldn't know the first thing about being a good mother."

"Being a good mother is about loving your kids. Plain and simple. There is no manual. Everyone has to learn as they go along."

"I'm terrified at the thought of having kids."

"I get that. But it's a long way off, isn't it? No one is forcing you to have kids right away."

"But you want kids, don't you?"

"Yes I want kids. We've discussed this. Can we get back to the job offer? What are you going to do?"

"I thought I would email Garry and ask him if I could work from here. Minimise the travel. See what he says. The money is really good."

"Do you think they will be open to you working from home?"

"I have no idea. But it is worth a try."

"I want you to be happy. But I don't hold out much hope for us if you are travelling overseas and back and forward to the city all the time. You know I can't leave here. I've made a commitment to my folks to keep the business going."

No matter how hard Lauren tried to shake the feeling of unease, Tommy's words kept coming back to haunt her all evening. Her mother sensed the tension between them and retired to her room to watch a movie after dinner. Tommy cancelled their visit to see his folks.

Even make-up sex could not diminish the tension in the air. She drifted off to sleep dreaming of walking a tightrope. Terrified of falling, but equally afraid of what was walking on the tightrope behind her, shrouded in mist.

MAYBELLINE LEFT LAUREN TO SET UP FOR BREAKFAST, NO DOUBT guessing a lover's tiff had attributed to the bags under her co-worker's eyes. Lauren battled though the morning, forcing a smile onto her face out in public and appearing as if the world was on her shoulders in the kitchen.

"I've let you stew all morning. It isn't getting any better. Do you want to talk about it?" Maybelline asked.

"Nope. I have to work it out on my own."

"Your shift is done in thirty minutes. Why don't you take off early? Here are some ready-made sandwiches. Go and visit Tommy. See if he can turn that frown upside down."

"I don't think he can."

"Take the sandwiches. Go have lunch with your guy. Have some afternoon delight. Get over it. Whatever it is." Maybelline shoved her towards the office where she stored her purse. "Get out of here."

TOMMY HAD ALSO BEEN IN A FOUL MOOD ALL MORNING. DON KEPT

out of his way and had occupied himself for a couple of hours dismantling the storeroom and checking the spare parts inventory.

When Lauren showed up at lunchtime, she had dark circles under her eyes, and looked as unhappy as he had been since their discussion the previous evening.

"I brought sandwiches." She held a paper sack out to Tommy. "Let's take these upstairs to the office. So we can talk." Tommy stepped out of his oil-stained coveralls, and washed his hands in the sink against the wall.

Lauren had begun to climb the stairs. Tommy wasn't far behind her when a dark-haired young woman dressed in well-worn jeans and a floral shirt, appeared through the open roller-door. She had a baby on her hip and carried a bulging backpack.

Tommy stopped in his tracks, halfway to the staircase. "Can I help you?"

"You don't remember me do you, Tommy?" The young woman adjusted the squirming baby, trying hard to balance the backpack on the opposite shoulder.

"No. Should I?"

"We spent the night together. You told me I looked beautiful. Like someone you knew when you were young."

Recognition appeared in Tommy's eyes. He looked from Lauren to the young woman. The similarity was uncanny. Lauren and this young woman could have been sisters. The dark hair colour, the physique, the high cheekbones, and approximately the same age by the looks of it.

"You took me to your hotel after the ballgame in Buffalo. Donna. Donna Washington. Remember me now?"

"Vaguely. What can I do for you?" Tommy's heart rate had risen.

"I saw your picture in the paper. Here in front of Slater & Son Garage. So I thought it was time for you to meet your son."

"My what? No way. I used protection."

"Well, it's not always failsafe. We have a child."

The air left his lungs with a whoosh, akin to having been struck in the solar plexus. Sweat popped out on his forehead and under his armpits, his skin became clammy.

"How do I know this boy is mine?" His voice had raised an octave. He cleared his throat.

"He's yours alright. But we can have a DNA test done if you need to prove it."

Damn straight we will. I have a son? A son! Tommy took a step forward. "What's his name?"

"Zach."

"Zach." *His son.* "Can I hold him?"

"Sure." Donna walked closer with the chubby baby. "He's pretty good with most people."

"Hello, Zach." Tommy lifted him from Donna's hip and held him under his arms, his bare little legs dangling, his pink, dimpled, chubby knees bent. He brought Zach close to his face, and stared at his features; looking for some resemblance, an indisputable sign of his own flesh and blood. Zach's tiny hand reached out to touch Tommy's face. Apparently Zach required some exploration of his own. A surge of something, be it recognition, affection, pride or the sudden revelation that he actually could be a father brought hot tears to Tommy's eyes. He blinked rapidly, forcing them down. A movement to his left brought him back to the present, and the knowledge that Lauren was descending the stairs. He glanced over and witnessed the shock on her face.

"You have a child." Lauren's eyes were filled with tears. She turned to face Donna. "He is a beautiful boy. You must be very proud of him."

"I am. And you're Lauren. The one they wrote the story about. It was your picture in the paper that brought me here. I saw Tommy in the background. I didn't know where to find him when he left the team. That article was a sign from God. He wanted me to bring Zach to meet his father."

"I'll leave you two to talk. Here." She pushed the bag of sandwiches into Donna's hands and left the garage.

When Tommy called out her name, she didn't turn back.

He has a child. A son. Dark hair, and big brown eyes. He looks like Tommy. Nothing had prepared her for that. She'd known he'd had relationships. A well-known baseball player, a good-looking guy: a chick-magnet, as they say, but she never thought that there was a child out there! *Face it, there could be more!*

The sick feeling in the pit of her stomach told her that the DNA test would come back positive. Then what? They were engaged, just starting out on a life together and now this complication. Because no matter how she looked at it, through no fault of this child, he was a complication in their lives.

Nausea threatened, her stomach rolled. Whether she liked it or not she was going to have to be a stepmother to a little child. She had no skills for this, and the thought terrified her.

She drove out of town to the lake, and pulled up at the water's edge. This spot held many favourite memories. They used to park here after school for a few precious minutes. To talk about their respective days in different classes, share gossip and homework and exchange hot fervent kisses full of promise. Before Tommy had to rush off to help his father in the garage, and Lauren to whatever after-school part-time job she had going at the time.

On the opposite bank of the lake, Lauren watched cars coming and going from Joe's Diner. Maybelline would be busy wiping tables and cleaning up after the lunch crowd. This morning, while she was wiping tables, she had no idea a photograph in a newspaper would bring about this change to their lives.

Her phone rang in her purse. She ignored it. A message flashed onto the screen.

Please come back. We need to talk.

She sure needed to talk to someone. But not Tommy.

When she pulled up in the driveway, her mother was stacking her belongings at the front door.

"Oh good, you're home. I was hoping you would be early. I have everything packed and I was hoping you would take me home today. . . Lauren, what's wrong. You look terrible." Alice followed Lauren into the kitchen.

"It seems that Tommy has fathered a child. And he's here in town with the mother. They haven't confirmed it's his, but he looks like Tommy."

"Oh dear. You must be devastated. And Tommy didn't know about this child? Is it a boy or a girl? What was his reaction?"

"A boy. His name is Zach. The mother's name is Donna. It was an accident, a one-night stand. Tommy had no idea until today. She saw his picture in the paper and recognised him. It was my picture taken in front of Slaters, and Tommy was in the background."

"Can I make you a cup of tea?"

"Tea won't fix this."

"Is there anything I can do to help you?"

"You can help me to understand why I am terrified when I think about having children."

"I guess I'm to blame for that. And your father. But you shouldn't let what happened to us put you off having your own children."

"Shit didn't just happen to you and my father. It happened to me. And it burns inside me still."

"I cannot undo the past. I would if I could. But I can tell you that you have a good decent man in Tommy. He will be a good husband and provider, and he will be a kind and loving partner. You need to trust that you will be happy and when children come along you will know what to do."

"Okay. Enough talking. Let's get you back home and settled. I've a lot to think about before Tommy gets home."

THE CURSOR BLINKED ON THE LAPTOP SCREEN. LAUREN HOVERED the mouse over the "send" button, while her heart thumped in her chest, her mouth became as dry as the Sahara Desert and her stomach clenched in protest.

Stop procrastinating. Send the bloody manuscript!

She tapped the send button. The email flew off. Her book was in the hands of the gods now. Or more precisely, the editor she had chosen.

She pulled up the other email from Garry, her old boss. Discussion had been cut short earlier at the garage. But now things were so very different. Lauren had more to consider, more weighing on her mind.

She sent off the application, and attached an updated copy of her résumé. She needed to know where she stood, if she had a chance. Or not. Then she could dismiss it from her mind.

I just need to know!

THEY HAD A LOT TO DISCUSS TONIGHT, AND SHE WANTED NO distractions. Lauren pulled meat and vegetables from the fridge and pots from the cupboard. She switched on the oven and set about making an early dinner.

She prepared the table, and decanted a bottle of wine. *We'll discuss our future like two reasonable adults. But a glass of wine can't hurt.* To boost her confidence, she changed into a pretty dress.

By the time Tommy arrived home, the mouth-watering aroma of a roast beef and garlic floated through the house.

She met him halfway between the kitchen and the front door. He appeared tired, shoulders hunched. He stopped when he saw her. His spine straightened. She realised he expected an argument.

"Before you say anything, I'm sorry I left today. I took my

mother back home this afternoon and I needed time to myself. Time to process what was happening."

"You could've called me. I was worried about you." His voice sounded strained. Frown lines etched into his forehead.

"I had some thinking to do. And you needed time with . . . your son and Donna."

"I took her to see my doctor. We sent off a DNA test. It should take a couple of days."

"Where are they now?"

"I called my folks. They took Donna and Zach home."

"Wow. It must've been a shock to them."

"You have no idea. There was a lot of yelling on the phone with my old man. Mom looked confused when she got there."

"Look, instead of us standing in the middle of the hall, why don't you take a shower and I'll serve up dinner. Then we can talk."

Dinner was tense and awkward. Lauren pushed down as much food as she could, and had drained the contents of a second glass of wine before Tommy spoke.

"Can we discuss what happened today? You left me to deal with it. I thought we were a team. Seems I was wrong." Tommy pushed away his plate.

"Can we go into the living room?"

Tommy and Lauren sat facing each other on either ends of the couch. Like opponents in a boxing match.

"I thought you needed time to talk to Donna. Be with Zach. It was a shock, but I could see the realisation on your face when you held him. You think he's yours. You *want* him to be yours. I couldn't breathe. You know how I feel about children. I panicked."

"I know what you said about being a mother. But this is different. Zach has a mother."

"You'll be expected to spend time with him. You'll want to have him stay with you. If we get married, I will be a stepmother."

"*If* we get married. What do you mean *If* we get married.

We're engaged. You're wearing my ring. We made a promise to one another."

"You might be rethinking that now."

"I had a one-night stand, Lauren. With someone who reminded me of you. A drunken one-night stand from all accounts. I am not rethinking anything. Are you?"

"I'm . . ."

"Why the hesitation? You're not sure, are you?" Tommy shook his head, and rose to his feet.

"Where are you going?"

"I'm going over to my folks. To see Zach. Take some time. I understand this has been a shock. It sure has blown me out of the water too. But you have to make up your mind. Are you in this relationship or are you looking for an easy escape? I don't know what I can do to prove to you that you are the one I want, the woman I want to spend my life with. And yes, have a family with. I didn't plan this but if Zach is mine, then we have a bit of a head start in the kid department."

Tommy left and Lauren sat still, immobilised by the emotions swarming around in her head, in her heart.

SAM OPENED THE DOOR WITH A CURIOUS EXPRESSION ON HIS FACE. "Hi, Lauren. We weren't expecting a visitor so late. Sarah's gone to bed. She hasn't been feeling well."

"Who is it, Sam?" Sarah called down from the top of the stairs.

"It's me, Sarah. I need to talk to you."

"Let her in, Sam. I'm up now." Sarah came downstairs tying her robe around her and put her arm around Lauren shoulders. "Why are you here alone? Where's Tommy?"

"That's what I need to talk to you about."

"Sam, honey, would you make some coffee please. Lauren, come into the living room. Now what's happened to bring you over here so late? Alone. Have you and Tommy had a fight?

Because it's normal when people get engaged, are living with each other and in each other's pockets. It will pass."

"I don't think this will pass, Sarah. A woman turned up at the garage today. With a baby. She says he's Tommy's."

"Was he seeing her back in New York? How does she know this baby is his? It could be a scam."

"They don't know for sure. Tommy took her to get a DNA test done. We'll know for sure in a couple of days."

"How are you feeling about this? Are you worried he has feelings for this woman?"

"No. She said they had a one-night stand. I don't think he has feelings for her. But I saw how he looked at the baby, at Zach. His eyes were full of wonder at the thought he could have created that child. I think he wants Zach to be his."

"So you're worried about his affection for the baby?"

"I am scared about having a family, Sarah. I don't think I can do it. And Tommy wants kids. I'd make a terrible mother."

"Why do you think that? Is this because you weren't treated well when you were growing up? Because you really need to rethink those feelings. I've been your friend since kindergarten. You had a happy childhood. Granted it wasn't all roses, but you weren't badly treated. It wasn't until your mother left when you were a teenager that things went downhill rapidly. We know what happened now, but remember you hated your mother all these years. And you have since found out that she didn't leave because of you. She loves you."

"This has brought all of my fears about having kids to the surface. Tommy and I had an argument tonight. He has gone to his parent's house. They took Donna and Zach to stay with them, until we can sort this out."

"I don't know what you are worried about. I have seen you with Jake and Milly. You are going to be a great mother. To this child, if it is Tommy's, and to your own, if you are lucky enough to have them. Believe me, when you create a child with the person you love, when you feel it growing inside you, when it depends on you for everything . . ."

"That's what I mean. It will depend on me. I'll have to be there twenty-four seven. I will be responsible if it has a cold, or if it is sick. What if I don't know what to do, what if it has a fever and I don't take it to the doctor, what if . . ."

"Honey, calm down." Sarah passed the coffee Sam had placed on the table. "Drink this. Maybe I should put a shot of brandy in it." She blew a kiss to her husband, and waved him away.

Sam retreated to the kitchen. Lauren picked up the cup with trembling fingers.

"Look, Lauren. You are having pre-wedding jitters. You seem to be focusing on the having kids part, imagining all sorts of scenarios that could go wrong. I am not trying to dismiss your fears, but I think that you need to talk to your mother. Get a clear picture in your head about why you are so afraid of motherhood. Or maybe you need to see someone professionally?"

"There was a shrink I used to see in the city."

"For God's sake go and talk to someone. Believe me when I tell you that having kids with the person you love is the best thing. The most important thing you can do. But we are jumping ahead. What if you can't have children? I don't want to be a negative Nancy here, but you may not be able to have kids, and you are twisting yourself into pieces over nothing. This child, if it is Tommy's may be the only child in your marriage. You wouldn't want to deprive Tommy of spending time with him then. Would you? And Tommy would want you to be there for him and Zach."

"You're right. Maybe it's time for me to go and talk to my therapist. And while I am at it, check out if I can have kids. I might be worried over nothing. Then I'll be handing my ring back to Tommy because he definitely wants kids, and he needs to find another fiancée."

"My God, you are a drama queen. He will not want another fiancée. You'll work this out. I'm sure of it."

Lauren's phone rang. Tommy's name flashed on the screen.

"I have to take this. I'll get going. Thanks for trying to knock some sense into me. I love you, you know."

"I know you do. And I love you too. Go talk to your fiancé." Sarah quickly hugged her, and closed the door.

"I'm at Sarah's. I'm just leaving." Lauren made her way down the path.

"Good. I'm home. I'll see you soon."

THEY WERE IN BED, WRAPPED IN EACH OTHER'S ARMS. APOLOGIES had been made, and tears had been shed. And at last they were talking. Rationally.

"Donna said she only wants me to be a part of Zach's life. Her family are supporting her, and they're comfortable, it seems. She's not after money from me. Although I will want to help provide for Zach. She just wants him to know his father. And when he's old enough, maybe he can spend time visiting us now and again. And we can visit him in Boston."

"So you're pretty sure the test will come back positive then?"

"Mom pulled out baby photographs. He pretty much looks like I did back then. Do you feel better now you've talked to Sarah?"

"Sarah made sense. I'm going to see to a therapist I worked with years ago. She thinks it will do me good to talk through my concerns. And while I'm in the city, I'm going to see a gynaecologist. This fear I have might be unwarranted. I may never be able to have children. Then you can find another fiancée."

"I don't want another fiancée, I want you." Tommy kissed her nose. "But I'm glad you have decided to talk to someone. For both our sakes."

He turned her around and tucked her into the spoon of his body, his arm over her chest, his hand cupping her breast.

"Now let's go to sleep and try to put this day behind us. I'm beat."

She couldn't argue with that. Tucked against Tommy's body, this was the place she felt most loved. She fell asleep to the steady beat of his heart, protected in his embrace.

AFTER TWO MONTHS WITH HER OLD PSYCHIATRIST, LAUREN HAD already made some amazing progress. Hypnotherapy had uncovered fear of abandonment when she was a child was the crux of her issues about motherhood. Now that she was engaged to Tommy, the care and attention she had received from the Slater family, along with her mother, had made a profound impact.

The DNA test had confirmed that Zach was indeed Donna and Tommy's son. Lauren had accepted the fact that she would be a stepmother to the little boy, and take care of him when he eventually came to visit them in Clearwater Springs.

Alice had bought the laptop she had talked about. Lauren was giving her basic lessons before signing up for computer classes at the local high school. Her first skin graft had been a success. Dr Bergin was thrilled with her progress, and equally impressed by her initiative to fund and run an art programme in the hospital burns unit, to help children deal with their trauma.

LAUREN HAD FINALLY COMMITTED TO AN APPOINTMENT WITH THE gynaecologist. Dr Bergin had recommended a colleague with private rooms at the same hospital. She left her mother to attend her regular check-up and travelled to the third floor to see Dr Lee.

The small waiting room was almost full. The receptionist gave her a clipboard with forms to fill in for their records, and asked for her health insurance details. She squeezed onto a seat between two very pregnant women, and balanced the clipboard on her knee. Surprise, surprise. She wasn't sweating or feeling nervous around these women. The sessions with her therapist had made a difference for sure. The woman on her right was called into the examination room. A movement to her left drew her eye. The T-shirt, stretched tight across the belly of the woman beside her, rose up. Lauren could see the baby move, pushing against the tight confines of the mother's skin. Her belly moved left, her belly moved right. The young woman noticed Lauren watching, eyes wide, as the baby pushed and extended its tiny feet and elbows. Bumps appeared on her swollen stomach.

"It's amazing, isn't it? To see him move inside. He's impatient to get out, I think." The woman rubbed her stomach, over the bulge, and the baby stopped kicking.

"Yes, it's amazing. How soon is he due?"

"I'm being scheduled for a C-section. He's overdue."

"No wonder. He's squashed in there." Lauren smiled as the baby pushed his feet out again. "Good luck."

The nurse called Lauren into the examination room. She handed over the clipboard. The nurse gave her a specimen jar for a urine sample, and opened the adjacent toilet door.

"When you're finished, come back here, undress behind that screen, slip on this robe, and hop up on the examination table. Dr Lee will be with you shortly."

The nurse passed through a connecting door to the patient in the adjoining room. Lauren could hear a muffled conversation. She provided the sample, undressed as directed and slipped on the cotton robe. The sheets on the table were cold underneath her bare thighs. She pulled the cotton waffle-weave blanket up over her. The nurse, accompanied by a short middle-aged Asian man with a kind face, appeared through the connecting door. He pulled on a fresh pair of disposable gloves.

"Good afternoon, Lauren. I'm Dr Lee. I see from your medical paperwork that Dr Bergin referred you to me."

"Yes, he's my mother's specialist."

"Excellent. Now just relax. How long has it been since you had a pelvic examination?"

"A couple of years now."

"And your health is good. No problems?"

"No problems to speak of. I've had issues with irregular periods. I'm on the pill."

Dr Lee palpated Lauren's stomach. "Hmmm." He turned to the nurse. "Would you run the sample please?

Dr Lee continued his examination. The nurse returned to stand beside the examination table. A look passed between them.

"Tell me, Lauren, when was your last period?"

"Mmm. About three weeks ago. But it was very light."

"And you made this appointment to check your fertility, I believe. Is that correct?"

"Yes. My fiancé wants to have children. I thought it would be wise to check."

"Very wise. I guess you won't have to worry about that now. You're pregnant. About eight or nine weeks I would say."

"No. I can't be. I'm on the pill. I've had my period."

"You can fall pregnant on the pill. You can still have a little blood. We checked your urine and the test was positive. I'd like to examine you to make sure all is well with the baby. Oh, and you can stop taking the pill now, my dear."

I'm pregnant? I can't be. I haven't felt sick. There has to be some mistake.

Someone was talking to her.

"Sorry, I didn't hear you." Lauren said.

"Everything seems fine, but since there was a little blood, I want to keep an eye on you. Can you come back and see me in two weeks? We can run a scan and check your baby then."

My baby! My. Baby.

"But I haven't been sick. I've felt fine. A little tired now and again. . . Oh, a little tired . . . was that because . . . ?"

"Yes, my dear, that was because there is a baby taking all your energy, getting bigger every day."

"And you're sure it's alright. I mean, it's normal?"

"We'll take some blood, and run some tests. The scan will tell us more in a couple of weeks. Don't worry. There are many women who don't know they are pregnant in the first couple of months. You are not alone. I'll leave you with my nurse. I have other patients to see. Make an appointment to see me in two weeks."

WHEN LAUREN RETURNED, ALICE WAS IN THE WAITING ROOM outside Dr Bergin's room. She put down the magazine she was reading, and gathered up her belongings.

"Shall we have a coffee downstairs before we head back . . . what's wrong? You look pale? What happened with Dr Lee? Is everything alright?"

"I had a bit of a shock. It seems we're going to have a baby in the family. I'm pregnant."

"You're pregnant! But I thought your appointment was to check your fertility."

"It was, and I am, it seems."

"That's wonderful news. Just wonderful. Wait and see. This will be the best thing that has ever happened to you." Alice pulled a tissue out of her purse and dabbed her eyes.

"Don't cry."

"Believe me, they are tears of happiness. Have you told Tommy yet?"

"No, I want to tell him in person."

"Well, let's go."

TOMMY SLIPPED OFF HIS BOOTS ON THE PORCH AND AMBLED INSIDE. The soft glow of the table lamp, the flickering candles on the dining room table, the smell of pot roast simmering on the stove, the soft music playing in the background, brought him up short. *Have I forgotten an anniversary? A birthday? No, it's not Lauren's birthday for a couple of months.*

Lauren appeared from the kitchen with a plate of hors d'oeuvres. "Is there a special occasion I've forgotten? "

"No, I wanted to have a romantic meal with my man."

He picked a savoury tartlet from the plate, and popped it into his mouth. "These are good." He mumbled.

"Have a seat, I have some news."

"I was going to have a shower before dinner. Can it wait?"

"I guess it can wait . . ."

"Good, I'll be right back."

"But not for long . . . in about seven months you'll have to have your shower when he goes to sleep."

"What are you talking about?"

"You'll be in too much of a hurry to hold him, or her, when you get home. Your showers will have to wait. I'm pregnant, Tommy. We're having a baby."

"A baby? *A baby.*" He grabbed her and lifted her off her feet. "I don't believe it. I sure wasn't expecting this. Are you okay? I thought you were on the pill." He put her down and stared at her stomach.

"Seems that isn't one hundred per cent foolproof. You must have super sperm. You've managed to impregnate two women who've been using protection."

Tommy couldn't stop smiling. "Yes, I have, haven't I? But are you okay with this. I mean, are you freaking out?"

"Strangely no, I'm not. I think I'm still in shock. I spoke to my therapist and she says she's very proud of me, and of the way I am handling this. I've made a breakthrough, it seems."

"Wait till we tell my folks. They'll be so happy. My mom has been fretting about her first grandson all the way over in Boston. We have to plan the wedding. I'm not having this baby born before we get married."

"Slow down. I've been thinking about the wedding today.

We can have a small ceremony with immediate family. I don't want a fuss. And a few friends. Sam and Sarah could be our witnesses. What do you think?"

"I think that I can't wait for us to be married and for this little surprise to come along." He placed his hand on her tummy.

"This wasn't the reunion I had expected when I came back to Clearwater Springs." Lauren said.

"No, this is so much better." Tommy pressed his lips to hers, with all the love he had to give.

THANK YOU FOR TAKING THE TIME TO READ LAUREN AND TOMMY'S story.

If you would like to keep up to date with my writing, please visit my website savannahblaize.com where you can sign up to my newsletter.

ABOUT THE AUTHOR

Savannah Blaize lives in Melbourne, Australia, after emigrating from Scotland many years ago. She enjoys writing stories in which the reader can step inside and visualise the world she creates. A member of the Romance Writers of Australia, and the Melbourne Romance Writers Guild, she is passionate about contemporary romance and engaging readers in the genre. The Class Reunion is her second published novel. Her first novel From Paris To Forever was published in 2017.

www.ingramcontent.com/pod-product-compliance
Lightning Source LLC
Chambersburg PA
CBHW071601110726
47908CB00007B/2194